The Blossom
Sisters

Books by Fern Michaels

The Sisterhood Novels

Books by Fern Michaels (Continued)

The Men of the Sisterhood Novels
Double Down

The Godmothers Series
Classified
Breaking News
Deadline
Late Edition
Exclusive
The Scoop

eBook Exclusives
Desperate Measures
Seasons of Her Life
To Have and To Hold
Serendipity
Captive Innocence
Captive Embraces
Captive Passions
Captive Secrets
Captive Splendors

Cinders to Satin
For All Their Lives
Texas Heat
Texas Rich
Texas Fury
Texas Sunrise

Anthologies
When the Snow Falls
Secret Santa
A Winter Wonderland
I'll Be Home for Christmas
Making Spirits Bright
Holiday Magic
Snow Angels
Silver Bells
Comfort and Joy
Sugar and Spice
Let It Snow
A Gift of Joy
Five Golden Rings
Deck the Halls
Jingle All the Way

Published by Kensington Publishing Corporation

FERN MICHAELS

The Blossom Sisters

ZEBRA BOOKS
KENSINGTON PUBLISHING CORP.
http://www.kensingtonbooks.com

ZEBRA BOOKS are published by

Kensington Publishing Corp.
119 West 40th Street
New York, NY 10018

Copyright © 2013 by MRK Productions
Fern Michaels is a registered trademark of KAP 5, Inc.

All Kensington titles, imprints and distribute... ..
at special quantity discounts for bulk purchases for are available
tion, premiums, fund-raising, educational or institutional use.

Special book excerpts or customized printings can also be created to fit specific needs. For details, write or phone the office of
the Kensington Sales Manager: Attn. Sales Department. Kensington Publishing Corp., 119 West 40th Street, New York, NY,
10018. Phone: 1-800-221-2647.

Zebra and the Z logo Reg. U.S. Pat. & TM Off.

First Kensington Books Hardcover Printing: May 2013
First Zebra Books Mass-Market Paperback Printing: May 2016
ISBN-13: 978-1-4201-0367-0
ISBN-10: 1-4201-0367-9

10 9 8 7 6 5 4 3 2 1

Printed in the United States of America

Chapter 1

GUS HOLLISTER COULDN'T REMEMBER WHEN he'd been so tired as he closed and locked the doors of his CPA firm. Well, yes, actually he could remember. It was last year at exactly the same time, April 16, the last day of that year's tax season. Not that it was totally over; he still had tons of stuff to do, extensions to file, but he'd made his deadline, all clients had their records, and he was going home. If only it were to a home-cooked meal and several glasses of good wine. Like that was really going to happen. But he was simply too tired to care whether he ate or not.

Instead of taking the elevator, Gus trudged down the three flights of stairs and out to the small parking lot. Exercise these days was wherever he could find it. He winced at the lemon yellow Volkswagen Beetle that was his transportation for the day. His wife had taken his Porsche, and he was stuck with this tin can. If only he were a contortionist, which he wasn't. Gus clicked the remote and opened the door. After tossing his heavy briefcase on the passenger-side seat, he struggled to get his six-foot-four-inch frame into the small car. He hated this car. Really hated it. He inserted the key in the ignition, then lowered the windows and stared out at the dark night, an anxiousness, which had nothing to do with taxes and the long days and nights he'd been putting in, settling between his shoulders.

For some reason, he didn't think it would be so dark. Regardless, it wasn't supposed to be dark at eight-thirty at night, was it? But he couldn't bring himself to care about that, either.

He was almost too tired to turn the key in the ignition, so he just sat for a moment, looking out across the small parking lot to the building his grandmother had helped him buy. A really good investment, she'd said, and she was right. He rented out the two top floors to other businessmen, and the rent money he received covered the mortgage and gave him a few hundred dollars toward his cash flow every month. He owed everything he had in life to his feisty grandmother Rose. Everything. And they were estranged at this point in time because of his wife, Elaine. He wanted to cry at the turn his life had taken in the last year. He banged the steering wheel just to vent before he started the Beetle, put it in gear, and roared out of the parking lot at forty miles an hour.

Fifteen minutes later, Gus untangled himself from the Beetle, a feat requiring extraordinary concentration and agility. Then he danced around, trying to work the kinks out of his body. The Beetle belonged to his wife. *She* looked good in it. *He* looked stupid and out of place sitting behind the wheel.

Today, Elaine had been out job hunting, and she wanted to make an impression, so she'd asked him if she could borrow his Porsche. Every bone and nerve in his body had screamed out *no, no, no,* but in the end, he had handed her the keys. It was just too hard to say no to Elaine, because he loved her so much. Especially when she kissed him so hard he was sure she'd suck the tonsils right out of his throat. When that happened, he could deny her nothing, not even his beloved Porsche.

Elaine had passed the bar exam six months earlier and was looking for gainful employment. *Or so she said.* For six months now, she been looking for a job. Citing the econo she'd told him that all the law firms w were slaves, not a qualified lawyer wh graduated at the top of her class. Tha reason she hadn't been hired. *Or s* She hadn't even been called back f interview by any of the firms. *Or s*

Sometimes he doubted her and instantly hated himself for his uncharitable thoughts, thoughts that had been coming more and more frequently of late. His gut was telling him that something was wrong; he just couldn't put his finger on what that something was.

Gus reached across the seat for his briefcase, then closed and locked the Beetle. *God, I'm tired.* No one in the whole world could or would be happier than he when today, April 16, turned into tomorrow, April 17. He was a CPA, a damned good one if he did say so himself, and he had been working round the clock since January 1 to meet his clients' needs. He'd made a lot of them happy and a few of them sad when he pointed to the bottom line that said, *refund* or *pay this amount!*

Gus walked across the driveway, wondering where Elaine was. It was eight forty-five, and she wasn't home. The jittery feeling between his shoulder blades kicked in again when he saw no sign of his car. He frowned as he walked toward the back entrance of his house, the house his grandmother had bought for him. It was a beautiful four-thousand-square-foot Tudor. He ‌ivered when he thought about what she would when she found out he'd added Elaine's ‌ to the deed in one of those tonsil-kissing ‌nts. For months, he'd been trying to find ‌rage—no, the guts—to tell his grand‌ ‍hat he'd done. He knew she'd go bal‌ ‍uld his two aunts. None of them liked Elaine. No, that wasn't right, either. They *hated* Elaine; they could not stand her. And Elaine hated them right back.

Elaine said his grandmother and the aunts were jealous of her because she was young and beautiful and had stolen his love away from them. He'd never quite been able to wrap his mind around that, but back then, if Elaine said it, he tended to believe it. With very few reservations. His grandmother and the aunts had been a little more blunt and succinct, saying straight out that Elaine was a gold digger. End of discussion.

The strain between him and his beloved zany grandmother and dippy aunts bothered him. He had hated having to meet them on the sly, then keeping the meeting secret so he wouldn't have to fight with Elaine and suffer through weeks of tortured silence with no tonsil kissing and absolutely no sex. Elaine held a grudge like no one he knew.

He owed everything to his grandmother. She'd raised him, sent him to college, financed his own CPA firm, then helped him again by buying him the beautiful house that he now lived in. With Elaine. And no prenup.

His grandmother had never once asked him even to consider paying her back, even when he'd tried.

He loved her, he really did, and he hated the situation he was in. Tomorrow or the day after, regardless of how it turned out, he was going to have a come-to-Jesus meeting with wife and lay down some new rules. Family was family, and it was time that Elaine realized that.

Gus opened the gate to the yard, and Wilson came running to him. Wilson was the one thing he'd put his foot down on. Elaine said dogs made her itch and sneeze. Well, too bad; Wilson was his dog, and that was that.

"What are you doing out here, boy?" Gus tussled with the German shepherd a moment before walking up the steps to the deck, which was located off the kitchen. The low-wattage back light was on. He didn't need Wilson's shrill barking to alert him to the pile of suitcases and duffel bags sitting outside the kitchen door. *His* suitcases. Six of them. And two duffel bags. All lined up like soldiers. Next to the suitcases was a pink laundry basket with Wilson's blanket and toys. He knew even before he put the key in the lock that the door wouldn't open.

"Son of a bitch!" He looked at the hundred-pound dog, who was barking his head off and dancing around the pink laundry basket. The jittery feeling between his shoulder blades had grown into a full-blown, mind-bending pain.

The words *gold digger* flitted through Gus's mind as he tried to peer in through the kitchen window. The only thing he could see was the faint greenish light coming from the digital clock on the microwave oven. So much for that glass of wine, never mind a home-cooked meal.

"You shoulda called me, Wilson," Gus snarled at the dog. As though what he said was even pos-ble. The big dog barked angrily, as if to say, *at do you think I'm doing out here?*

"Let's check the front door." Wilson nudged Gus's leg, then slammed himself against the door. The envelope stuck between the door and the jamb fell to the floor of the deck. The dog backed up and sat on his haunches. "Aha!" Gus said dramatically as he ripped at the envelope. He held up a single sheet of computer paper toward the light.

> Gus,
> I'm sorry, but this just isn't working for me. I don't want to be married anymore. I'm going to file for divorce. I packed all your things, and they're on the deck, along with your dog. As you can see, I had the locks changed. I don't want to see you anymore, so don't come here, or I will file a restraining order against you. I'm keeping the Porsche to show you I mean business.

The signature was a scrawled large *E*.

"Son of a bitch!" Wilson howled at the tone of his master's voice. "And she's keeping my car! My pride and joy! Next to you, that is, Wilson," he added hastily. "How the hell am I supposed to take all my stuff in that tin can she calls a car? I damned well do not believe this!"

Wilson's shrill barking told Gus that he had damned well better believe it.

Gus sat down on the top step and put his arm around the big dog. His wife didn't want to be married to him anymore. But she wanted his house and his car. *Gold digger!* So, his grandmother and the aunts had been right all al

His thoughts were all over the map as he tried to figure out exactly how and when it had all gone wrong. There must have been signs. Signs that he'd ignored. How far back? The start of tax season? Before? October, maybe?

Elaine had been looking for a job for over six months, so that would take it back to October. What happened at that time? He racked his brain. Elaine had wanted to go on a cruise, but he'd been too busy to go. She'd pouted for two whole weeks and only gave up when he bought her a diamond bracelet. November was a disaster, and they'd eaten out at Thanksgiving because all Elaine knew how to cook was eggs and pasta. He'd wanted to go to his grandmother's, but she had refused, so he hadn't gone, either. A real man would have gone.

Then came Christmas. Elaine said Christmas trees made her sneeze and itch the way Wilson did. So, no Christmas tree. He'd had a hard time with that as he remembered how his grandmother and the aunts went all out for the holidays. Elaine had gladly accepted presents, however. Lots and lots of presents, was what she'd said. And jerk that he was, he had complied.

He had mentally kicked himself and lost weeks of sleep because he'd kowtowed to his wife and not gone to see his grandmother and the aunts for Christmas. Now, right this moment, he felt lower than a snake's belly. If possible, he'd felt worse on Christmas Day. Here was, nearly four months later, and he still n't so much as spoken to his grandmother or his aunts. He really did have a lock on stupidity. His shoulders heaved. Wilson was on top of him in a heartbeat. Man's best friend. Damned straight. Right now, his only best friend.

"I'm thinking I need a lawyer, Wilson," Gus said, getting up from the steps. He swiped at his eyes. "Real men don't cry. Bullshit!" he said, swiping at his eyes a second time. Wilson howled his misery as he waited to see what Gus would do.

"Okay, my tail is between my legs, so the only game plan I can see at this point is to pack you up in that tin can, take you to my grandmother's, and beg her to let us stay there until I can get my head on straight. If I'm lucky, maybe she'll lend me that farm van of hers so I can come back to get our stuff. Let's go, boy!"

Wilson ran down the steps and over to the yellow Beetle. He scratched at the door, leaving long gashes in the glossy paint. "Chew the damned tires while you're at it, Wilson!" Gus said as he opened the door. Wilson leaped in and tried to settle himself on the passenger seat, but his legs hung off the seat and actually touched the floor. He barked and howled in outrage.

"It's just for five miles, so relax. We'll be there before you know it."

Wilson threw his head back and let loose with an unholy bark that made the fine hairs on the back of Gus's neck stand on end.

Gus clenched his teeth. "Yeah, you're right, Wilson. We're going to be damned lucky if my grandmother doesn't kick our asses to the curb, and I wouldn't blame her one bit. I've been a real shit. She really pulled the wool over my eyes, Wilson. Meaning Elaine, of course, not my grandmother. I'm even worse than a shit!"

Wilson whimpered.

Ten minutes later, they were at the turnoff to Blossom Farm, which his grandmother had renamed after his grandfather, Brad Hollister, had died, and her sisters, Iris and Violet, had come to live with her. For the sake of simplicity, his grandmother had also taken back her maiden name, Blossom.

"Okay, get ready, Wilson, we're coming to the driveway. Look, this is serious, so pay attention. If it looks like Granny is going to kick my ass off her property, you have to step in and whine. However she feels about me, she loves *you.* You know what to do, so just do it!"

Wilson whined to show he understood his master's words as he tried to untangle himself from the seat. The moment the car stopped, he was pawing the door to get out.

Inside the old farmhouse, the three residents were gaping out the window. "Rose! It's either that gold digger or Gus! What are they doing here at this time of night? Oh, my God, lock the doors! Is the door locked? Of course it's locked, we always keep the door locked," Violet, Rose's sister, squealed.

"We need to hide," Iris, the third sister, said. "Rose, you can't let him in, even if he is your grandson! We can't let him find out what we're doing."

Rose Blossom peered out into the darkness. It was indeed her grandson and his dog coming up to the front porch. In full panic mode, she crouched next to her two sisters under the front bay window. "He knows we're in here. Something must be wrong," she hissed.

"Who cares?" Violet hissed in return. "If you let him in, we go up in smoke. Is that what you want?"

"Good God, no! We could go out on the porch. I'll just tell him . . . *something* will come to me," Rose dithered.

"No, something will not come to you, Rose. I say we just hunker down and wait him out. Unless, in one of your stupid moments, you gave Gus a key. Did you, Rose?" Violet snarled.

"He's always had a key, you know that. I don't see him using it. We are, after all, estranged," Rose reminded her sisters. "Anyway, the key won't work because we have a deadbolt inside. All he can do is bang on the door. Let's just stay put and see what he does."

"Why is he driving *her* car?" Iris hissed.

"Maybe *she's* dead," Violet whispered.

"You wish. Highly unlikely, or we would have seen the obituary," Rose said.

Violet clapped her hands over her ears when she heard the first bang on the front door. Her sisters did the same. Outside, Wilson howled and barked, the sound loud and shrill enough to set the sisters' teeth on edge.

"My legs are cramping," Iris grumbled.

"Mine, too," Violet added.

"I know you're in there, Granny, so open the

door. Wilson needs a drink. I'm sorry! I really am. Please, open the door!"

Winifred, the sisters' basset hound, took that moment to waddle up to the door. She barked, a charming ladylike sound that pretty much said, *Welcome.*

"Damned dog! Now for sure he knows we're in here," Violet hissed. "I really have to get up *now,* or I'm going to faint."

"If you're going to faint, do it quietly," Rose shot back.

More banging and more apologies ensued. The sisters turned a deaf ear.

Winifred turned and started to waddle toward the kitchen. "Oh, my God, he's going to the back door. All he has to do is smash the glass, and he can open the door," Iris said, momentarily forgetting all about the cramps in her legs.

"Gus wouldn't do that," Rose said. But her tone of voice indicated that she wasn't sure if what she had said was true or not.

"He's not going to give up," Violet said. "That has to mean the reason he's here at this hour is important, at least to him. Maybe you should just open the door and talk to him through the screen. Tell him you were just getting ready for bed or something. You and he *are* estranged, Rose. I don't think Gus is here just to make nice. Just open the door and tell him to make an appointment to see you. That way we can, you know, just let him see what we want him to see."

"That sounds like a plan. For God's sake, do it, Rose," Iris said.

"Do I have a choice?"

"No, not really," her sisters said in unison.

Rose heaved a mighty sigh as she made her way through the dark house to the kitchen, her sisters following behind. She didn't even bother to turn on the light when she opened the door. She tried to make her voice as cold and unfriendly as she could when she said, "Please stop banging on my door, Augustus Hollister. Why are you here? What do you want?"

"I need to talk to you, Granny. It's important."

"Well then, young man, I suggest you make an appointment," Violet, the bossiest of the sisters, said coolly. "In case you hadn't noticed, we've retired for the evening."

"It's not *that* late. You guys are night owls. Look, I need to talk to you; it's important. If it weren't, I wouldn't be here, especially in that yellow sardine can that masquerades as a car." The desperation in Gus's voice was getting to the sisters, but they held their ground.

"Tomorrow afternoon around five-fifteen will work for us. I hesitate to remind you, but you do have a wife. Shouldn't you be discussing *your* important business with *her?*" Rose asked defiantly.

"That's why I'm here. She kicked me out, stole my car, and is threatening to get a restraining order against me. I need to borrow your van to bring my luggage here. Elaine packed it up and left it on the deck. She changed the locks on all the doors and said she'd call the police if I went back. Elaine does not want to be married to me any longer. So I need to stay with you until I can find a place of my own."

"You *have* a place of your own! I know because I bought it for you and put your name on the deed. So *now* we're good enough for you! What's wrong with this picture, Augustus? You cannot stay here with us; stay at your office if you have to." Rose reached behind her for the keys to the van, which were hanging on a hook. She opened the screen door a crack and dropped the keys on the stoop. "Be sure to bring it back in one piece." Her tone was troubled but not unkind.

"Will you at least let Wilson stay here with you?" Gus pleaded, his voice cracking with emotion.

The sisters looked at one another. Iris and Violet shrugged, which meant, okay, open the door and let Wilson in. Rose opened the door, and Wilson bounded into the kitchen. Rose closed and locked the door, then turned to face her sisters.

"Girls, that was so cruel, what I just did. Gus is my grandson."

"Need I remind you that he is the grandson who turned on you after all you did for him and chose that gold digger over you?" Iris said.

"He's young, and he was in love. We all make mistakes at some point in our lives. Gus just made his mistake earlier than most people," Rose insisted as she tried to defend her grandson.

"Give it up, Rosie," Violet said, wrapping her distraught sister in her arms. "Let's get Wilson settled and have some cheesecake. We need to talk this over and come up with a plan where Gus is concerned."

"We can't let him in the house, that's the bottom line," Iris said. "Not tonight, not tomorrow, not anytime soon. If we do, it's all over."

"We know all that, so will you please stop reminding us?" Violet grumbled.

Chapter 2

GUS HOLLISTER LITERALLY TOOK THE TURN into the driveway of the house he had shared with his wife on two wheels. *Wife? Ha!* His grandmother and the two aunts were absolutely right, and he was totally wrong. Gold digger was Elaine's new name. It had probably been her name all along, and he had just been too stupid to see it. God, how had this happened? When he'd gotten up this morning to leave for work, Elaine had kissed him with such passion. What a sap he was.

"Well, baby, my eyes are open now, you . . . gold digger!" he snarled as he ran around to the back deck and started to haul his six suitcases down the steps, across the yard, and over to the van. Damn, who knew he had so much stuff? Four trips later, carrying the last duffel bag and dragging Wilson's pink laundry basket, Gus stopped to catch his breath. Sweat dripped from every pore in his body. Talk about being out of shape. He took a moment to wonder if he was going to have a heart attack. If that happened, the gold digger would get all his insurance money. Screw that! First thing tomorrow, he was going to change his will and the beneficiaries on his insurance. He'd leave everything to Wilson. "Bitch!" he seethed.

How did undying love go to deep hatred in sixteen hours? He needed to read up on the rules of gold digging.

Gus settled himself behind the wheel of the rickety van. *Rickety my ass,* Gus thought when he turned the key in the ignition. The engine purred like a kitten. He frowned when he realized it sounded better than the engine on his beloved Porsche.

Gus sat for a moment, the soft purr of the engine almost lulling him to sleep. He reached across the seat, but Wilson wasn't there. He wanted to cry at what was happening to him. All in the name of love.

The roads are quiet tonight, Gus thought as he steered the cumbersome van down the highway. As if by rote, he finally took the turnoff that led to his office. The thought of lugging his suitcases and the duffel bags up the steps to his office almost made him turn around and leave. *Damn, I am tired.*

An hour later, all his belongings were stacked up in his office. Wilson's laundry basket remained in the van, to be dropped off at his grandmother's house. It would have to wait until morning. That's when it hit him like a bolt of thunder. He hadn't done his own taxes!

Shit! Shit! Shit!

Gus fired up his computer, tapped furiously, and hit the PRINT button. He filed for an extension. And his gold-digging wife could just file her own damned taxes. No more joint anything where she was concerned.

Gus turned off the computer, ripped off his suit jacket, wadded it into a ball, and lay down on the floor. He was asleep in a nanosecond.

It was dark out when Gus rolled over and groaned. He was disoriented, and then he remembered where he was. He groaned again as he struggled to get up. He peered down at his watch: five-ten. His only option under the circumstances was to head for the Hampton Inn and rent a room. Every muscle in his body screamed as he opened his suitcases and pulled out casual clothes, clothes that were wrinkled and messy. He jammed the clothes and his toiletries into a duffel and left the building. He'd given all his employees the rest of the week off in appreciation of all their hard work during tax season, so he had no worries about his staff seeing the disarray in his office.

As he was making his way down the stairs, Gus made a mental note to call a locksmith to change all the locks on the office building. It was going to be a pain in the butt, but there was no way he wanted his gold-digging wife to have access to the building.

Since it was just the beginning of the early morning rush-hour traffic, Gus made good time to the Hampton Inn. The drive over, registering, and trekking to his room took all of twenty minutes before he was headed for the shower in his new home away from home. He used up another twenty minutes showering, shaving, and dressing before he headed downstairs to order breakfast. He was starving, which surprised him. *How can I eat like this with a broken heart?* He amazed himself at how he wolfed down three eggs, two rashers of bacon, six pancakes, and a dish of fresh fruit. By the time he ordered his second cup of coffee, he felt almost normal.

Gus's thoughts were all over the map as he sipped at his coffee. He had shifted mental gears so many times, he was forced to pull a pen out of his jacket pocket along with the little notebook he always carried. More often than not, he never scribbled anything in the little spiral book. But, for some reason, it was comforting to carry it. Within minutes, he had a long list of things he had to do. He scribbled the word *IMMEDIATE* in capital letters. First, though, he had to go out to the farm and drop off Wilson's gear. Then he had to sit down and have a talk with his grandmother and the two aunts. He felt a lump the size of a lemon lodge itself in his throat. He had to make things right with the three of them, no matter what.

Gus called himself every name in the book as he contemplated his list. He loved those old gals more than life itself. Then he turned on himself, and he was back to square one. If they refused to listen to him, to forgive him, he didn't know what he would do. Dig a hole, crawl in, and wait for his gold-digging wife to toss in the dirt? "Well, that's not going to happen," he muttered to himself as he signed the bill the waitress set in front of him.

It was seven minutes past seven when Gus exited the Hampton Inn and crossed the parking lot to where he had parked his grandmother's van. He climbed in and headed out to the farm.

The Blossom sisters, Rose and the twins— Violet and Iris—stood in the kitchen eating cooked oatmeal with raisins and brown sugar and real cream. The dogs sat at their feet as the women ate, mumbling and muttering among themselves.

Rose, the oldest—Gus's grandmother—waved her spoon in the air. "Augustus will be here shortly, I guarantee it." She reached for a strip of crisp bacon and broke it into two pieces. She handed one piece to each of the dogs.

Violet, two minutes older than her twin, Iris,

said, "We agreed that we weren't going to let him in. Please tell me you aren't having second thoughts, Rose."

"You aren't, are you, Rose?" Iris hissed.

"No, I am not having second thoughts, but I don't see why he can't at least come into the kitchen. We do need to talk to him; at least, I do. If we don't talk to him, he's going to keep coming around until we do. Do you all want to live in fear of that happening? We won't get anything done. Who knows what he'll *see*."

"Rose has a point," Violet said. Violet liked to think that she was the voice of reason among the three of them. "I say we allow him into the kitchen, tell it like it is, and send him on his way."

The pessimistic one of the threesome, Iris, looked at her twin and said, "And you think Augustus is going to settle for that? He *needs* us now. No, that's not right, he *wants* us, now that his gold-digger wife put the screws to him. Just remember how we all felt at Thanksgiving and Christmas last year. You play, you pay," she said heartlessly.

"Well, that's not very Christian, Iris," Rose said.

"Do I have to remind you that you were inconsolable during those two holidays?" Iris asked in the same heartless tone.

Rose sighed. Her plump body started to tremble as she remembered how distraught she'd been without even a phone call or a card from her grandson during the holidays. "All right, all right! I am hearing you loud and clear. Let's just finish our breakfast and get on with the day."

Violet wasn't about to let up on her sister, knowing sooner or later she'd waffle one way or the other. "Easy for you to say. Do I need to remind you that your grandson has our van? We need the van, Rose. Read my lips. We-need-the-van! Henry will be here at eight-thirty to take the first load to the post office. He does not like to wait, as we all know."

Iris slammed her fist on the table. Both dogs reared up at the sound. "The girls will be coming to work at nine o'clock. Lulu took the golf cart with her when they left yesterday. What are we going to say if Augustus is here when they arrive?"

"Just say we're having an old-lady bingo day," Rose huffed as she dumped the rest of her oatmeal down the garbage disposal.

Wilson raced to the kitchen door, Winnie hot on his heels. Both dogs barked.

"I think your grandson has arrived." Violet sniffed as she, too, disposed of her uneaten cereal at the sink. Unlike her sisters, Iris finished her cereal before proceeding to load the dishwasher. "Shall I make another pot of coffee?"

"Don't bother, Iris. Augustus won't be here long enough to drink it," Violet said. "Right, big sister?"

Rose wanted to cry, but she bit down on her lower lip. "Let's just hear him out. Then we'll send him on his way. We don't want to have any regrets later on, do we?"

Gus knocked on the kitchen door. Rose

opened it. She had to fight with herself not to reach out to hug her grandson. "Come in, Augustus. We have fifteen minutes to talk, then we're expecting some friends. Please be quick."

Gus stepped into the old familiar kitchen. He noticed that it had been upgraded at some point. He should have known that, but he didn't. Everything was bright and cheery, with spanking-new, state-of-the-art appliances. He marveled at the built-in coffee machine.

"Coffee?"

"No, we don't drink coffee; we drink herbal tea. It's supposed to be good for old people's digestion. With lemon," Violet said, frost dripping off her words.

"Okay, I'll take that," Gus said, sitting down at the table.

"We're fresh out. Today is grocery-shopping day," Iris said.

Gus shrugged. He could see the three of them weren't going to give an inch. "I brought the van back. Here are the keys. Thanks for the loan," Gus said, sliding the keys across the table to where his grandmother was sitting. "The van sure runs nice."

"We had it tuned up recently," Rose said flatly.

Gus stared at the unfriendly faces of the three sisters glaring at him. Once, those same faces had been full of love. For him. Once. He cleared his throat and folded his hands. "I . . . I want to tell you that I love you all. My love has never wavered. I got derailed and . . . and I'm sorry. I don't expect you to believe me, but I had this plan that I was going to make our situation better this week, regardless of what Elaine said. I just needed to get through yesterday. I know I hurt you, but that was never my intention. I was so . . . so blinded, I just couldn't see straight. Elaine became my world, twenty-four/ seven. She was my siren, and, unlike Odysseus, I didn't have any protection against hearing her song.

"I can't unring the bell. I would if I could, you know that. If you want me to get down on my knees, I will. All I can say is I'm sorry. And, I have a confession to make as well, and when I do, I know full well that you are going to boot my ass out of here. But I'm going to tell you anyway."

"Then maybe you shouldn't tell us. Maybe you should just leave before we do boot your ass out of here," Violet snapped.

Before anyone could say anything else, Gus blurted out that he'd put Elaine's name on the deed to his house.

The three women rose from the table as one and leaned across until their faces were inches from Gus's.

"You did *WHAT*?" the sisters said in unison.

"She . . . she had this . . . this way of kissing me that . . . it was like I had no will of my own. I just did it."

"This is just too pitiful to listen to," Iris said. "I cannot believe you turned into such a *wuss*. I can't deal with stupid; I'm leaving."

"I don't expect you to understand; you're old," Gus said.

The Blossom sisters were on him then like fleas on a dog, pummeling Gus as they attempted to yank him from his chair and push him to the door. All three of them were screeching at the top of their lungs about being old, working their fingers to the bone so he could have a good life, and how they knew what sex was all about because they'd had some of the best sex in the universe during their earlier years. It was Rose's voice that drowned out everyone else's. "And you gave it away to that . . . *that person!* Shame on you, Augustus Hollister! Now leave my house!"

"I will not leave this house until . . . until . . . Okay, I'm going." Tears burning his eyes, Gus got up from the table and headed for the kitchen door. He turned around and said, "Will you at least keep Wilson until I can find a place that will accept dogs?" His eyes were wet and burning so badly, he could barely see.

"Yes," Rose said. "Did you bring his things?"

"I did. I put them by the back door. I'll get them. Granny, I'm sorry, really sorry. I don't know what else to say. If you need me for anything, you can reach me at the office or call me on my cell phone. If you still have the number."

"Don't you have that all a little backward, nephew?" Iris said. "Why would *we* need you? You're here. That means, as usual, you need us. Does it look to you like we need you? Not from where I'm standing, it doesn't. Do we need him, girls? Tell us, what's wrong with this picture?"

Gus struggled to find his voice. Why in the

damned hell had he thought his family would welcome him with open arms and make his world right side up again? Why? Because they had always done it before. They were his cushion, his buffer, his safety net. In a million years, he never thought they would turn their backs on him. The realization that they had just kicked him to the curb hit home like a freight train running over him at a hundred miles an hour.

Gus opened the door and picked up the pink laundry basket. He set it inside on the floor near the door. He waited a moment to see if Wilson would attack the basket. He didn't. The shepherd stayed where he was, with Winnie, on the little rag carpet by the sink. That hurt almost as much as his aunts' and grandmother's unbending attitude. "See ya," he said in a strangled voice as he closed the door.

Rose sat down at the table and buried her face in her arms. The twins rushed to console her. Their voices were soothing as they tried to ease their sister's anguish. "We have options, Rose, if we want to pursue them," Iris whispered.

"No, we don't have options, Iris. It would take us *months* to relocate. It simply is not feasible. Actually, it's impossible. We have a system that works. Remember the last time we deviated, and what happened," Violet said. "It took us almost a year to recover. I, for one, don't want to go through that again, and I'm sure Rose doesn't, either. I suppose it's possible to make some adjustments, but, at this time, I don't see how we can even do that. There are too many people who count on us and are involved now. Rose, look alive here. We need to talk seriously now."

Rose lifted her tear-stained face to stare at her sisters. "Did you see his face? It just about broke my heart. He's just a boy."

"He's not a boy, Rose. Augustus is thirty-two years old. He's a married man. He has to take responsibility for his actions. My conscience is certainly clear. We gave that young man a good life, we raised him properly, we sent him to the best schools, we were there for him every step of the way. We helped him start his own business. You bought and paid for that fancy house he is now going to lose to that gold digger. We did not do anything wrong, so get over whatever guilt you're feeling," Violet said, as she continued to rant.

"Maybe we could help him without his knowing we're doing it," Rose said.

"Get that idea right out of your head this very minute, Rose. We are going to go on with our lives, more alert than we've been, and we'll let this play out however it's meant to play out," Iris said softly.

"I don't want to rain on anyone's parade here, but have either one of you given a thought to *the wife*? What if she files for divorce, which I'm sure is her intent, and her lawyer starts asking questions on her behalf? She'll hire a real sleazebag, we all know that. I'm thinking ahead here. We might need to hire some security or shore up this place. Maybe build a security fence, hire someone with guard dogs to patrol at night, things like that. Before you know it, some smart-ass lawyer will be wanting to take our depositions, then they'll want to see our tax returns. Try explaining those to anyone, Rose," Violet said.

"Oh, for God's sake, Violet, will you give it up already? That's not going to happen."

"It could happen," Iris said. "I saw that same scenario on television last week. We need to move our money offshore. Liechtenstein is where they sent their money on the TV show."

"Stop it right now!" Rose shouted so loud, Wilson barked to show his displeasure. "We are not moving our money to Liechtenstein or anyplace else. Because, we do not know how to do that. We can, however, take it all out of the bank and the brokerage house and bury it in the root cellar if you want."

"That's stupid!" Violet said.

"So is Liechtenstein!" Rose snapped back.

"I hear Henry," Iris said, and ran to the door. Everyone knew that Iris was sweet on Henry. Everyone except Henry, that is.

Chapter 3

GUS HOLLISTER ACCEPTED THE BOX OF NEW keys for his office building from the locksmith. He promised to call if anything went awry. With the rest of his mental to-do list taken care of, he was about to head out of the office. He had no idea where he was going to go or what he was going to do. He slapped at his forehead. He needed to change the code to the security system on the off chance he might have mentioned it to Elaine at some point. No sense in taking chances at this stage of the game. When he was leaving the building, he would turn over the new keys and the new code to his two tenants. Thank God the doors were self-locking.

His last chore taken care of, Gus turned off the lights, took one last look around, and was about to close the door when the office phone rang. He walked back to the reception area and looked at the caller ID. His fist shot high in the air. Barney! His best friend in the whole wide world. Best friend since the age of four, when they had met in a sandbox at the park. Good old Barney. He blasted out a loud hello and waited.

"Hey! How's it going, buddy?"

Instead of answering the question, Gus let loose with a volley of his own. "Where are you? When did you get back? How long are you staying? Can you meet me someplace, Barney? I'm just leaving the office now. I really need to talk to you. The long and short of things . . . never mind, I'll tell you when I see you. Can you make Gilligan's in, say, fifteen minutes? I'll wait for you, all day if necessary."

"That bad, huh?"

"Yeah, that bad, Barney."

"Make it forty-five minutes, and I'm all yours."

Gus stood for a few minutes, staring at the phone console after he disconnected the call. His world was suddenly looking a tad brighter, with Barney back in the picture. Barney, he was sure, would have some words of wisdom for him.

Best friends since the sandbox days, they'd gone through school together. Barney was the nerd, and Gus was the jock. He'd lost count of the jerks he'd popped for tormenting his best friend. They'd gone to the same college, graduated, and gone on to get their master's degrees together, after which Barney took off in the financial world and set it on fire. At age thirty-two, Barney was the youngest hedge-fund manager on Wall Street, and he was worth billions. Not to mention, he had a sterling reputation. No shortcuts for him.

Outside, in the April morning sunshine, Gus looked around. To the east, he saw a bank of dark clouds heading his way. What was it his granny always said? April showers bring May flowers. Yeah, that was it.

His shoulders slumped at the mere thought of his grandmother. Barney was going to have a fit when he found out that Granny Rose wanted nothing to do with Gus. Barney loved Gus's grandmother and dippy aunts as much as Gus did.

Gus went through his contortionist routine as he struggled to get into the Beetle. Barney was going to laugh his ass off when he saw the Bug. Gus winced in pain. Then again, Barney could be diplomatic at times. He might not say a word. *Yeah, right.*

Gus peeled out of the parking lot—as much as a Beetle could peel—and headed for the main drag of Sycamore Springs, Virginia. Population: eighty thousand. He loved this town. He'd grown up here. Knew every store, every nook and cranny of the town. He knew all the shortcuts, as did Barney, because they'd ridden their bikes all over when they were kids.

He was partial, as was Barney, to the old section of town, where the drugstore still had a soda fountain, where the hardware store still set out its wares on nice days, where you could still get penny candy at the Emporium, only it was a nickel now.

Then there was Eva's Café, with her home-made everything. The candy shop, the hat shop, and, of course, the filling station that served lunch to anyone in a hurry. All the shops, he still patronized, as did his grandmother and the aunts.

The new part of town was high tech, with Internet cafés, a Starbucks, it seemed, on every corner, and boutiques. There were trendy eateries and a few high-end bistros for the younger crowd like himself, but he rarely patronized them. Barney didn't frequent them when he was back, either, preferring the comfort of old town. And yet, Barney was as high-tech as they come. Well, that was business. And he was never in town long enough to do much of anything but kick back until it was time to catch a plane to somewhere else. Usually no more than forty-eight hours, barely time to pound a few beers, visit with Granny and the aunts, catch some sleep, and be off again.

Gilligan's was a ramshackle building by design, at least a hundred years old, a family business with the grandkids waiting tables—and doing their homework at the back tables—while aunts and uncles cooked and saw to the customers. Everything was homemade from scratch, all baked goods the envy of every house-wife in Sycamore Springs.

Many a husband had been duped over the years, thinking it was his wife who had baked the delectable pastries she served him while, in truth, they came boxed from Gilligan's, the boxes ground into bits in the trash compactor so as not to give away the housewife's little se-cret.

Gus sighed as he played gymnast again and crawled out of the Beetle. He checked the skies once again. He made a bet with himself that it would be raining in less than an hour. Then the day was going to get even more depressing. He missed Wilson and wondered how the big dog was doing. Probably very well and being spoiled rotten in the bargain. What if his best friend didn't want to come back to him when he finally found a place that would accept an animal? What would he do then? God alone knew the answer. His thoughts turned to his wife, to Elaine, the gold digger. *Where in the hell did I go wrong?*

Gus realized he wasn't going to find answers standing here in Gilligan's parking lot. Better to go inside and wait for Barney.

When Gus opened the door, he was greeted like a favorite customer and called by name. Even the grandkids doing homework called him Mr. Gus. He often took the time to help the kids with their math. He smiled and waved and was ushered to his favorite table in the back.

Gilligan's wasn't a nautical restaurant by any means. It didn't have any kind of theme or specialty other than home-cooked food and a place that generation after generation took pride in running. There were no celebrity pictures on the walls, but there were plaques from Little League baseball and Pop Warner football, along with pictures of the various teams that Gilligan's sponsored. Hanging from the rafters were green plants that the grandkids watered from stepladders when business slowed down. The tables were rough plank but sanded and polished, the scars of years of use evident. The captain's chairs were oversized, with green-and-white cushions. Gus was thirty-two, and as far as he remembered, the cushions had always been green and white. There was a counter with stools, where people who popped in for a homemade cinnamon bun and coffee or a slice of pie sat. The tables were for parties of three or more, or two if the restaurant wasn't busy.

Gus loved the smell of Gilligan's because it reminded him of his grandmother's kitchen when he was growing up. It smelled of cinnamon, vanilla, celery, and a touch of garlic. Today there was spaghetti and meatballs, according to the chalkboard, so that accounted for the scent of garlic. The soft garlic twists were every bit as famous as the spaghetti and meatballs. There were never more than two specials on any given day, and today the second special was chicken potpie. He was going to get the spaghetti and meatballs, and he knew that Barney would opt for the potpie. They'd top it off with a big slice of blackberry pie with homemade vanilla ice cream.

One of the grandkids he'd helped with homework carried a large glass of frosty ice tea and set it down in front of him. Gus ordered a second glass for Barney, who came in just as the tea arrived. Gus got up. Manly hugs were followed by ear-to-ear grins, and they were back to the good old days, at least for a few minutes.

"You look like crap, Gus," Barney said as he settled himself in the chair, which just fit his girth. It was then that Gus realized it had been almost a year, and fifteen pounds, since he had last seen Barney. Make that twenty pounds.

"You look a little heavier, Barney," Gus retaliated.

"You're right about that. I have to go on a diet, and I will. Too much rich food. What's your excuse?"

Gus told him.

Barney blinked, then blinked again. "Now, you see, that's why I never got married and will never get married."

"Get off that bullshit, Barney. The reason you won't get married is you don't like to share, you're selfish and materialistic, and no woman will agree to your prenup."

"That, too," Barney said cheerfully. "You should have listened to me about the prenup. Oh, no. You said you were in love, and it was forever and ever and into eternity. What's it been, a little less than a year?" Barney laughed at his own wit. Gus scowled.

"That's got to hurt that she took your Porsche. I know you loved that car. At least she let you keep the dog; that says a lot." Barney laughed again.

"The only reason she let me keep the dog is that Wilson makes her sneeze and itch. Granny has him. She's going to spoil him rotten, and he won't want to come with me when I finally find a place to light that will take animals. I'm staying at the Hampton Inn right now. Granny won't even talk to me. Well, that's not quite true. At first she talked to me through the screen door; then I was allowed into the kitchen. But she won't let me move in. She has all that room at the farm, but I'm definitely persona non grata right now to my family."

"You don't think that extends to me, do you?" Barney asked anxiously. "I was planning on going out to the farm. I brought Granny and the aunts some presents from Paris and wanted to give them to them."

"Nah, they'll let you in. They love you. It's me they hate," Gus said morosely. "Maybe you can plead my case when you go out there. Give Wilson a hug for me. I'm going to spend the afternoon looking for an apartment I can afford. I have to get a lawyer on board pretty quick. Stop looking at me like that, Barney. I know I screwed up, and I take full responsibility. I sure hope she can't come after my business. I busted my ass to build it up, and I don't want her to have any part of it. Damn, I was stupid. Why didn't you warn me or say something?"

Their food arrived. Gus stared down at his plate and couldn't remember ordering. He shrugged as he shook out his napkin.

"I did try to warn you, and you told me to mind my own business. If you recall, I tripped you as I handed you the ring, and told you not to do it. Did you listen to me? No, you did not. I rest my case; my conscience is clear. Having said that, now is the time for you to be in the bosom of your family, but since that isn't going to happen, what are your plans?"

"I'm just glad tax season is over. My head is above water." As he chewed on the delicious meatballs, Gus explained what he'd done about changing the locks, his will, and the insurance policies.

"None of this is computing for me, Gus. Weren't there signs? Did you see them and just ignore them? Something must have triggered this. Was it the last three and a half months of tax season? Did you ignore her? Women don't like to be ignored."

"I was working eighteen hours a day, so, yeah, I guess I ignored her. She was sleeping when I got home, and when I left at five in the morning, she was still sleeping. One does not ever, as in *ever*, disturb Elaine when she is sleeping.

"But, come to think of it, yesterday, before I left for the office, she kissed me good-bye. I suppose she only got up because I let her have the Porsche for her so-called job hunting. As for the kiss . . . ?"

"So there was no sex in three and a half months?"

"You got that right."

"And you didn't think that was a clue?" Barney gasped.

"I was hoping and dreaming for a spectacular April 17. It was spectacular all right; she booted my ass and my dog out of *my* house. On top of that, she stole my car!"

Barney wanted to laugh, but he somehow managed not to. "Let's get serious here. Tell me what you know about Elaine. Not the marriage part, but before. Who is she? Where did she come from? What's her background? You're going to need a private detective to get the goods on her in order to have a fighting chance. I know a guy, and when I tell you he is good, he is good. We use him all the time. He can find stuff you would never believe could come to light. I can call him for you and bill it to the firm. No sweat there. And you can use one of our lawyers. I know just the one, too. She is hell on wheels. You need a female lawyer, because she'll know how your wife thinks. She's tops. She's on my payroll, just like the detective, so don't worry about that, either. You can stay at my place as long as you want. I'm leaving for Hong Kong tomorrow and will be gone six months. And you can bring Wilson with you. Built-in maid service, gardener, and you can drive one of my cars. I'm serious, Gus. I can't go off and leave you in the mess you're in. We're friends, remember? You'd do it for me, so just say yes, and let's shake on it."

"Barney . . . I . . . Yeah, okay, thanks. I'll pay you back, you know that."

"Hey, who's the guy who loaned me his last three thousand dollars to start up my own business? I never even paid you back because, jerk that you are, you wouldn't take it. Just so you know, Mr. Smart-Ass, I started a fund for you with some of that three grand, and someday I'm going to tell you what you are *really* worth financially. And there's no way that person you were married to can ever get near it. Whatever happens with *that* person, your future is secure, my friend."

Gus's eyes started to burn. All he could do was nod.

The blackberry pie and ice cream arrived, again, without being ordered. Gus ate while Barney sent text messages that went through at the speed of light. He smacked his hands together before he dug his fork into the pie. "They're on it, and you are now officially represented, my friend. Let's finish up here, get all your stuff, and take it out to my house. Then I'm going to go and plead your case with Granny. You okay with that?"

Gus nodded again, not trusting himself to speak. He knew he was in good hands with Barney's people. It still didn't make him feel better.

The bill paid, the two friends left the restaurant. It was starting to drizzle, and the day had turned as gray and gloomy as Gus felt. He looked at the yellow Beetle and groaned.

"I have an idea, Gus. Get in that hunk of junk and drive it to the first fireplug you see and park it. Let the cops tow it and have Miss Elaine fight with the town over it. I think—and this is just a suggestion—but I think you should park it as close to the police station as you can. And, when you get out, wipe off all your finger-prints, just to be on the safe side. It is registered in her name, right?" Gus nodded.

"You won't need it anymore, so that's one less thing on your list to worry about. My de-tectives will find where your car is, and they'll heist it for you. Since the car is in your name, there is nothing she can do about it. Unless you were dumb enough to put that in her name, too. Were you?"

"No, I didn't put her name on it. But I have to be honest with you, I did think about it; the business, too. She was harping on me about that, last fall, but I just didn't get around to it."

Barney laughed as he climbed behind the wheel of a snappy Mercedes-Benz. "I'll follow you, and, Gus, you're in good hands now."

Two hours later, Barney's car was loaded with all of Gus's belongings. After a forty-minute drive, they set about unloading the car at Barney's place. Gus was never sure what to call Barney's digs. Was it an estate? A mini-castle? A palace fit for a king named Barney? Barney said it was just a house to sleep in that happened to have a six-car garage, with a high-end car in each bay. A house that sat on five pristine, manicured acres, which held a tennis court, an Olympic-size swimming pool, a four-bedroom guesthouse, and another building where his live-in housekeeper and gardener resided.

The inside of the palatial house was just as spectacular as the outside, but in a different way. Inside, it was all home and hearth, with comfortable furniture, fireplaces that worked, and a kitchen that would have been any chef's idea of perfection. It was homey, and it smelled like Granny's house. Barney had told Gus once that one of his rules was he always wanted his house to smell like something was cooking or baking, and he had succeeded.

Gus looked over at his pudgy friend—at his owlish glasses, his thinning hair, his kind eyes—and got all choked up. "I don't know what to say, Barney."

"Then don't say anything, okay? You know I hate it when you go all mushy on me. I have an idea. Let's pitch a tent and sleep out tonight. We can make a campfire and roast some wee-nies and marshmallows. We can tell ghost stories, or you can tell me horror stories of your marriage, whatever pleases you. It will be like old times, but now we're legal to drink beer. What do you say?"

"I say let's do it. Barney, did you ever have anyone kiss you until you thought your tonsils were going to pop out?"

"Yep."

"And you didn't marry her?"

"Nope."

"But why?"

"Well, for one thing, I wanted to keep my tonsils. So I won't get sore throats. You get sore throats once your tonsils are removed. For another thing, when a woman kisses me, I want it to be because she loves me and wants me to be the father of her children."

"Ah."

Chapter 4

GUS ROLLED OVER, UNCERTAIN FOR A MOMENT as to where he was, something that it seemed was becoming a habit. He reached out, thinking he was in bed with Elaine, until he felt the stubble on Barney's face. He whooped and sat up, waking Barney.

"What the hell!"

"Bad dream, Barney. Sorry. Damn, it's raining."

"Granny always said April showers bring May flowers," Barney said, sitting up. "I feel like crap. Been awhile since I downed six beers, a bag of marshmallows, and four weenies. Do ya think we're too old for this crap, Gus?"

"Nah! You're never too old for your memories. They just come out different in real life. We never did get around to the ghost stories. That's probably why we feel like shit this morning. We didn't complete the ritual."

"Yeah, well, we aren't ten years old anymore, either," Barney groaned. "Let's pack up the sleeping bags and head on into the house to get cleaned up. Then we can sit down and have a good breakfast. After that, I'm heading out to the farm to see Granny and the aunts. What are you going to do?"

Gus thought about it. What *was* he going to do? "Guess I'll sit around here and wait for you to get back. Bring Wilson with you, okay?"

"Yeah, sure. You should hang out in my office in case the detective or lawyer fax something over. You need to be on top of everything from here on in. Phil Ross is the detective, and Jillian Jackson is the lawyer. Everyone calls her Jill. You're going to like them both. They're both animal lovers, so that's a plus. Unlike Elaine, who does not like animals. Does she like anyone except herself, do you know?" Barney asked as he rolled up his sleeping bag and stuffed it into a sack, then pulled the drawstring. "We don't have to worry about the tent. Tim will take it down, dry it out, and pack it away."

Gus finished with his sleeping bag and waited until Barney pulled down the zipper of the canvas door. The rain was coming down in sheets. They made a run for the house but got drenched in the process.

"We're wet to the skin. You want to stomp in some puddles before we go in? Fling some mud the way we used to?"

Gus grinned as he kicked off his shoes, which were already soaked, and ran like a crazy man around the yard, Barney whooping and hollering right behind him. Twenty minutes later, they rolled in a huge pile of mud beside a flower bed that one day soon would be sprouting with blooms. They were ten years old again, yelling at each other and pelting mud pies in every direction. Finally, exhausted, they lay down on the grass and let the cool rain clean off the mud.

"I needed to do that, Gus. I really did. I think you did, too. Now we have to go back to being the responsible adults everyone thinks we are."

Gus was the first one up on his feet. He reached down for Barney's hand. "I don't know what I would do without you, Barney. I'm sorry if I don't say it often enough, but I love you. I couldn't love and respect you more if you were a blood brother."

"I feel the same way. The only difference is I *have* a brother who isn't worth a good spit. Hell, I don't even want anyone to know he's related to me. C'mon, I'll race you to the house!" Barney bellowed.

Gus grinned as he wondered what Barney's millionaire clients would think of him if they could see him now. They'd probably run for the hills or pull out their hair. The visual was so funny to Gus, he burst out laughing. And Barney wouldn't give a good rat's ass. Anyone worried about their tonsils simply wouldn't care. Gus was still laughing when he stripped off the soaking-wet clothes and stepped into a shower with twenty-one jets to pummel his sore body. For sure, he wasn't ten years old anymore.

Wilson leaped up, hopped over Winnie, and raced to the front door. Company!

"Oh, Lord, who is it this time? Don't tell me Augustus has returned," Rose said as she ran after Wilson and Winnie, who had finally woken up long enough to wonder what the commotion was all about. She let loose with two sharp barks to show she was still in the game.

They came from all corners of the house: Iris and Violet from the packing room, Myrt and Gert, Shady Pines star ambulatory residents bounding down the steps, their aprons flapping in the breeze they created. Henry, another resident of Shady Pines—and their driver—stuck his head out of the doorway to the dining room to see what was going on. Six other residents of Shady Pines hung over the upstairs balcony, peering down into the foyer.

"This can't be good," Violet hissed.

"Augustus is sending in his big gun to plead his case," Iris hissed in return.

"We have to let him in," Rose said. "We don't have any other choice. We'll give him fifteen minutes, that's it." Rose then waved her arm to indicate that all the other spectators should disappear.

Rose waited till the house turned silent before she opened the door. She smiled, but it was more like a grimace. The three sisters greeted Barney warmly and headed for the kitchen. That's when Rose remembered the ledger she had been working on. Well, she'd just close it and hope for the best. Wilson and Winnie continued to bark now that a friend had come to visit, a friend who always had treats and was good for a few belly scratches.

Right off the bat, Barney knew he had interrupted something of major importance. The Blossom sisters were nervous and jittery, and it took them a full five minutes before they offered him coffee. Their expressions clearly showed they hoped he wouldn't take them up on the offer. He didn't.

I should have shoved the ledger in the oven to hide it, but Violet is baking two peach pies, Rose thought. Talk about cooking the books, had she done that. She sucked in her breath and said, "It's so nice to see you, Barney. How long are you staying this time?"

"Actually, I'm leaving early this evening for Hong Kong. I'll be there for six months. I just wanted to drop off these presents. French perfume!" Barney said, holding out the shiny black bag he'd brought with him as though it were the Holy Grail.

"Well, that is just so sweet of you, isn't it, girls? We'll be sure to wear it on Sunday when we go to church. Right, girls?" Iris said as she sniffed the expensive perfume. Rose and Violet nodded.

"My pleasure. It looks like I interrupted something," Barney said, eyeing the ledger on the kitchen table. "I won't keep you if you're busy. I just wanted to pop in and say hello." The relief he saw on the women's faces was almost comical.

Rose shrugged. "Household expenses, that kind of thing. I hate to let things go because then I can't remember to make the entries."

"Gus is a CPA, Granny. Why don't you have him take care of that for you?"

"Because . . . well, we started out with an old friend who does our taxes. We can't just take that away from him because of Augustus. It wouldn't be right."

"And Augustus doesn't need to know our business," Violet snapped. "That young man has loyalty issues," she snapped again.

"Whoa! Whoa! Are we talking about my friend Gus, your grandson, Rose, and your nephew, Violet and Iris?" Barney spread his hands wide to show he wasn't buying whatever it was the Blossom sisters were trying to sell him.

"One and the same," Rose said smartly. "We do thank you for bringing us the perfume. I know how busy you must be, since you said you're leaving this evening. You did say that, didn't you?"

Barney knew he was being dismissed, and he didn't like it at all. *What the hell is going on here?* Suddenly, he felt like he were ten years old again and had just failed his social skills test given by three stern taskmasters. In spite of himself, he shivered, and he didn't like the feeling. Not one little bit.

"We know Gus sent you!" Violet blurted out.

"He did not send me. I came here on my own. I come to visit each time I'm in town, and the three of you know it darned well. Whatever your issue is with Gus, it shouldn't have anything to do with me." Barney waited to see if he'd get a slap upside the head. He was so relieved when it didn't happen, he felt weak. "He does know I'm here and asked me to bring Wilson back with me."

Three sets of eyes stared at Barney. "Ask Wilson if he wants to go with you. If he does, he'll drag his basket to the door. If he doesn't, he's staying here," Rose said coldly.

Barney felt like a fool, but he leaned down and said, "Wilson, Gus wants me to take you to him. Get your basket and let's go."

Wilson showed Barney his teeth before he trotted over to the handmade rag carpet by the stove, where Winnie was watching what was going on. He plopped down, showed his teeth again, then barked.

"Guess that's your answer, Barney. Wilson is smart. He knows he was dumped here by Augustus just the way Augustus dumped us."

Barney threw his hands in the air. "You all need to have a meeting to clear the air. Gus loves you three more than anything in life. Can't you cut him a break? He's miserable."

"Young man, tell that to someone who cares. We-do-not-care! You probably should leave now before the three of us pitch a hissy fit. Thank you for the perfume," Violet said.

Iris reached for Barney's arm and escorted him to the front door.

Barney looked around over his shoulder, and was certain eyes were watching his every move. Many eyes. Too many eyes. Unfriendly eyes. Shit!

At the door, Iris opened it and literally shoved him outside. "Thanks for stopping by, Barney. It might be wise to call for an appointment the next time you feel the need to visit."

Bang! The door slammed shut. Barney heard the deadbolt snap into place. He could hear Wilson and Winnie barking their heads off. *What the hell is going on inside that house?*

If I were a cat, my tail would be between my legs, Barney thought as he pulled up to one of the bays of the garage attached to his house. He pressed the remote, and the door slid upward. Gus was going to be devastated when he saw that Barney didn't have Wilson with him. He'd personally known Wilson since the day Gus got him at the age of six weeks. He considered himself the dog's godfather and had bought him his first collar and leash. Never once had Wilson showed him his teeth. *How am I going to explain this to Gus?*

Gus practically flew out the door as Barney pulled his car into the garage. He whistled for Wilson, who always came at the sound. When nothing happened, Gus felt his shoulders slump. Even his dog had abandoned him.

Barney lowered the garage door. He stood

with his hands on his hips, the rain pelting him for the second time that day. "He showed me his teeth, Gus. He didn't want to come with me. I wasn't about to force him, and those old ladies were in no mood for me today, French perfume or not. I gotta tell you, something is going on out at that farm. And, yeah, you are part of it, but that's not what I'm talking about. Those ladies are up to something. I felt like I was being watched the whole time I was there, and they could not, I repeat, could not, wait for me to leave. They have a hate on for you right now. They said you had no loyalty. I tried to defend you, but they didn't want to hear it. I wouldn't go out there for a while if I were you. Maybe never!" Barney said dramatically as he stomped in a puddle and ruined a second pair of shoes. "C'mon, let's go in and get some fresh coffee. They were baking pies at the farm. Among other things," Barney said through clenched teeth.

"What should I do?" Gus asked as he held the door open for Barney.

"Hope for a miracle, would be my advice. I told you not to marry that gold digger."

"That's what Granny called Elaine. Well, they all did," Gus said as he followed Barney through the house and up the stairs. He, too, had to change his clothes and shoes again.

At the top of the steps, Barney bellowed to Maggie, his housekeeper, to make fresh coffee. Gus hoped she heard from wherever she was, because he was chilled to the bone.

Gus was the first one down to the kitchen.

He marveled at the place setting Maggie had laid out. He knew he could get used to being waited on like this in no time. And he liked the roly-poly little housekeeper with the laughing eyes. He wondered if, in the days to come, he'd ever be able to afford a housekeeper. By the time Elaine got through with him, he'd be lucky to eat at Burger King five days a week and starve the other two days. His eyes burned then when he remembered his grandmother telling him that God never gives you more than you can handle. That was easy to tell a little kid who didn't understand that his parents didn't want him because he was a burden. They'd just dumped him at his grandparents' when he was four years old and took off. He'd never heard from them again. God must have been out to lunch that day, because it was more than he could handle, just like now.

Gus was finishing his first cup of coffee when Barney appeared in the kitchen doorway with a pile of papers in hand. "The first report from Phil Ross. It is not pretty, Gus, so be prepared. There's a fax from Jill, too. She's coming out here later this afternoon. I invited her to dinner on your behalf. More casual that way, and you two can get to know one another.

"I'm going to gulp this coffee and head out. I have meetings right up until it's time to head to the airport, so this has to be good-bye for now. Man, I hate leaving you like this, Gus. I really do. But, the good thing is, I'm leaving you in good hands. That much I do know. I'm just a phone call away, and if you really need me, I can be on the first plane home. I mean it, Gus."

Gus nodded, his eyes on the papers lying on the table. He wondered exactly what was not pretty and what he needed to be prepared for. What could be worse than his wife claiming his house and stealing his car? And being mean to Wilson—that was the biggie for him. He looked up at Barney, waiting to see if his friend had more to say. He did.

"Phil said he is going to drop your Porsche off in the parking lot behind Gilligan's, and you can pick it up later, or he can have someone bring it out here. He had to hot-wire it, but he did get your car back. If I were you, I'd drive one of the cars in my garage and park yours in there, at least for now. Elaine still has a key to it, so if you take it into town, and she spots it, then it's gone again. By the way, Phil also said that her Beetle was taken to the impound lot, and she hasn't picked it up yet."

"Damn! He actually got my Porsche back! That's great. Good idea, too, about me not driving it, as long as you don't mind me driving one of yours."

"What's mine is yours, you know that, Gus. So we're good here, right? At least for now. I can go off knowing you're in good hands and not worry too much."

"I don't know what to say, Barney. I just wish there was something I could do for you to repay you. You have everything. What's a guy like me supposed to do?"

"I'll tell you what you're supposed to do. You

need to find a way to make peace with those old ladies. I don't care if you have to slither on your belly to make it happen, just do it. This whole thing is killing them, Gus. So work on that, and we're square."

The two old friends hugged, both their eyes burning. "See ya when I see ya," Barney said, popping open his umbrella, which was as big as one of those monstrosities one sees at the beach. Gus watched from the kitchen as his best buddy in the whole world approached a large puddle. A very large puddle. He knew before Barney knew that he'd stomp in it. Once a kid, always a kid. He would have done the same thing.

Gus closed the door, poured a third cup of coffee, then sat down at the table to read Phil Ross's report on his wife—soon-to-be ex-wife—Elaine Ramsey Hollister.

The only thing missing was Wilson. God, how he missed the big dog. He felt like crying. He shook his head to clear his thoughts. He knew he had to be alert and in the right frame of mind to read what was written in Phil Ross's report. Knowing it wasn't going to be pretty, according to Barney, before getting started, Gus steeled himself for a very tough read.

Chapter 5

ELAINE RAMSEY HOLLISTER CURLED UP IN THE window seat under the bay window and watched the storm rage outside. She hated storms, but she knew she was safe from the elements. She leaned back and hugged her knees to her chest. Next to her was a notebook and pen. It was one of those black-and-white-marble-covered ones, the kind she'd used back in grade school. She'd found it at one of the dollar stores years ago when she first decided to keep a diary to chronicle her journey to becoming rich. She clearly remembered buying a dozen because they were two for a dollar, and she'd thought that was a real bargain. She was on her last notebook. If she'd written her words smaller, condensed them more, she probably would have several virgin books left, but her childish scrawl was big, and she had felt the need over the years to write *everything* down.

Elaine flinched when a limb snapped off one of the old sycamore trees. It hit the ground with a loud thump. She peered through the driving rain to see how big the branch was. It looked huge, meaning she'd have to call someone to come and take it away. If she tried to do it herself, she'd ruin her French manicure and possibly pull a muscle in her back. She shrugged. Worst-case scenario, her attorney would require Gus to pay for the removal. She moved on in her thoughts.

Elaine picked up the black-and-white notebook and flipped to the back. She only had four blank pages—eight actually, if you counted the fronts and backs. Not nearly enough pages to continue with the intriguing details of her life saga. She panicked then as she bolted upright and swung her legs off the window seat. *Where in this day and age am I going to find these old-fashioned notebooks? They have to be the same as the rest of them.* She really hated to admit how superstitious she was, but, despite her cool and calculating personality, she was easily spooked. And she was really spooked now.

Later, she would go on the hunt for the black-and-white notebooks. Maybe eBay or that Web site she'd found a year ago for a company called Initial B Enterprises would have them. She'd really lucked out that day, and she'd been a loyal customer ever since. She'd purchased the company's voodoo kit, purchased an assortment of spells and black candles. She'd utilized their adult sex course, and she'd had more astrology readings than she could remember. She knew she was the company's best customer because they constantly sent her freebies to make sure she came back to order, which she did.

And Gus never knew a thing about it. She kept all her secret doings in a huge suitcase in the attic, someplace Gus never ventured. He had balked, though, when she insisted he install a pull-down ladder, but when she'd kissed him, he capitulated the way he always did. It made it so much easier to be able to cast her spells in the attic, where she was alone with all the paraphernalia she needed. Rituals were time-consuming, spells even more so, but she had become a pro at them. She could probably teach a course on witchcraft if she wanted to.

The only problem was making a payment to Initial B Enterprises. She didn't want to use a credit card or check, so, because she was such a good customer, the kind folks at Initial B Enterprises had agreed to money orders and the use of a post office box number. She used the household money Gus gave her for food and whatever she needed, to buy the money orders. And, from time to time, she helped herself to the bills in Gus's wallet, always careful not to take too much. For a CPA, Gus was pretty stupid when it came to money. But then, she had him *wrapped*. She corrected her thought: *All* men were stupid about all things. If they weren't, she wouldn't be where she was now. In the cat-bird seat, sitting in a half-million-dollar house that was paid for and would be all hers shortly. Not to mention a high-six-figure bank account in the Caymans. As would half of Gus's business, and half if not all of everything in the Hollister coffers. Even his inheritance down the line, when the old battle-axes finally kicked the bucket.

An evil smile on her face, Elaine made her way to the second floor and pulled down the ladder that would take her to the attic, where she would perform one of the daily rituals guaranteed to make her rich beyond her wildest dreams, all thanks to Initial B Enterprises.

Gus Hollister woke with a raging headache. He knew instantly why his head was pounding like a bongo drum. Phil Ross's report on his wife. And his meeting with Jill Jackson and her less-than-encouraging assessment of his current predicament. Then there were the two bottles of wine he'd consumed.

Gus swung his legs over the side of the bed, appalled that he was still wearing the same clothes and shoes he'd worn yesterday. Damn, he must have really been out of it. He hadn't fallen asleep in his clothes since his college days. He wondered if he was on his way to becoming an alcoholic.

That's when he squinted to look out the

bedroom window. Shit! It was raining, thundering, and lightning like it was the Fourth of July. He squeezed his eyes shut as he tottered toward the bathroom. Maybe a shower would help, followed by aspirin and coffee. Lots and lots of black coffee. Maybe.

His head pounding like the thunder outside, Gus turned on the water and waited for all the showerheads to bombard his body. He felt like he was participating in a paintball exercise. He hopped and danced around the massive shower as his head continued to pound. He had to get out of here before he exploded. *Now!*

He obeyed his own instructions and barreled out of the shower. He yanked at a thick, thirsty robe hanging on the shower door and put it on. He toweled his wet head, the hair standing straight up. He tried to smooth it down as he made his way gingerly down the hall to the staircase that would take him to the kitchen, where, hopefully, coffee waited for him.

The first thing he noticed was a place setting at the kitchen table. Obviously, Maggie planned to cook breakfast for him.

Gus looked at the neatly stacked papers that made up the background check on his wife and felt sick to his stomach. If Phil Ross had been standing next to him yesterday when he'd read the report for the first time, he knew without a doubt that he would have pummeled the man into the ground. By the time he'd read it six or seven times and had it committed to memory, he knew he would have pummeled himself into the ground for having been so damned stupid. His head continued to pound.

Maggie entered the kitchen and opened the refrigerator. He shook his head and said, "No breakfast, thank you. Just coffee." Gus looked around the kitchen, but it was neat and tidy, the two wine bottles gone. If ever there was a time for a cigarette, this was it. He'd given up the disgusting habit when he married Elaine, because she said she wasn't sleeping with a chimney stack. But Barney smoked on occasion, usually when he was under the gun on something or other.

Gus rummaged through the kitchen cabinets until he found a pack of Marlboros. He could hardly wait to light the cigarette in his hands. It felt unfamiliar. But at that moment, he didn't give a good rat's ass about the surgeon general's report or all the horror stories he had read about smoking. This was *now,* and he needed *something* to get him through the mess he was wallowing in. And if it was a cigarette or multiple cigarettes, then so be it.

Maggie had disappeared somewhere in the house, leaving him alone in the kitchen. A good thing, Gus decided as he fired up still another cigarette. He was on his third cup of coffee, surprised that it had stayed in his stomach, and on his fourth or fifth cigarette as he tried to come to terms with the stack of papers on the table.

What really got to him, aside from the in-depth report, was the detective's personal note to Barney saying he'd done a background check on the same individual for someone else and, at Barney's insistence, had included it in the report, which he followed up with a current update. The previous client's name was Rose Blossom. His grandmother had hired Phil Ross to check out Elaine before the wedding. Granny had known all along, had tried to tell him, to warn him without actually telling him about the report, and he had pretty much told her to mind her own business. No, not pretty much told her, he *had* told her to keep her nose out of his love life. Talk about being a total screwup. *If they gave an award for biggest chump in the Commonwealth of Virginia, I'd take that prize hands down,* he thought. *Hell, I'd probably win if the territory expanded to cover everything east of the Mississippi.*

How disappointed his grandmother must be in him, deservedly so. *I am never going to be able to make this right. Never.* Gus massaged his temples, hoping to ease the pounding headache. *Why hasn't the aspirin kicked in?*

Gus reached over to the counter for his reading glasses. Like he really needed to read this crap again. He'd memorized it, every single word, last night. What he couldn't remember was if it was before the two bottles of wine or after he'd emptied them.

Gus eyed the ugly, hateful dossier on his wife. His stomach crunched itself into a hard knot. Maybe it was better to think about the powerhouse lawyer Barney had presented him with, Jill Jackson. He hadn't been impressed at first. Nor had he been impressed midway through dinner. It wasn't until the end of dinner, when he'd started to really listen to her and look at her. He'd always gone for the flash when it came to women, much to his own detriment. He liked eye candy, he really did. He liked it when other guys looked at him with envy, which didn't say a whole heck of a lot for him. Hell, it didn't say anything about him other than that he was nuts. What good was a pretty package if the contents were downright ugly?

Right up front, the minute he'd shaken hands with Jill Jackson, Gus knew she despised him and the situation he was in. He'd cringed at the look in her eyes, which said he was worse than gum on the bottom of her shoe. To his credit, he'd done nothing to change her opinion of him. Probably because, if he was honest with himself, it was that Jill Jackson was not a looker, not even close to eye candy.

Gus drank more coffee, fired up another cigarette, and blew a perfect smoke ring as he let his mind wander back to the meeting with his brand-new attorney. His headache was now a drumlike throb. He tried to ignore it.

Jill Jackson. Short had been his initial assessment. Good things come in small packages. Sometimes. Not this time, though. Then the word *squat* came to mind. Then another word, *fireplug*. A short fireplug. Based, of course, on the clothing she wore. Cargo pants with stuff in the pockets, a Harvard sweatshirt that had seen years of wash and wear. Hair skinned back into a tight ponytail. No makeup. Granny glasses.

His spirits had plummeted during dinner, when he realized she wasn't all that great at small talk or conversation in general. He cursed Barney then for hooking him up with such a dud. He remembered her healthy appetite. He'd struggled to keep the conversation going, but he knew that he had failed. Jackson had cleaned her plate and had two helpings of baked Alaska. He'd only picked at his food, preferring the vintage wine, which she had only sipped. And to think she'd been given the task of getting him out of the mess he was in.

What bothered him more than anything was that this plain Jane fireplug hated his guts on sight. You didn't need to be a rocket scientist to see the lack of respect she tried, though not all that hard, to hide. She had spent a lot of time extolling Barney's wonderful qualities, saying how admirable, how smart, how kind and generous he was, and how *he would never get himself into a mess like the one you find yourself in, Mr. Hollister.* He'd bristled over that zinger, but he'd bitten his tongue, because it was true.

After that, it had been one zinger after another, her mantra being, you need to get over yourself, Mr. Hollister. Twice she'd said, you reap what you sow. And then she really went at it about his grandmother and aunts. She'd told him in no uncertain terms she could never respect anyone who was unkind to old people or animals. She called him pond scum. He had almost leaped across the table to strangle her, but that statement was true, too. Except for Wilson. The only time he'd been unkind to his dog was when Wilson wanted two Pop-Tarts or when he gave him blueberry when he wanted strawberry. Surely that didn't count. Bullshit; she'd send him to the gas chamber, if she could, for the Pop-Tarts.

When they'd finally called it a night, at nine-thirty, his new attorney hadn't bothered to shake his hand. Instead, she'd looked him in the eye and said, "I detest you and people of your ilk. I'm only representing you as a favor to Barney Beezer, whom I happen to adore. You will get the best representation I can possibly give you because of Barney. Just so you know, Mr. Hollister. One last thing. I am in control, not you. If I tell you to jump, you *WILL* jump. Are we clear on that, Mr. Hollister? And do not ever be presumptuous enough to call me Jill, because if you do, I will cut off your balls and shove them where the sun doesn't shine. Thank you so much for dinner. You also need to stop drinking. I refuse to defend a drunk. If I ever again smell alcohol on your breath, I will tell Barney to get you a new lawyer. Not to mention the word *free* representation. That alone should tie you in a knot. Now, Mr. Hollister, tell me you understand everything I just said, and we can say good night."

Gus had offered up a sloppy salute. *People of your ilk.* Now, that really hurt and was a shot below the belt. "Yes, ma'am, I understand everything you just said. And, for the record, I already hate *your* guts, and I just met you. I think that levels the playing field."

Jill Jackson had laughed. Gus thought it was the most evil sound he'd ever heard in his whole life.

Dammit, why am I thinking about that crazy-ass drill sergeant posing as a lawyer? Because he didn't want to go back to the papers on the table, that's why.

Gus worked at his temples, trying to lessen the drumroll in his head, which was doing its best to match the thunder outside. He couldn't help but wonder if the storm meant impending doom.

How in the hell is that four-eyed, squirrelly fire-plug going to get me out of this mess? Maybe I need to call Barney and voice my disappointment in his legal appointee. Yeah, yeah, I really need to call Barney.

Gus pressed in the digits that would connect him with Barney. His BFF answered on the third ring. "Talk to me. Time is money. Bet you're calling to tell me you love Jill. Don't bother. I knew she would be the perfect choice. She hates your guts, right? You hate her even more, right? She told you to stop drinking and also told you that when she says jump, you will jump and not even presume to ask how high, right? Don't even bother trying to thank me, buddy. What are friends for? Just a word of advice, don't take her to the brink, where she will cut off your balls and shove them you know where. It won't be pretty, and it's damned painful in the bargain. Nice talking to you, buddy. Gotta go and make some money."

Gus looked at the phone he was holding and cursed in a whole new language. His head continued to pound. A bolt of lightning ripped across the sky. He shivered. Elaine hated storms and always hid out in the bathroom. Bitch!

Gus took a moment to wonder if he was the most hated man in Sycamore Springs. He wished Wilson were with him. On a whim, knowing full well his grandmother would probably hang up on him, he called. When she answered, he asked how she was, then said he was calling to see how Wilson was and did she have enough Pop-Tarts on hand and reminded her to give him only one and just the strawberry.

"Augustus, I have more than enough Pop-Tarts, and I give him two strawberry just the way you do, or he pouts, then Winnie gets upset. Is there anything else?"

"Just that I love you and the aunts and want to tell you again how sorry I am for what happened."

"You need to tell that to someone who cares," Gus heard Violet shout in the background. Gus ended the call, reached for a cigarette, and lit up again. If he kept this up, he'd use up all of Barney's stash. He made a mental note to replace the cigarettes and quit smoking after today.

Elaine's dossier beckoned him. He really had to deal with it. Or did he? Now that the fireplug was on the case, let her deal with it all. It was making him crazy, however, that it was another woman who was going to get him out of the mess he was in. His grandmother and the aunts had a saying when he or Barney had gotten into trouble when they were kids: Don't think I'm pulling your chestnuts out of the fire.

Gus swallowed hard. When did he turn into such a loser, such a misfit? He answered himself before he bolted for the bathroom off the kitchen.

When he returned to the table and Elaine's dossier, he felt drained and empty. Maybe now, when he read through the papers, he'd absorb it all again, even though he already had it committed to memory. This time he was going to read it out loud to the empty kitchen so he could hear the words and really, really see what a fool he'd been.

Gus squared his shoulders and tossed the remaining cigarettes into the trash. He didn't need a crutch for this. *This* called for cold-turkey awareness. He took a deep breath, held it as long as he could, then let it out with a loud swoosh as he picked up the first typed piece of paper. *This is your life, Gus Hollister.*

Chapter 6

A wicked streak of lightning zipping across the sky followed by a loud roll of thunder startled Gus to the point where he dropped the papers he was holding. He shivered, knowing that the loud sound was an omen of some kind. He just knew it. He thought his head was going to spiral right off his neck when he bent down to pick up the papers and put them in order. Just another diversion, so he could postpone reading again about his perfidious wife.

Gus settled his reading glasses more firmly on his nose.

Elaine Sara Ramsey was born in Newark, Delaware, to parents Helen and John Ramsey, twenty-seven years ago on January 3, 1985. Subject resided with parents until the day she turned sixteen, when she left and hitchhiked out of town, according to parents. Parents say they have had no contact with subject since that day.

Subject was a poor student because of lack of home supervision and barely made it from one grade to the next. There are no records to indicate any type of further education. Parents appear to be honest, hardworking people. They said subject was promiscuous starting at the age of thirteen. Father said subject was a bad seed. Mother just cried at interview. Father said subject was a beautiful girl and used her beauty to get what she wanted. Said subject could pass for eighteen at the age of fourteen. He also said she was a liar and a thief, that there was no controlling her, and that they eventually gave up because they had three other children who were good and decent and needed to be cared for, too.

Tracking subject by Social Security number and work history, subject worked many jobs, mostly in the food industry—waitressing, hostessing, or tending bar. Mostly in upscale establishments where she could meet well-to-do men. At the age of nineteen, she married her first husband, Ian Larsen, a young dentist just starting his practice in Richmond and loaded with debt. Before divorcing him, she hung around long enough to use him to meet other white-collar professionals who did have money. Divorce record states that Dr. Larsen took out a loan and paid her $25,000 to get out of his life. When interviewing Dr. Larsen, who is now happily married and has a thriving practice, he said subject was a living nightmare, and refused to discuss details. The only thing he would say was that she pretended to be going to college and had stacks and stacks of books. Once she married him, she refused to work. They were married for fifteen months.

Husband number two was a man named Clayton Mitchell, a stockbroker to whom she had been introduced by one of Dr. Larsen's colleagues. Subject married him fifty-five days after her divorce from Dr. Larsen was final. According to personal interview with Mr. Mitchell, it was anything but a marriage made in heaven. Same MO with this guy—said she was about to graduate, lied to him about her age, lied about everything. Nothing domestic about her. Wanted to dine out every night and meet his wealthy clients. She flirted with them all and hit on some of them. She drove him to the brink of bankruptcy with her outrageous spending.

Things went from subject's being verbally abusive to becoming physically abusive. Mr. Mitchell moved out of their town house to get away from her. She came to his office, threatened him, and made wild scenes. He paid to get rid of her. She got the town house and the mortgage that went with it. She promptly sold it and netted $146,000. He still doesn't know how that happened, because he said the town house wasn't worth anywhere near that much. He, too, is happily married now, lives in New York, and is quite successful on Wall Street. He also said subject pretended to be studying and she said that she would graduate from the University of Virginia the following year. It was, of course, a lie on top of an elaborate charade. They were married for seventeen months.

Subject then married Hugo Hintermyer—a real-estate broker who had aspirations of becoming a real-estate tycoon—three months later, although she had moved in with him two weeks after he sold the Mitchell town house for her. When they married, HH bought her a Mercedes convertible. They lived in what he told her were properties that he *owned*. Actually, the properties were investment properties belonging to people who were out of the country and never bothered to check on them. HH was conning her in much the same way that she was conning him. This marriage only lasted nine months. Subject kept the Mercedes convertible and HH gave her $78,000, so she wouldn't turn him in to the licensing board. He had to raise the money from friends and by helping himself to several escrow accounts.

Despite what had happened, he said in some ways he was sorry to see the last of her because she was so good in bed, even if she was a bitch on wheels. He also said she pretended to be a student and, from time to time, when she wasn't out charging up a storm on his credit cards, she actually looked like she was studying. HH hopes never to see her again.

There are no records to indicate subject has ever personally filed state or federal income taxes, even though she worked and drew a paycheck. (Check last page of this report for the establishments where subject worked.)

Subject did not remarry for three years. She worked, and pretended to go to school; law school, to be precise. Had tons of law books, carried them with her. Sold her Mercedes convertible the second year after the divorce from HH, as she was short of funds. Hooked up at this point with the manager of an Avis rental-car franchise. She moved in with him and drove the cars on the lot while she went on the prowl to find someone better than the manager, who showered her with gifts and allowed her to use his credit cards. His name was Leroy Denvile. She cleaned out his bank account, took off with one of his rental cars, and left him holding the bag. He said he wanted to marry her, but she told him he had no potential. He was devastated.

This relationship lasted four and a half months.

Two weeks after leaving Mr. Denvile, subject hit on a circuit court judge old enough to be her grandfather. Name was Nathan Perry. People thought subject was his granddaughter. He was a widower. His children became estranged from him when he married subject. Within three weeks, she had a brand-new Mercedes, candy-apple red; new credit cards; and plenty of cash. They lived in a fancy Tudor home complete with swimming pool and tennis court. They went out every night to dinner. The judge suffered a stroke; he was eighty-two. He died a week later. His children swooped in and swooped her out. One of them just happened to be an FBI agent. They paid her off with a three-hundred-thousand-dollar check, and she signed a ream of paperwork promising never to darken their doorstep again. The judge had been in the process of changing his will but had the stroke before he could sign off. If he had, she would have been set for life. They were married for nine weeks.

Gus rubbed at his eyes. It was all so unbelievable. And he hadn't had a clue. He knew that if his grandmother had handed him this report back then, he would have refused to read it. He felt sick to his stomach. He shuffled the papers in front of him. There was no need to read the rest of them, since they picked up with his meeting Elaine at his health club, where he exercised after work.

For weeks, he had watched her on the equipment. He liked the look of her toned body, her classy workout clothes. He liked that she was serious about her workouts and didn't mess with any of the male members. He liked seeing her leave the gym with her arms full of books and her gym bag. He'd slipped one of the attendants fifty bucks to let him see her application. All he got out of it was that she was single, was going to law school, worked nights as a bartender in a trendy joint in New Town, and drove a bright yellow Beetle. His kind of girl. He'd made it his business to visit the trendy joint two or three times a week, have one beer, then go home. He'd thought at the time that he was being clever, but she told him later that she had his moves down pat. Then she'd laughed at him when he approached her at the health club, saying, "Don't I know you?" The most tired pickup line of all time.

A month later, in June of last year, they were

married. But before that happy event, at her insistence, he'd given her a tour of his business, the building he owned—along with the bank—and his paid-off house. They had gone to the farm where his grandmother lived with the two aunts. She didn't like Wilson from the get-go, but she'd given in on the dog when he'd told her he would never ever part with Wilson even if he did make her itch and sneeze. Wilson hated her and stayed out of her way.

Elaine Sara Ramsey Larsen Mitchell Hintermyer Perry Hollister. He wondered how she fit all those names on her driver's license.

Yessireee, he was one damned lovesick puppy back in those days.

Gus shoved the papers back into the manila folder. *Now what am I supposed to do?* It was still raining, but it wasn't as dark as it had been. The thunder and lightning seemed to have abated, along with his headache. Maybe he should go into the office instead of just sitting around sucking his thumb. If he did that, he could get a jump-start on next week's work. Yeah, yeah, he'd go to the office. The only question was, which one of Barney's cars should he take? Maybe the vintage Jeep Commander.

Leaving from Barney's house meant that the usual ten-minute drive to his office now took forty minutes, then another ten to wade across the parking lot to the back entrance of his building. He let himself in, climbed the back steps to his office, and opened the door with his brand-new office key. After he locked the door behind him, he turned on the lights and headed to the minikitchen, where he started a pot of coffee. While he waited for it to drip, he checked his e-mails and the voice mail. Two voice mails from his tenant on the top floor asking him to call. He did, and was told a client had come by earlier and said he would be back around noon. No, he didn't leave a name, and the tenant hadn't asked, saying just that the man had said he was a new client. Gus shrugged. He really didn't need any new clients; it was all he could do to provide the ones he had with first-class service. Still, tax season was over, so it wouldn't hurt to see what kind of help the guy needed. Plus, it would be someone to talk to.

Gus scrolled through his e-mails. A few from friends, some forwarded jokes, some political cartoons some nitwit thought he would enjoy, an invitation to speak at next week's chamber of commerce luncheon. He typed OKAY and sent the e-mail off after he marked it in his day planner and copied it to his secretary/receptionist.

Gus walked back to the kitchen, poured his coffee, and returned to his office, where he decided to read the morning news online. Normally, he read the real newspaper while he had his coffee because he didn't like reading online, just the same way he didn't like reading a book with a Nook or a Kindle. When he realized he had forgotten his reading glasses, he turned off his computer, propped his feet on the desk, and drank his coffee. His headache was totally gone by now, thank God.

He should have stayed home. He tried to shift

his mental gears to pleasant thoughts, happier times, but it didn't work. He thought about Wilson and how he missed him. Did he dare risk his grandmother's wrath again by going to get the dog and forcefully taking him from her? He wondered if he had the guts to threaten his granny with the cops if she didn't hand over his dog. That was a no-brainer if ever there was one.

Before he could change his mind, he pulled the desk phone closer and pressed in the digits that would connect him with Blossom Farm. His grandmother answered. He identified himself politely and said he would be there within the hour to pick up Wilson, and to have him ready.

"In that case, Augustus, you will have to take Winnie, also. Wilson won't leave without her, and Winnie will cry, and I cannot stand an unhappy animal."

Gus loved Winnie almost as much as he loved Wilson. "Are you sure about the little lard bucket? She never objected before when you kept Wilson, and we left."

"I'm sure," Rose said curtly. "And stop calling my dog a lard bucket."

"Okay, I don't have a problem taking Winnie. But, Granny, she is *fat*, and she waddles."

"I'll have them both ready in an hour. Goodbye, Augustus."

Maybe Granny was relenting a tad. She loved Winnie, and for her to let him take her dog had to mean something. Gus felt almost happy as he looked around to see where he'd left his umbrella. He was checking his computer one last time and turning off the lights when the buzzer outside his office sounded. The new client, he supposed. Well, since he didn't have an appointment, he would just have to come back later on or next week. Right now it was more important for him to pick up the dogs. He opened the door, the dripping umbrella in his hand.

The man was a nice-looking guy, a little damp, but he smiled. "Are you Augustus Hollister?"

"I am. Are you the new client? Look, I'm just leaving, and I can't stay right now. Can you come back next week, and we can talk then?"

"I don't think I need to come back as long as you're Augustus Hollister. Here! You have been served, Mr. Hollister."

Son of a bitch! "That's a lousy way to earn a living!" Gus shouted to the process server's retreating back. He winced at the man's laughter. He'd earned his sixty-five bucks first crack of the bat. "New client, my ass!" Once a fool, always a fool. There should be a law about those guys lying just to make $65. He had to hand it to his wife; she worked at the speed of light. Then again, maybe not, if, as he suspected, she'd been planning this for some period of time. Everything could have been drawn up and just waiting for her to kick him out. Out of his own goddamned house. *Bitch!*

Gus folded the summons and shoved it in his hip pocket. He'd read it when he got back to Barney's house.

Chapter 7

GUS WAS SOAKING WET BY THE TIME HE CLIMBED behind the wheel of the Jeep Commander. And he'd just ruined another pair of shoes. It was black outside, and lights were on everywhere as far as he could see. What the hell kind of April shower was this, anyway? Like none he'd ever seen. A worm of fear crawled around his belly as he goosed the Jeep through the water in the parking lot and out to the main road. Maybe it was the end of the world. Well, if so, he wanted to be with his granny and have his dog at his side when he went to meet his Maker.

Gus crawled along behind the cautious driver

in front of him, the taillights a faint, pinkish color. Since Gus was driving one of Barney's prize cars, he tried to stay a good car length behind the other car in case the driver braked suddenly. Barney did like his toys.

As Gus drove, his eyes straining to see ahead of him, his headache came back. He was too tense; he needed to relax, to take deep breaths—inhale, exhale. He prayed then, something he didn't do on a regular basis even though his granny had taught him to pray. She had taught Barney, too.

Gus did pray sometimes, but more often than not when he wanted something to go his way. *I really am a shit of the first order, no doubt about it.*

Forty minutes later, Gus turned off the road onto a service road that would take him to Blossom Farm. He was driving through water that was midway up his tires. At the first sign of the post lamps—which were like beacons—that started at the entrance to the farmhouse, Gus knew he was less than a mile from the front door and safety. He crawled along, saying all the prayers he could remember, one after the other. When he finally stopped in front of the house, he had a bad moment wondering if the Jeep Commander would start up when he was ready to leave. Would his granny let him stay until the storm eased off, or would she kick his butt out the door? More than likely, she would let him stay since he would be taking Winnie and Wilson with him. He needed to calm down. He sat quietly, the spring storm raging all about him as he struggled with his breathing. It was hard because he was chilled to the bone.

That's all I need now, to get sick. His wild thoughts took him to a wicked place in his mind, his own funeral, with no one in attendance but Barney and his dog. Maybe Elaine, dancing on his grave while his grandmother and aunts hid behind a tree watching the proceedings. Old people got off on funerals, didn't they? Happy to attend one as long as it wasn't their own. Maybe Barney wouldn't make it home from Hong Kong in time, and they'd keep his body in a freezer until he arrived. Maybe someone would give the order to fry him. Elaine! They were still married, so she could do whatever she wanted with his cold, dead body.

"Enough!" The single word exploded from Gus's mouth like a gunshot. He opened the car door and stepped down into water that was almost up to his knees. He slogged through the water to the steps and raced up like a runner, lightning crackling and thunder booming overhead. He couldn't believe that the power was still on. Maybe that was a miracle. But, if it went out, Granny had a kick-ass generator that would take care of all her needs. He and Barney were the ones who had insisted on the generator, and she hadn't balked at the cost or the installation. He mentally patted himself on the back for that one.

Gus rang the doorbell. Iris opened the door and handed him a towel. He kicked off his shoes and did his best not to drip on the floor.

Wilson bounded into the foyer, took one look at him, barked, then rushed him. Gus dropped to his knees and hugged the big dog as he whispered in Wilson's ear. Winnie waddled over to them and managed to wiggle next to Wilson. His happy little family. Gus wanted to bawl at what he was feeling. That little ditty that you never knew what you had until you lost it rang in his ears. Just more confirmation that he was a real shit.

"Come along, Augustus, you need to change your clothes before you catch cold. Violet brought down some of the clothes that you left behind in your old room. You can change in the laundry room. Your grandmother is making you some hot tea."

All Gus could do was say thanks. He was shivering so badly, he could barely make it to the laundry room. He closed the door and looked at the contents of the dryer, which were tumbling around. He could see a pair of his old boxer shorts. He stripped down in record time, goose bumps all over his body. He stopped the dryer and couldn't get into his old clothes quick enough. Then he put the clothes he had been wearing in the dryer and turned it on. Nothing ever felt as good as warm clothes next to his body. Who but his grandmother would think to put his clothes in the dryer for him? His eyes burned. He swiped at them as he made his way out to the kitchen and the hot cup of tea that waited for him. His eyes continued to burn.

As Gus took his seat at the table and saw the huge mug of tea, he knew that if some fairy godmother came along and offered him one wish, his wish would be that he could unring the bell and go back to the day he'd first seen Elaine Ramsey. But that was wishful thinking, and it wasn't going to happen. He cupped his hands around the heavy mug and sipped at the blackberry currant tea that his grandmother loved. He loved it, too. Wilson lay down by his feet, Winnie next to him.

They all made small talk, mostly about the crazy storm raging outside, the flooding that was taking place, and, of course, worrying that the power was eventually going to go out. There was no real concern for him on their faces. They were just doing what they perceived to be their duty. He missed their open smiles. He was definitely not out of the woods where they were concerned. Maybe he'd blown it all for good. The thought was so awful, Gus had trouble swallowing the tea. He wanted to say something, something meaningful, but he couldn't find the words. Finally, he blurted out, "I love you all so much, I don't have the words to tell you. I know you're disappointed in me. Hell, I'm disappointed in myself. I know those are just words, and, like you guys have always said from the time I was little, actions count more than words. Can't you see it in your hearts to give me a second chance? Please."

Violet was the first to chirp up. "Well, that is not going to happen anytime soon, young man."

"You can't just trample on a person's feelings, flip them the bird, then expect to waltz back into their lives when you get a boo-boo. We are no longer in the lifesaving business," Iris said so coldly, Gus shivered. He thought that was the most he'd ever heard Iris say at one time.

Two down and one to go. Gus looked at his grandmother. "Drink your tea before it gets cold, Augustus, so you can take the dogs and leave us. We have things to do today that we only do on bad-weather days."

They weren't going to give him an inch. Not even half an inch. His eyes still burning, Gus gulped at the tea as instructed. Time to get out of their lives. He finished his tea, stood up, and realized he wasn't wearing shoes or slippers. He did have on socks, a pair knitted at some time in his youth by his grandmother. He looked toward the laundry room, where Violet stood holding his old Bass moccasins. He'd had them since he was a senior in high school. He'd bought them with his own money from his job clerking at the supermarket. They were old, soft, and broken in. He couldn't remember why he hadn't taken them with him when he'd moved out eons ago. Out with the old, in with the new, or something like that, most likely.

Gus shook his head at Violet. "I don't want to ruin them. I'll just take my clothes and shoes. Maybe I can still save the shoes." Violet shrugged as she yanked clothes out of the dryer and stuffed them in a white drawstring trash bag. Trash. Well, he felt like trash. Who in the hell ever thought that these three women, the loves of his life, could turn on him like this? (Probably the same way they wondered how he could cut them out of his life for Elaine.) *Certainly not I,* he thought to himself. He had a bad moment then, where he just wanted to curl into himself and bawl like a baby, so they would rush to him and hug him, smother him with kisses as they assured him in their gentle, loving voices that they would make it all right for him. He wanted that so bad he could taste it, could feel their warm arms around him, hear the soft words being whispered.

Instead, he heard a noise that shook the house and rattled the windows. He saw the alarm on the older people's faces, heard shrieks and howls coming from all parts of the house. The kitchen door leading into the dining room burst open. He saw a sea of white hair as senior citizens came on the run, their voices fearful. What the hell was going on?

His grandmother sighed mightily, looked around, and said, "I think lightning hit the old sycamore out by the front porch, and it hit the ground or the verandah."

Gus looked around in a daze. "Who are all these people?" he finally managed to ask.

Violet ran to the front of the house and was back in a minute. "You were right, Rose, it was the old sycamore. It's gone. The good news is we'll have firewood for the next ten years once we get Mr. Younger to come and split it for us. Oh, the left side of the verandah is gone. We'll need to use the back door until we can get it repaired."

"Who are these people?" Gus asked again, pointing to the group of chattering seniors with white hair who had barreled into the kitchen from all directions in the house.

"Not that it's any of your business, young fella, but we work here," Oscar said, his dentures clicking as he tried not to lose them in his excitement.

"Doing what?" Gus demanded.

"Don't concern yourself with our friends, Augustus. Just take the dogs and go, so we can do what we have to do," Rose Blossom said. "By that, I mean putting in calls to people to get the best price on repairs, and, of course, the insurance company. We need to be first because I'm sure other people will have damages, too, and we don't like to wait. As you know, I like keeping the house in tip-top shape."

"And that would be what, exactly?" Gus demanded again. He threw his hands in the air. "You know what?" He sat down and planted his feet firmly on the floor. "I'm not going anywhere until someone tells me what the hell is going on here. Like, *NOW!*" he bellowed at the top of his lungs.

Suddenly it was bedlam, a Chinese fire drill gone bad as the little group that wasn't so little anymore started to chatter and grumble. Gus watched in fear as one old man shook his fist in his direction and called him a young whipper-snapper. It took all of Rose's persuasive powers to calm down her little group once she clearly interpreted the look on her grandson's face. Augustus meant exactly what he said. He wasn't going anywhere until he got some answers. She felt defeated, as did her twin sisters, as they all glared at Gus.

"You need to wait right here, Augustus. Wilson, do not let him move. We're going to have a wee meeting in the dining room. If you so much as move a muscle, Augustus, I will personally take the broom to you. Do you understand me?"

"Yes, do you understand your grandmother?" the dude with the loose dentures asked, his voice filled with menace.

"I won't move a muscle," Gus promised. He looked down at his dog, who was taking his orders seriously. Wilson sat up on his haunches, his ears straight up, the fur on the nape of his neck as straight as his ears. Winnie growled so loud, Gus itched at the sound.

Gus watched as the seniors literally pushed against each other in their haste to get to the dining room. He could hear voices, loud and angry, but he couldn't make out the words, and if someone had offered him his weight in gold to go to the door and listen, he would have turned them down. Instead, he looked at Wilson and hissed, "Traitor!" Wilson showed him his teeth. So did Winnie.

"Yeah, well, guess what, Wilson? From now on it's Milk-Bones, and no more Pop-Tarts for you. See how you like *that!* What the hell kind of guard dog are you? You let those old ladies brainwash you. You did, Wilson! I'm going to have to take you for therapy, and I have too damned much on my plate right now as it is." Wilson showed him his teeth again. Winnie backed him up, but her heart wasn't in it; her tail wagged.

Wilson noticed. He lifted one paw and smacked her on the side of the head. Winnie's tail stopped wagging in midswing.

The moment the dining-room door opened, Gus sucked in his breath. He watched as the seniors filed into the kitchen. They formed a circle around the table and chair where Gus was sitting. He had never in his life felt so intimidated.

Gus let his breath out slowly as his grandmother advanced, looked him in the eye, and said, "Come along, Augustus. It's time to take a walk on the *wild side.*"

Suddenly, Gus didn't want to get up off the chair. He would have stayed glued to it, but Wilson nudged his knee and showed him his teeth for the third time.

Gus didn't know what made him say the words or where they came from, but they shot out of his mouth at the speed of light: "I'm not going to like this, am I?"

"No, nephew, probably not," Violet snapped. Gus wasn't sure, but he thought the dude with the clicking dentures said, "We should have just killed him. It's not too late, you know. Or we could shackle him to the tractor in the barn if you're all too squeamish. We vote on everything else. Why didn't we vote on *that*?"

Gus felt his blood run cold when no one responded.

Chapter 8

THE BLACKNESS OUTSIDE THE OLD FARMHOUSE turned blinding white. And then the earsplitting sound of the lightning striking something close by brought everyone to a standstill. The old house rumbled again as Gus ran to the front door, his grandmother and aunts right behind him. "It hit the old sycamore again!" He could feel the anxiety of the three women as he opened the front door to stare at the destruction in the front yard.

Gus loved that old tree. Once, a long time ago, there had been a fort nestled among its branches, with a sturdy ladder some handyman had built on his grandmother's orders. He and

Barney had practically lived in the fort during good weather. His grandmother would bring out food, and they'd hoist it up in a bucket from a pulley that same handyman had installed. He'd fallen out of the tree when he was nine and had his first broken bone, his arm. Five days later, Barney had fallen out and broken his ankle. Both of them wore casts, and they'd played tic-tac-toe on both casts for the six weeks they'd had to wear them. They'd staked claims to the old sycamore that same year and carved their names in it along with the date. Now it was gone. Gus could feel his eyes start to burn. Gone. The way his old life was gone. And the new life he had, just plain old sucked. Big-time.

"There's nothing left to it. Nothing at all," he said sadly. "Do you think when they come to chop it up, you can ask them if they can save the bark where Barney and I carved our names? I'd like to . . . what I mean is . . . never mind. I know you three aren't in the business of doing me any favors. I can't believe it's gone." The lump in Gus's throat was the size of a golf ball, making it hard to swallow.

"We'll ask," his grandmother said curtly. "Close the door, Augustus, the rain is coming in." Gus slammed the door shut and shot the deadbolt.

"We should get on with this," Violet said. "We're losing valuable work hours with this tour."

"Violet is right; let's just do it and get it over with." Rose nodded as she opened the door to what had once been her beloved husband's library. It was a handsome room, with wall-to-wall bookshelves, a massive fieldstone fireplace, and a stunning oriental rug, which seemed to grow more beautiful with the years. Gus remembered sitting in that room and listening to his grandfather read to him. His grandfather had died when Gus was twelve, and he remembered that his mother and father had not even come home for the funeral. It was after that that his aunts had come to live with him and Granny Rose.

The drapes were gone, replaced with shutters, which seemed to throw the room off kilter even though they matched the bookshelves. The books were gone now, packed away in boxes in the attic. The shelves held manila folders, mailing envelopes, files of every color and description. There were boxes with lids on and initials scrawled on the sides for easy identification.

Gus looked around as he tried to understand what he was seeing. His grandfather's antique desk was gone. He and Barney used to hide under it. In its place were long folding tables that held six computers. Another table held four fax machines. A third table held four copiers. A fourth held nine telephones, the old-fashioned landline kind. Gus blinked. His first thought was wild and crazy: Were these ditzy oldsters running a bookie joint? He didn't mean to blurt the words out, but he did. His grandmother looked at him like he'd sprouted a second head. "That's too silly to dignify with a response."

"What is all this?" Gus insisted, waving his arms about.

"Hit it, Iris!" Rose said.

Iris smiled and sat down at one of the computers and clicked away for several seconds. She got up and motioned for Gus to take her seat. "Check it out! Just scroll down, and everything is there." She moved off to stand to the side with her sisters. "I almost wish we smoked, because we could light up now. We don't even have any gum," she whispered as she eyed her nephew, who looked like he'd gotten caught in a horror movie.

"He isn't going to take this very well," Rose whispered to her sisters.

"And do we care about that?" Violet said out of the corner of her mouth. Her sisters ignored the comment.

Ten minutes went by, then three more, before Gus swiveled his chair around to stare at his grandmother and the aunts. "It's an impressive Web site. Whoever did it knew what they were doing. What is Initial B Enterprises?"

The three sisters' chests puffed out. "*We* are Initial B Enterprises—us, and all the people you saw earlier. It's our business," Rose said. "Iris, show Augustus our financial records."

Iris moved to another computer and clicked the keys. "Even you, nephew, should be able to understand this, you being a certified public accountant and all." She got up and waved her arm with a flourish to indicate Gus should take her seat.

The fine hairs on the back of Gus's neck stood on end as he eyed the screen in front of him. The sisters huddled, not taking their eyes off Gus as they waited for his reaction.

When it came, it wasn't what they expected. "Who handles the accounting? Do you have a lawyer? What am I, chopped liver? You didn't trust me to help you? For God's sake, is this even real? Most important, is what you're doing legal?"

Rose sucked in her breath and tried to straighten her round shoulders and stand tall. "You are in no position to ask us any questions, because what we do is none of your business. But because my sisters and I do not want you storming around here trying to ruin our lives, I will respond. Yes, of course it's legal. We have one of the best lawyers in the state working for us. And our accounting firm is top-notch, one you used to lust after but where you couldn't get hired. I don't know if you're chopped liver or not, Augustus. None of us know what you are anymore. We did not want to involve you. You young people are so irresponsible, and you proved us right. And, yes, it's real."

Gus threw his hands in the air. "What is it you do? I mean . . . how did you generate so much money? What exactly are you selling? It was hard . . . this does not make one bit of sense to me. No offense, but you're old ladies. This is . . . who invests your money?"

"Goldman Sachs! And a fine job they've

done for us, as you can readily see!" Violet said smartly. "We're all millionaires. You certainly can't quibble with the numbers, now, can you?"

Gus rubbed at his temples. His headache was back.

"And you never told me. Even back before . . . well, before."

"You wouldn't have understood. You were young, full of spit and vinegar. You thought then the way you think now. That because we're old, we should be put out to pasture. We were going to tell you at one point, but then you got yourself involved with that gold digger, and we couldn't take the chance. Can you even imagine what she would do if she knew about all of this? That's why we took you out of our wills," Rose said.

"You took me out of your wills!" Gus yelped in horror.

"Oh, this is just too much. I can't deal with stupid," Violet said as she made her way to the door.

"Wait! Hold on here! I wasn't talking about money. I don't care about that. I thought we were family. You're all I have. If you take me out of your wills, that means I'm practically an orphan. I don't want to be an orphan!" Gus realized how ridiculous he sounded, but he didn't care. "I don't have any parents. You three were my parents. So, are you saying you disowned me and didn't even tell me?" There was such hurt, such outrage in Gus's eyes, the sisters backed up a step.

"Well, maybe you aren't so stupid after all," Violet said, her faded blue eyes sparkling. "We thought of it as a temporary thing that could be corrected at some point in time. We're leaving our money to no-kill animal shelters across the nation, to shelters for battered women, and, of course, to children's agencies."

"That's great. It's your money, you can do whatever you want with it. But couldn't you at least leave me a dollar so I'm in the will?"

"We did leave you ten dollars," Iris said. Gus deflated like a pricked balloon.

"I know this sounds stupid, but does Barney know about all of this?" Gus asked.

"No, not really, but he is the one who got us the people who made up the Web page. He got us the best of the best. Barney never asked why, he just said okay, and his people contacted us. He had the good sense not to ask questions," Rose said.

"We're wasting time," Violet said. "Are we going to give him the tour, or is this it?"

"I want the damned tour," Gus blustered. "I want to know everything about Initial B Enterprises. In case you get arrested and go to jail. I cannot believe what you are doing is legal."

The sisters rolled their eyes, and they all trooped out the door and down the hall. "Well, here we go. This is Door Number One. Enter please, but stand still," Violet said.

Gus thought his eyes were going to pop out of his head. He saw four sewing machines and boxes stacked almost to the ceiling. There was only a small space that could technically be called a path. The lights were on not only because it was dark outside but because cartons had been stacked up against the windows. "What . . . what do you sew in here?" he asked.

"Underwear. We monogram it," Rose said.

"*Thongs* to be precise," Violet tittered.

Gus turned pink. His thoughts turned to all he'd seen on the Initial B Enterprises Web site. He struggled to work his tongue around the question he needed to ask. "Whose underwear, excuse me, *thongs*, and what initials are you monogramming? OMG! OMG! You're selling Anna Nicole Smith underwear? And you're monogramming it?"

The sisters crossed their arms over their chests and stared at Gus. "We can see how you would think that, but it isn't true. We are selling Alice Nolan Sanders underwear. She was a resident of Shady Pines until she expired. We're selling it in her memory. A percentage of sales goes to her family. It's not our fault if people assume, and the key word here is *assume,* that we are selling Anna Nicole Smith underwear. She's dead now, you know, God rest her soul!" Rose said virtuously.

"And you're telling me some dumb-ass lawyer signed off on this?"

"What's not to sign off on? We told him we were selling Alice Nolan Sanders underwear. There's nothing wrong with that."

Gus slapped at his forehead. "Just how the hell old was Alice Nolan Sanders when she . . . expired?"

"I think she was ninety-two," Violet said, "but

she died almost twenty years ago. We didn't
start the business until shortly after you and Barney entered high school. And even then it was
difficult keeping you and Barney from finding
out about it."

"And she wore thong underwear?"

"No, actually, she wore Depends. She wanted
to wear a thong, but it wasn't practical," Rose
said. "This is one of our biggest sellers. We can't
fill the orders fast enough. In fact, it was the
first product we ever sold, well before Web sites
and the like. Although, when we first started
selling them, orders were soft. Then we decided to monogram them, and we couldn't fill
the orders fast enough, as you can see by our
inventory reports. We had to buy extra machines, but we have a staffing problem. We're
looking to expand by recruiting from other assisted-living facilities."

"Expand?" Gus was in a daze as he followed
the sisters out of the room.

"Yes, expand." Rose stopped in her tracks
and turned around to glare at her grandson.
"Where do you think the money came from to
raise you, send you to college, buy and pay for
the house that is no longer yours, and set you
up in business? We don't farm the farm. Your
grandfather left just enough insurance to get
us through the first few years. And this farm
has to be maintained. Well?"

"I don't know, I'm ashamed to say. You never
discussed money with me. Never, Granny. Even
when I asked, you wouldn't discuss it. I sure as
hell never thought you put me through school

selling Anna Nicole Smith thong underwear. I'm never going to be able to get that out of my mind."

Violet was heartless. "Easy for you to say after the fact. You'll get over it! Can we just get this show on the road? We're losing valuable work hours."

"Door Number Two. Fortune cookies. We get the fortunes. We bake the cookies, too. But, again, it's a problem keeping up with the demand. We supply all the Chinese restaurants within a twenty-mile radius."

"Well, at least that looks legitimate." The sisters shot Gus a glare that could have melted candle wax.

"Door Number Three. This is our voodoo and spell room. Or *witchcraft,* if you prefer that word. I think it's self-explanatory. This is very profitable, and we have tons of repeat customers, though we only started this service about five years ago. We craft spells designed to a person's wish. A lot goes into this part of the business. We have a newsletter that goes out once a month. We sell candles, incense, and anointing oils to go with the spells. It's quite lucrative. The referrals are astounding, and we have thousands of repeat customers. Again, a staffing problem. We could be making three times as much money if we had more people to help us," Iris said.

"Door Number Four. This is our astrology room. Big dollars in astrology. We have a newsletter for this, too. Personal horoscopes at a hundred thirty dollars a pop. We have two-hundred-dollar-a-year memberships, and we had to cut it off because we simply can't keep up with the demand. That's another way of saying we know what we're doing," Rose said.

Gus followed the sisters in a daze. He pinched himself to see if he was dreaming. It hurt, so, no, he wasn't dreaming.

"This is Door Number Five, or the parlor. We needed the biggest room in the house for this portion of Initial B Enterprises. We closed off all the pocket doors to keep the room airtight. We have to keep all the vents closed. All we can do for you right now is to open the door a crack so you can see inside. If we open the door all the way, the feathers will start flying, and it is impossible to catch feathers," Violet said.

Gus let his mind go back to the Initial B Enterprises Web page. At the top and at the bottom, there was a duck quacking across the screen. He hadn't thought much about it until this very minute. "You're selling the Aflac Duck's feathers?" he asked in horror. "You could go to jail for that! I'm sure that duck is protected. Oh, my God!"

"Will you stop being so damned dramatic, Augustus. No one said we are selling the Aflac Duck's feathers. You are *assuming* again. We're selling Audrey's feathers. As you know, we have ducks down in the pond. And we get tons of feathers shipped from Taiwan. Ethel made a dress out of the feathers and put it on our blog, and, yes, we have a blog. Well, that little number sold to a starlet in Hollywood for five thousand dollars. Before you could say *feather,* we had so many orders we were going crazy. Again, supply and demand, and we don't have enough staff.

"Then, the day we saw on the news that Prince William was going to get married, one of our ladies from Shady Pines said we should start making fascinators. Those are the little feather things ladies in England wear in place of a hat. We got right on it, and we were the Web site from which to order for the nuptials. We cleaned up handsomely on that, and the overseas shipping was almost nil because feathers weigh next to nothing. It almost killed us filling the orders because the feathers from Taiwan are white, as are Audrey's feathers, and we had to spray them different colors. But not only did we persevere, we prevailed. We made a killing on those fascinators."

"Because of the Aflac Duck?"

"The duck just runs across our Web page. We never claimed to be selling his feathers. The insurance company the duck represents has no quarrel with us; we're giving them free Web press, or whatever you call it. We cannot be held accountable for what people presume or assume."

"I think I've seen enough," Gus said.

"Really! We were just getting started. We wanted you to see why you can't stay here," Violet drawled.

"How much more is there?"

"Well, there is the entire upstairs. We have an over-sixty sex hotline, an over-seventy hotline, a newsletter, and an advice column that is beyond active. Then there is the foot room. Old people for some reason get purple feet as they age. We have lotions and creams, all kinds of stuff. Right now, though, we're having a bit of a problem with one of the lotions. Never mind, you wouldn't understand."

"I think I've heard enough. Okay, okay. If your intention was to blow my socks off, you have certainly succeeded. I don't know if I should congratulate you or cry for you. I just don't want you all to get in trouble. Tell me again that this is all legal, and I'll be okay with it."

"Our people tell us we are doing nothing wrong, Augustus. We stand behind all of our products and services. Customers have access to us twenty-four/seven. If a problem crops up, we take care of it immediately. We're giving people what they want, and, at the same time, we're not just sitting around waiting to die. We're busy, and we're active, and wc all love what we're doing. Even during the hectic times. Now that you know what we do, are you okay with it?" Rose asked anxiously.

"Well, yes and no, Granny. I'm glad that you're all happy. I'm going to worry, no matter what you say, about the legalities of what you're doing. I won't be able to turn that off. Look, all I want is for us to go back to the way it was. I want you to love me again the way I love you. I screwed up. I'm sorry, but I can't unring that bell. I'm going to try like hell, though. I'd lay down my life for the three of you. I just want you to know that."

And then he started to bawl the way he had when he was six years old. The sisters looked at his miserable face and rushed to wrap him in their arms, tears streaming down their faces.

A good cry was had by all. As if on cue, the sun peaked through the window of the front room.

"I think it's an omen of some kind," Iris sniffled. Violet and Rose agreed. Gus just hung on tight, not wanting to leave the comfort of the warm arms that were wrapped around him.

Finally, Gus was able to say, "What can I do?"

"Are you serious? Do you really want to help?" the sisters asked in unison.

"Damned straight I do. And, no, I do not want your accounting business, but I really need to know one thing for sure. Did you really put me through college selling monogrammed underwear belonging to God only knows who?"

"We did," the sisters said solemnly.

"Well, then, hot damn. I was never first at anything, so I think I can now claim a title of some sort. Not that anyone will ever know, right?"

"Right," the sisters said.

"So, what do you need me to do? I have all kinds of free time now that tax season is over, and I have a lawyer handling my legal affairs. Just spit it out!"

"Recruit for us. Find us people our age who are withering away, old people who have given up and want their lives back, the forgotten ones. Can you do that for us, Augustus? We have a list out in the kitchen, friends of our staff, and, of course, some friends of our own who for one reason or another are residing at other assisted-living facilities. We hesitated to out-and-out recruit, but if you're serious, we'll give you the list, and you can see what you can do. Next to each person's name is the name of the friend who works here, and you can use that as a recommendation. Are you okay doing that, Augustus?"

Gus couldn't remember the last time the sisters had smiled at him the way they were smiling now. At that precise moment, he would have agreed to anything to keep those smiles on their faces. "I'll give it my best shot or die trying. How many?"

"At least twenty. I think we have only eleven names, but I'm sure that each one of those has a friend whom they themselves can recruit. I guess what I'm saying is, get as many as you can get. And if you want to sweeten the pot, tell them they can relocate to Shady Pines. We run a shuttle service between the Pines and here. Meals are free. Nice clean rooms, a bonus every year. Paid vacation."

"All of that plus a shuttle service! Now, why doesn't that surprise me? Okay, I'm in."

"We thought you'd see it our way, Augustus," Rose said happily.

And he did.

Chapter 9

JILL JACKSON, GUS'S ATTORNEY, LEANED BACK IN her ergonomic chair and surveyed her domain. It was a beautiful corner office, with two huge bay windows. Barney Beezer had given her carte blanche on the decorating, telling her to order whatever she wanted because he wanted her to be happy and to stay with his company forever. Being an orphan, she'd always been on the frugal side, so she hadn't gone overboard. She'd shopped and bargain-hunted until she found exactly what she wanted, though it had taken her months to get the office to where she was as comfortable in it as she was in her own home.

Barney had been so impressed with her choices, he spent hours in her office when he was in town. He professed to love the buttery-soft camel chairs, the matching sofa nestled in a corner for clients. He said he loved the fish tank, found it so soothing he nodded off a time or two. He'd complimented her endlessly on her green thumb with the two ficus trees, which were full and glossy, and the luxurious ferns she had on matching pedestals. He always kicked off his Brooks Brothers loafers and walked barefoot on the sand-colored carpet. She'd chosen eyeball overhead lighting that bathed the entire room in a soft glow so that clients didn't feel the need to wear sunglasses. Almost against her will, she'd added a small entertainment center along with a minibar and a built-in coffee machine.

She'd brought blankets and pillows from home for the times when she was too tired to make the trek home late at night. All in all, with her own personal bathroom complete with shower and linen closet, she had been more than happy to sign on with Barney Beezer, and she hadn't regretted it even for a second.

Jill turned her chair around to stare out at the magnificent landscaping Barney insisted on. Nestled in the intimate gardens were colorful tables and chairs, where employees took their coffee and lunch breaks or snatched a few minutes to read an actual paper newspaper. She loved it here. Absolutely loved it. What she didn't love at the moment was her new client,

Barney's oldest and dearest friend, Gus Hollister. Jill knew in her gut, in her heart, and in her mind that if she screwed up on this case, she would be out the door in a nanosecond. While she didn't like it, she understood the politics of such a friendship.

Everything looked so cleaned and scrubbed now in the bright sunshine. The storm of the century, as the newscasters were calling it, was finally over. It would take at least a week of dry weather before the ground would be dried out enough for her and the other employees to enjoy the garden again. More than likely, she wouldn't really miss the time, because she had a full plate, and that meant eating on the run or at her desk while she saw to business.

Jill swiveled her chair back to the desk. She looked down at her little notepad and interpreted her own squiggles. Appointment in thirty minutes with Lynus Litton, her favorite private investigator. It wasn't that she didn't like Phil Ross; she did like him. As a person. What she didn't like was inheriting other people's staff, and, anyway, Phil had retired and done the report on Hollister's wife as a final favor to Barney. She preferred to work with people she was comfortable with and had trained to her liking. Lynus Litton was such a person.

She'd met Lynus in college, and they had become fast friends because she didn't object to what Lynus called his "gayness." Lynus came from a blue-blooded Ivy League family who couldn't accept his gayness and paid him huge sums of money to stay out of their lives, which he did happily, with his partner of many years, Lewis Lippman.

After college and law school, Lynus further angered his blue-blooded Ivy League family by opening a private security firm. He gave quality service at cheap rates, further annoying his upper-crust family; and then he added insult to injury by having Lewis Lippman, the top pastry chef at a five-star hotel, provide pastries for his clients, which arrived fresh three times a day. Lewis Lippman also came from a blue-blooded Ivy League political family that could not accept his gayness, either. His family, however, chose not to pay him to stay away; they insisted on it and disowned him. Jill adored Lewis as much as she adored Lynus. Lewis had even signed a note saying he would make her wedding cake if she ever decided to get married. "Don't go there," she'd said of the offer, "because that isn't going to happen," to which Lewis had responded, "Never say never."

Lynus had a swanky suite of offices in New Town, where he knew everyone and everyone knew him. He never lacked for clients. When Jill called, he immediately put her and whatever she needed at the top of his list and made sure she had his best investigators, which wasn't hard because everyone he worked with was the best.

Jill gathered up her jacket, her backpack, and her Wellington boots and left the office. She needed the yellow Wellingtons to get across the parking lot—unless she was willing to go barefoot, which she did not want to do. If she showed up either barefoot or wearing the Wellingtons, Lynus's sense of fashion would be offended.

Jill was surprised to see how warm it was. Just three hours ago, when she'd practically canoed into the parking lot, certain the engine of her truck would stall out, it had been around forty-five degrees. Now it felt like it was approaching seventy. The sun was exceptionally bright after the monster storm. She loved days like this, when everything looked like someone had scrubbed the world with a brush and soap and water. The day smelled as wonderful as it looked.

Jill made it out of the parking lot and onto the main road that would take her to New Town and Lynus's swanky offices. The trip, which under normal circumstances could have been made in fifteen minutes, took forty-five minutes, what with the flooded roads, downed trees, and drivers unsure where the detours would take them. When she finally arrived at Lynus's building, she was glad she had worn the yellow Wellingtons. She slogged across the parking lot to the front door, where Lynus was waiting for her.

Jill smiled. Lynus could have posed for *GQ* or *Town & Country* in his elegant attire, and the truth was, he had been on the cover of each of these magazines twice, to the absolute mortification of his family. Today, he was wearing a charcoal gray Armani suit with a pristine white shirt and red-striped power tie. Lynus never wore anything but Armani because he said the suits draped his slender body to perfection, something Armani himself attested to. Lynus had even modeled for his buddy Giorgio Armani on more than one occasion.

They hugged. "You smell good," Jill giggled.

"It wouldn't hurt you to spritz yourself with something. Don't you get tired of smelling like grass and fresh air? Those boots have to go!" They bantered back and forth as they walked arm in arm back to Lynus's suite of offices, which had, of course, been professionally decorated, no expense spared.

It was a black-and-white experience. Stark white, pitch-black, yet soft and comfortable at the same time. She didn't know how that could be, with all the chrome and glass, but it was. The carpet was ankle deep and coal black, with not a speck of lint anywhere. The plants were glossy and green, healthy and luxurious. The glass-top modern-looking desk was virtually bare, except for a phone console and a laptop. Jill knew there was a state-of-the-art recording system, somewhere in one of the drawers, which Lynus used instead of taking notes. Lynus was a one-man shop indoors. He did have a reception area, where he had a blowup Betty Boop doll sitting behind the desk. Just for fun. He preferred to greet his clients at the door himself and did not accept walk-in appointments. The foyer door was kept locked at all times, but he did have a remote control in one of his desk drawers that he could activate in case law enforcement showed up regarding clients.

The two old friends made small talk on the leather sofa. In between bites of the delectable pastries and exceptional coffee—made from some exotic beans Lynus had shipped to him from someplace far away that she couldn't pronounce—Jill outlined what she needed from Lynus. Lynus listened, committing it all to memory, knowing that his recording system was his backup.

"Let me make sure I understand all of this. You want Elaine Hollister followed twenty-four/seven. You also want *your client,* Gus Hollister, followed twenty-four/seven. Because . . . you want to know if he lies to you, because all clients lie to their lawyers. You want to know if Gus meets up with his wife for whatever reason."

"Precisely," Jill said, reaching for another pastry.

"In addition, you want to know everything there is to know about your client's family, meaning, of course, the Blossom sisters, Rose, Violet, and Iris. You want all the paperwork on the farm, their holdings if there are any, the whole ball of wax. I'm assuming you want to know about any inheritance down the line that the soon-to-be-ex might think she's entitled to."

"Precisely," Jill said.

"You faxed me Phil Ross's report. I read it; I was not impressed." Lynus sniffed.

"Neither was I. I want all her financials; my client's as well. I want you to pretend that you never saw Phil Ross's report and do your own. You'll bill the firm the way you always do. Stan-

dard expense account. Check with me for anything outgoing over a thousand bucks. I want
video as well as stills. Check in with me every
forty-eight hours. Did I miss anything?"

"I don't think so. If you did, I'll let you know
as we go forward. Tell me something, just between you and me. You don't like your client,
do you?"

"Does it show that much?"

"Oh, yeah," Lynus drawled. "Why?"

"Because he chose a gold digger over his family, a family that raised him, gave him the best
they could. And, when push came to shove, he
chose the gold digger over them. They're old
ladies and he broke their hearts after all they
did for him."

"People do silly things when they're in love,
Jill. Even you know that," Lynus said softly.

"Silly, yes. Silly, I can understand. I don't understand blatant stupidity. What he did to
those old ladies and the way he treated them is
unforgivable in my eyes."

"That's because you've never been in love,
Jill. I'm not saying I'm on Hollister's side. I'm
just saying Hollister might turn out to be an
okay kind of guy who stepped off the rails and
didn't know how to get back on, and this is the
outcome. You really shouldn't judge people
until you know *all* the facts. You know what
else? If you'd fix yourself up, you'd be a knock-
out."

Jill was on her feet in a second, her face dark
pink, her eyes blazing. "Don't you dare go

there, Lynus Litton, or I'm out of here, along with my business."

Lynus smiled. "Testy, aren't we? Must mean I hit a nerve. Okay, peace, my friend. I mean it, though. I know this guy who could turn you into a bombshell in four hours."

"Four hours!" Jill screeched at the top of her lungs. "Did you say *four* hours? I need four whole hours to bring me to the bombshell level or whatever you call it?!"

Lynus grinned. "Okay, maybe I was a bit hasty. Three and a half. Not a second less."

Jill burst out laughing. "Well, that's not going to happen, but if it does, I'm going to hold you to the three and a half hours. Give up on the fixer-upper business and do what you do best, spying."

Jill looked up at Lynus, who towered over her. She thought he was one of the most handsome men she'd ever seen, with his wavy dark hair and soft brown eyes. He had a killer smile that she knew had bought beachfront property for some orthodontist. Lynus was also the kindest, the gentlest, the most caring person she'd ever met in her life. She also knew he was one of those rare people who would always be in her life because he knew, as she did, how important friendships were.

"Okay, big guy, I'm outta here. Keep me posted and give Lewis a hug for me. Tell him those pastries were awesome."

"Those boots have to go, Jill! Lose the backpack, too. Tell Barney you need a raise, and I'll take you shopping for shoes and handbags. I can get them for you wholesale."

Jill laughed all the way to her car. She called over her shoulder, "You know that is never going to happen, Lynus, so give it up already."

Lynus laughed along with her. "Someday you are going to beg me for those three and a half hours. Mark my words." He locked the door, then made his way back to the office, stopping only long enough to salute the blowup doll at the reception desk.

Gus Hollister clicked the remote on the visor and waited for the garage door to open. He sailed in, parked, cut the engine, and hopped out. Wilson was next, but he waited, like the gentleman he must have been in his former life, for his master to first lift out Winnie, who was protesting at being groped.

Gus walked the dogs around to the door that led to the kitchen and waited till both dogs were inside before he carried in Wilson's pink basket and Winnie's treasures. He set the baskets down in the kitchen, then whistled for the dogs, who ignored him completely because they were too busy sniffing out their new digs.

Gus eyed the pile of dog things and decided Maggie might not appreciate having all their treasures in her kitchen, so he lugged their beds and the baskets into the family room and placed everything by the hearth. Maybe tonight he'd make a fire. The last thing he'd heard on the car radio before he turned off the engine was the weatherman announcing the evening temperature, a chilly forty-four degrees once the sun went down. Wilson loved a good blazing fire. Gus kind of liked it himself. He wasn't sure about fat little Winnie. She might have to waddle off to the side if the heat was too much for her.

Gus made his way back out to the kitchen, where he saw that the coffeepot was full, and there was a plate of sandwiches along with a bowl of cut-up fruit in the refrigerator just waiting for him. He helped himself.

He tidied up the kitchen before he headed to Barney's home office, where he sent off text messages, an e-mail, and a fax to Barney, apprising him of what he had learned at Blossom Farm and asking for advice. He was certain Barney would respond to either the text or the e-mail, but he wasn't sure about the fax. The main question, however, was, "Were you aware of any of this?" Right now, though, he needed to think, to come up with a game plan to help his granny and aunts.

Gus trudged back to the kitchen for a second cup of coffee, which he carried into the family room. He was not surprised to see both dogs sacked out in their beds. Wilson offered up a feeble wag of his tail and went back to sleep. Winnie was already snoring, her paws wrapped around a ragged doll that might have been a Raggedy Andy at some point in time. He smiled.

He settled down in Barney's favorite recliner to wait for his friend to get in touch. He closed his eyes and drifted off to sleep.

Chapter 10

GUS BOLTED OFF THE RECLINER WHEN HE HEARD the three-note cell-phone ring. He shook his head to clear away the muzziness from his interrupted sleep. He answered and mumbled a sleepy greeting.

"Well, hi there, sleepyhead," Barney said. "What the hell are you doing sleeping at this time of day? Now, me, I should be pounding out some z's considering the time difference, just so you know."

"I'm stressed, okay? Cut the bullshit, Barney, I'm not in the mood. All I want to know is did you know what my family was doing?"

"No! You spell that, n-o! They came to me and asked my advice about finding someone to construct a Web site for them and I recommended someone. When I asked if they needed any other business services, like a good CPA, they said that they already had an accounting firm. I tried to talk them into switching their business to your firm, but they were adamantly opposed. Said you didn't need to know their business. I had to respect that, and there was no way in hell I was going to go up against the three of them. And, obviously, I could not say anything to you about whatever was going on.

"That is the sum total of my involvement in their activities. I have to say I didn't think anything in this life could surprise me, but you did one hell of a job. Did they really make all that money doing . . . ah . . . what they've been doing?"

"Oh, yeah, and they have the capacity to make twice that much if I can manage to recruit more help for them. I didn't tell you this, but some dude named Oscar, who works with them, wanted to take me out to the barn and kill me. To keep me silent. Did you hear what I just said, Barney? They were actually considering it."

Barney laughed. "Well, they didn't, that's the important thing. What are you going to do? Do you have a game plan?"

"Not exactly, but I will do what they want me to do if that's the only way they're going to let me back in their lives. I have a list of . . . potential employees. I just have to go visit them and give them my spiel. That means I have to snatch them away from their current digs and get them to Blossom Farm."

"I'm thinking that might be kidnapping, Gus." Barney laughed again.

Gus fumed. "You have a better idea? And it's not kidnapping if they come willingly. Oscar, the dude who wanted to kill me, said they have minds of their own and can do whatever they want to do. Wait. Maybe that was Fred. They all look alike to me. And I was worried about my well-being. So that's your advice. You know what, Barney, that wasn't even advice. You just made a comment."

"I can't believe they didn't want me to invest their money. Goldman Sachs, my ass! That really hurt!" Barney said, all trace of his earlier laughter gone. He sounded wounded to his very core.

"Ha-ha! Guess they didn't trust you, either. Now you know how I feel. *Felt.*"

"Well, if that's all your news, I'm going to shut down and go to bed. I have a full day ahead of me."

"There is one other thing. Elaine had me served today. She's charging me with everything under the sun."

"They always do. Just turn it all over to Jill and let her deal with it. You have more pressing things to deal with right now."

"She hates me. Don't you know any other lawyers? Like a man, for instance."

"I do, but they won't work for your situation. Trust me, she will give you superior representation. She doesn't have to like you, and you don't have to like her. The end result is all that counts. And she knows *everybody* and uses all her contacts. Suck it up, buddy. Keep me posted on how you're doing. I can't believe they didn't want me to invest their money. I seriously doubt I'll ever be able to sleep again knowing that."

"Guess they didn't want you knowing their business, either," Gus jabbed. Instead of a reply or remark, Gus realized he had nothing but dead air on the line. He ended the connection and flopped back into the recliner. Neither dog so much as cracked an eyelid.

Gus sniffed the air as he looked at his watch. He'd slept away the better part of the afternoon. He was smelling the tantalizing aroma of garlic and . . . spaghetti sauce. Maggie was cooking dinner. He could hardly wait to chow down.

Four o'clock! If he hustled, he could make a trip to the Sea Crest facility, where he might be able to recruit someone named Elroy Hitchens. Sea Crest was, at the most, seven or eight miles as the crow flies, from where he was standing. But first he had to fax the papers the process server had handed him to the fireplug.

Gus trudged to Barney's office, ripping papers away from the staple, not caring if the paper ripped at the corner. He caught snatches of the legalese and still couldn't believe what he was reading. The words *brutality* and *physical violence* locked on his eyeballs. No way was he going to read this piece of crap again.

Gus scribbled a note on the cover sheet before he shoved the papers into the fax machine and punched in the numbers that would send them flying to Jill Jackson. He dusted his hands dramatically and left the room. His work here was done.

The Sea Crest Adult Living facility was nestled behind a colorful hedge of glossy greenery. Gus parked Barney's Jeep Commander and got out to walk up a flagstone path that would take him to the reception area. A pleasant-looking woman greeted him cheerfully when he said he wanted to visit with Elroy Hitchens.

"Elroy is on the deck. He likes to sit out there and read before dinner. Go down the hall, and the second set of doors on the right will lead you to the deck."

Gus thanked her, followed the instructions, and found Elroy Hitchens without any problem because he was the only one on the deck. He was reading a copy of *Moby Dick*. Gus introduced himself and sat down. "Fred sent me."

Elroy Hitchens peered at Gus over the top of his glasses. "Why?" He marked the page he was reading by turning down its corner.

Gus told him.

"How do I know you aren't some kind of slick con artist who preys on old people in assisted-living facilities? All that you just said, it sounds too good to be true. When something sounds too good to be true, most likely it isn't true. You following me here, young fella? How'd that all happen?"

Gus told him everything, even his part in what had been going on. He didn't hold anything back.

"You should never turn your back on your family, young fella. In the end, that's all that's left to us. I should know. So now you think you can step up to the plate and make all that sadness and sorrow go away. Is that what you're telling me?"

"I guess I am." Gus had the good grace to look ashamed.

"Well, women are more forgiving than men, so I can see that maybe happening in your case. Before I give you my answer, I need to call Fred. Why don't you go into the dayroom and fetch us some coffee while I make my call."

"Okay. How do you like your coffee?"

"Black, how else?"

That wasn't so hard, Gus thought as he made his way to a huge coffee urn sitting on a table in the corner of the dayroom. It was a cozy room, with wraparound windows on two sides. A giant seventy-six-inch television was mounted on the wall. The chairs and sofas were colorful and looked comfortable. The carpet was a neutral color and flat, for easy wheelchair mobility, he assumed. He looked around. Two men were playing checkers. Two ladies were watching

Oprah reruns, and a fat, lazy-looking cat was sitting on the lap of a woman who sat in a wheelchair. She was stroking the cat, her eyes blank. Gus looked away.

Back on the deck, Gus handed over the coffee. He waited.

"Okay, young fella, Fred backed up everything you said and added a bit more. I made a call to another old friend, who is over in Sunrise, who said he knew a few others. It's in the pipeline as we speak. By the time I finish this coffee, I think you'll have enough commitments to make everyone happy. Now, how are you going to get us all out to Blossom Farm? You're going to need a bus, young fella. And we'll be ready to go by ten tomorrow morning, I guarantee it. Give me your phone number, and I'll be calling you sometime this evening. We have things we need to get in order. There is one hitch. We all want a *contract*; otherwise, we ain't buying no pig in a poke."

Contracts. He hadn't thought of that. "I don't see a problem with that. I'll bring them with me tomorrow if it's a go. What about your families, your bills here?"

"I'm no problem. I don't have any family. I signed myself in here so I can sign myself out. I can do my banking online here. I'll take care of that this evening. As for the others, when it comes to family, while they might be lurking out there, they won't even notice our friends have moved. That's a pretty blanket statement, but ninety-nine percent accurate. All the others have to do is notify their Social Security office and the state that they are no longer responsible for payment to their facility. I can almost guarantee there won't be a problem, but if there is, you can deal with it, young fella. Does that work for you?"

"It does," Gus said happily. He could hardly wait to get home to call his grandmother to report in on his progress. He'd come through for her, and he really hadn't had to sweat it out. A piece of cake.

"Well, it was nice meeting you, Mr. Hitchens. I guess we'll be seeing each other tomorrow. If anything changes, tell me when you call tonight. I'll see about renting a . . . bus or some kind of vehicle to get you all to Blossom Farm. If I can't get a bus, I'll just make several trips. Before I leave, is there anything else you need to know? Any questions?" Gus stood up and offered his arm for a handshake.

"Call me Elroy, everyone else does. There is one thing. What are you going to do about the gold digger? I'm just being nosy here, so that means you don't have to answer me."

Gus sat back down. "I don't know. I have a lawyer. Nothing my wife said in the complaint was true. This is all about money. I don't think she ever loved me. That's pretty hard for me to swallow and accept. I feel like a fool. I must have been blind, is all I can say in my own defense."

"What do you feel about her now?"

"What? You planning on writing a book, Mr. Hitchens?"

"I told you I was just being nosy. See! You still have feelings, and you need to let them go. You need to deal with what's going on in your life, and you can't let her drag you down. Put it behind you and move on. Really move on. In the end, actions speak louder than words, and your family will be watching to see how you handle it. Guess you know that, don't cha, young fella?"

"Yes, I do know that, Mr. Hitchens." Gus was on his feet again, his hand extended for a second time. Elroy offered up a bone-crushing shake. "I'll see you tomorrow. Have a nice evening, Mr. Hitchens."

"I plan to, young fella. See ya."

Gus was back in Barney's house by six o'clock. Just in time, according to Maggie, to sit down and enjoy his dinner. "Do you want me to stay and clean up or to come back later?" she asked.

"I can do the cleanup. It smells wonderful. Did you make some extra meatballs without the sauce for the dogs?"

"I did, and they're in the covered bowl on the counter. The garlic bread is in the warming oven. Just cover the leftovers, and I can either freeze them or you can have them for lunch tomorrow."

"Thanks, Maggie. Have a nice night. Oh, were there any calls?"

"Just one. Well, actually four, but it was the same person. Miss Jackson. She sounded . . . perturbed."

"I bet she did. Is she going to call back, or did she want me to call her back?"

"She didn't say. Each time she called, all she said was, 'Is he back yet?'"

"I'll call her after dinner."

Gus knew he wouldn't be able to enjoy his dinner until he fed the dogs theirs. Winnie was looking at him with adoring wet eyes. Wilson glared at him. "Okay, okay, I'm getting it, Wilson. I forgot to give you guys a Pop-Tart, so you'll get two after you eat your dinner. Cut me some slack here, okay?" Wilson's tail gave a half wag as he sat back on his haunches to wait for his dinner.

Gus mashed up the meatballs, added some wet and dry dog food, and set the bowls down on the floor. The dogs practically inhaled their food and then trotted over to the door to go out. They scratched on the door to be let back in just as Gus sat down to eat. He handed out the two Pop-Tarts, and the dogs scurried back to their beds in the family room.

The phone rang six times as Gus ate his dinner. Knowing it was the fireplug, Gus refused to answer it. Just the sound of the ringing phone was already giving him indigestion. He had a wonderful, tasty dinner in front of him that he should have been enjoying. He knew he wasn't going to be able to enjoy the peach cobbler, either. So he'd save that for later.

The phone continued to ring as Gus finished his dinner, packed up the leftovers, and tidied the kitchen. He turned on the dishwasher and sat back down to enjoy his after-dinner cup of coffee. Just as he brought the cup to his lips, the phone shrilled for the umpteenth time.

"That's it!" He picked up the phone and barked a single one-word greeting. "What?!"

"When I call you, Mr. Hollister, you WILL answer the phone. I can't represent you if we don't communicate. Is that clear?"

Gus grimaced as he pictured the fireplug venting her venom at him. "Tell me how to answer the phone when I'm not here. If you don't want to represent me, then quit. This world is flooded with lawyers. I can take my pick. I faxed you the papers I was served. I included a message saying it was all lies. Do you want me to repeat the message? It *is* all lies. Now it's your turn to do whatever the hell it is Barney pays you to do. Now, here's another message for you. You only need to ring this number once and leave a message, the way normal people do. Now here's my third message. Sit on a pointy stick and twirl around until it comes out that mouth of yours. Goodbye, Miss Jackson, have a nice evening."

Gus sipped at his coffee as he waited for Barney to call him. He knew in his gut that the fireplug would have called Barney as soon as she hung up, to tell him she was quitting, then Barney would call him and ream his ass. He waited as the minutes crawled by.

When the only phone call that evening was the one from Elroy Hitchens, Gus was almost disappointed.

With nothing else on his agenda, Gus went

upstairs, showered, and changed into warm sweats. He returned to the family room, made a fire, and sat down to watch reruns of *NCIS*, his favorite television show. The dogs were snoring contentedly by the hearth.

Tomorrow is another day.

Chapter 11

GUS BOLTED UPRIGHT IN THE RECLINER. HE wasn't sure what had woken him. A bad dream? The pain in his neck from sleeping in the recliner? He looked over at the hearth, where Wilson and Winnie were snoring. Maybe the last log that fell over, shooting sparks up the chimney? He was inclined to go with the bad dream. What the hell was it? Nothing came to mind. He looked at his watch: three a.m.! He must have dozed off around eight, which meant he'd slept seven or so hours, his regular sleep pattern. It also meant he was done sleeping for the night, so he might as well get up, shower, shave, make some coffee, and get a head start on the day and whatever it was going to bring his way.

Gus leaned his head back and closed his eyes, not to sleep but to think. His last conscious thought before falling asleep had been that he had to call the fireplug and apologize for his rudeness. They needed to start over from square one and stop with the one-upmanship. Like Barney said, he didn't have to like her. All he had to do was let her do what she does best, represent him. Well, he could do that. Or die trying.

He made a mental list of things he wanted and needed to do for the day. First, he had to arrange contracts to bring with him when he picked up the seniors. Next, he had to get a bus from somewhere to pick them up and take them to Blossom Farm. Then he had to come up with a work plan for everyone on his grandmother's staff. A daunting job to be sure, but he was good at organizing, or at least he thought so. And he needed to call Barney again at some point today. And he had to get in touch with a Realtor to find him a place of his own. Otherwise, he was going to have a neurotic dog on his hands. Wilson liked routine—his own place, his own things—and for sure he did not like to be shuffled from one place to another. He understood that because it was exactly how he himself felt.

Gus heaved himself out of the recliner and looked at the dogs. Wilson cracked one eyelid as if to say, *it's not time yet to get up*, and promptly went right back to sleep. Winnie simply continued to snore.

Gus was back downstairs and in the kitchen making coffee. The clock on the Wolf range said it was four-thirty. His grandmother and the aunts would be up at five. He could call then and ask about contracts and if they had any ideas as to how and where he could get a bus.

While the coffee dripped, Gus toasted a bagel he didn't really want. He spread apple butter on it and wolfed it down as he waited for the coffee to finish dripping. He looked around to see where he'd dropped his briefcase yesterday. He saw it sitting by the laundry-room door. He opened it and withdrew a legal pad and pen. He needed to make a list. Phone calls first. Then physical things he needed to do. When he was done, he had the page almost filled, and not because he wrote big. *Awesome*, he thought.

The coffee, when he poured it, was dark and strong, just the way he liked it. So strong it almost curled the hair on his chest. He grimaced. *What man in his right mind would want curly chest hair?*

Gus went back to rummaging in his briefcase until he found the fireplug's office number. If he called before office hours, he could take the coward's way out and leave a message, and he wouldn't have to talk to the irritating lawyer. Yeah, yeah, that's what he'd do. But he'd wait till six o'clock. Six o'clock was a decent hour to call and leave a message. Okay, done. He crossed that chore off his list.

Gus yanked his laptop out of his briefcase and booted up. He scrolled down in his address book until he found the name of a Realtor with whom he'd done business before. Marsha Dewey. He fired off an e-mail stating his requirements and said expediency was paramount. He added a P.S. that he needed a fenced-in yard for Wilson.

The next thing he did was to check his business account. He didn't like tapping into it for his personal use, but the way he saw it, at the moment he had no other choice. There was enough money in the account for a deposit on a small house of some kind and some new furniture if he only furnished a bedroom and bought a few chairs and a television. Later on, he could finish furnishing it. If there was a later on. Worst-case scenario, he could always borrow money from Barney. Marsha would do her best for him, that much he knew. He scratched Marsha off his list.

Gus spent the next hour tapping out e-mails in response to clients concerning their filing extensions. He liked to stay in touch and give what he called his own personal touch to his clients. It worked well for him, and he rarely lost a client; when he did, it was because the client had either passed on or moved out of state. That taken care of, he e-mailed his insurance agent and a few other people to bring them up-to-date about his present circumstances.

The last e-mail that he sent off was to his office manager, apprising her of his current status, which was, "You will see me when you see me," and "I'm only a phone call away."

Bus. He needed a bus. As far as he knew, car-rental agencies did not rent out buses. Schools had buses. Churches had buses. But then there was the question of insurance and liability. He groaned. Well, hopefully his granny would have some ideas, or else it was going to be trip after trip in the Blossom Farm van.

Wilson appeared at his side and nosed his leg, his dark eyes asking for forgiveness. At least, that's what Gus wanted to think. Winnie offered up a soft *woof* of an early morning greeting. Gus opened the door, and, gentleman that he was, Wilson waited until Winnie waddled through. He followed her out to the gray of early dawn. While the dogs sniffed the new territory, marked it, and sniffed some more, Gus got their food bowls ready. He always fed Wilson twice a day, breakfast and dinner. Winnie he rather thought got fed three or four times a day, a rule he was about to break. He fished out a Pop-Tart and broke it in half. First step in cutting back on the dog's food intake. He wasn't worried about Wilson, because Wilson ran off the calories, while tubby little Winnie preferred to laze about. He hoped her bad habits didn't rub off on his dog.

Ten minutes later, Maggie came in with the dogs, looked around, and asked if Gus wanted breakfast. He said no, and she disappeared, probably to make his bed, which hadn't been slept in. God only knew what the little house-keeper thought about her newest guest.

At six-forty, Gus had both dogs loaded into the Jeep and was on his way to Blossom Farm. Winnie moaned and groaned the whole way, while Wilson poked his head out the half-open window to enjoy the early morning air.

Before he got out of the Jeep, Gus checked his cell phone to see if the fireplug had sent a text. She had not. His fist shot in the air. "Okay, guys, let's hit it!" Wilson hit the ground, ran to the kitchen door, and barked. Gus was left to carry Winnie into the house, where all the seniors made a fuss over her. He watched in horror as they all fed the dogs bits of bacon, waffles, and scraps of sausages and toast.

"Keep this up, and that dog is going to have a heart attack. And don't for one minute think dogs can't have heart attacks. She's too fat, Granny. You need to stop giving her extra food. I already fed her kibble and her regular food plus half a Pop-Tart, which I am going to cut back to a quarter, then just a pinch," Gus said half under his breath. He waited to see what the seniors' reaction would be.

"He's right; my old springer spaniel had a heart attack," Fred said. "What are you doing here so early?" he groused.

"Getting ready to get this show on the road. I need to get a bus. Do any of you know where I can get one?"

"As a matter of fact, I do. I'll call Pastor Evans at Sycamore Baptist Church. How long do you think you'll need it, Augustus?" his grandmother said.

"At least till noon. Depends if your new recruits are ready, and how long I have to wait for them at each stop. Noon, and I'm being conservative. Ah, what time do you all start to . . . ah, work?"

"We like to be at our workstations by seven a.m. We get up at five. We were busy last evening trying to set up accommodations at Shady Pines for the newcomers. A few of us got up late this morning as we had only a few hours of sleep last night. We were just trying to figure out how to do kitchen duty. We're going to have a lot of mouths to feed. And a lot of food to order," Rose said softly. To Gus's ears, it sounded like he was back in the fold with his granny.

"You should have called me. I would have helped."

"We thought about it, but decided against it," Violet said in her most unforgiving tone of voice.

"Well, I'm here now, so is there anything you want me to do? I don't have to pick up Elroy Hitchens until ten. He's at Sea Crest."

"No, not right now. Besides, you're on probation," Iris said.

"Probation! You put me on *probation?* When did that happen? No one said anything about probation!" Gus exploded. Wilson was at his feet, not liking the tone of his master's voice. Winnie whined from the rag carpet by the sink.

"We told you that yesterday morning. You were so busy grumbling and complaining about the old sycamore, you probably didn't hear us," Violet said. "Or else you simply tuned us out. Now, which is it?"

"I didn't tune you out. I didn't hear you. Yes, I was grumbling and complaining about that old tree because I loved it. It was part of my growing-up years. Barney's, too. How long is the probation?"

The Blossom sisters looked at one another. "Ninety days! You have to prove yourself. Then we'll vote on whether to make you a permanent employee," Rose said. "In the meantime, you will receive a stipend of sorts. We still have to vote on that."

"Ninety days! That's three months! And then you're going to *vote* on me? I don't believe this! I'm your grandson." Gus looked at his aunts and bellowed, "I'm your nephew!" The Blossom sisters shrugged.

"While we're talking about making people employees, Elroy Hitchens said that the seniors would not be coming to, as he put it, buy a pig in a poke, unless they had contracts. I told him I would bring them with me this morning. I assume that you have contracts for your new hires," Gus said.

"Certainly," Rose said. "I'll just get them before you leave."

Having paid no attention to the discussion of contracts, Oscar of the clicking dentures said loud and clear, "Well, you better belicve that you're on probation, young fella, because that's the way it is. How do we know that you can measure up? This is not some Mickey Mouse operation we're running here, just so you know. We have to take that into consideration." Clickety-clack went the dentures.

"Okay, okay, I get it! I accept your terms. I will prove myself. Granny, if you call the pastor, I'll be on my way to pick up your new . . . staff . . . as soon as you get me those contracts. Is there anything else I can do for you wonderful people before I leave?"

"Well, you got one thing right. We are wonderful," Fred said. Gus eyed him to see if he was being sarcastic. He wasn't.

Gus felt like a ten-year-old, waiting to hear about the bus. All the old people were staring at him. He didn't know if he should smile, grin, or stare down at the floor as he waited for his granny to say yeah or nay on the bus.

"Okay, it's a go. It's bus number two, and it's parked to the left of the front door that leads into the school. The keys will be on the visor. You are to fill the gas tank before you return it. We have a company gas card," Rose said, rummaging in the cookie jar for the credit card.

"Thank you. I'm on my way. Do you want me to report in on the way, or should I just, you know . . . show up? Should I bring them here first or take your new staff and their belongings to Shady Pines?"

Violet drew herself up to her full height, which was awesome in itself. "This is what we meant about you proving yourself: taking the initiative. We'll be grading you on your performance."

Gus didn't know where it came from or why he said it out loud, but the words were out of his mouth before he could stop them. "I get it, like a sexual encounter when you have to perform, then you get a grade from your partner."

Clickety-clack. "Right on, young fella."

Gus decided to quit while he could still walk. He was out the door in a flash. Wilson howled. Gus stuck his head back in the door and yelled, "You can go next time. There'll be no room in the bus."

Gus slid into the Jeep and drove up the hill and out to the main road. He stopped, took a deep breath, and yanked out his cell phone and called Barney. The moment he heard Barney's *What now?* he started to babble.

"They fucking put me on *probation*. I have to prove myself in ninety days, then they're going to *vote* on me. Did you hear what I just said, Barney? Will you say something, for Christ's sake?"

"They didn't mention my name, did they? Just you, right?"

"What? You're concerned for yourself and not me! I called you for . . . Jesus, I don't know why I called you."

"Well, the way I see it, this isn't about me, for which I am very thankful. This is about your making things right. I'm glad it's you and not me. Probation for ninety days. Damn, that's three whole months. That really sucks.

That's going to take you right into the middle of July. And then there's all that worry about how they're going to vote on you. Man, I am so glad I am not you. Oh, and you need to stop calling me unless it's an emergency."

Gus ended the call. He was tempted to pitch his cell phone out the window, but he knew in his gut that would show up some way, somehow, on his performance record. He did his best to shift his thoughts into neutral and concentrate on his driving.

Fifteen minutes later, Gus pulled into the Sycamore Baptist Church parking lot and saw the bus right where his grandmother said it would be. He parked the car, got out, and jogged over to a big yellow bus with a bright-colored rainbow painted on the side. He opened the door, got in, and saw the keys on the visor. That's when he realized he didn't know how to drive a bus. Gears! More gears than the ones in the Porsche. And the bus was *BIG!* He had to back up this baby. Maybe he could pull it off if he didn't have to park anywhere. *Or I could call someone and ask how to drive a bus.* The thought was so stupid, he cringed. It all came down to two words: *performance* and *vote.*

Gus called Barney a second time. "Do you know how to drive a bus?"

Barney's laugh was so evil that Gus clenched his teeth as he turned the key in the ignition and waited for something to happen. Maybe there was a manual in the bus. Or . . . maybe Elroy Hitchens knew how to drive a bus. It might be worth a call, he decided, when he

couldn't find a manual. Performance, performance, performance.

Somebody should have asked him if he
could drive a bus. Aha, it was a test. They were
testing him for his performance record. Well,
by God, he'd just figure this out on his own
and drive this damned bus or bust wide open.
He was going to perform if it was the last thing
he did.

Chapter 12

Elaine Hollister looked at herself in the ornate mirror hanging on the back of the closet door. She'd chosen a jonquil-colored suit and a silk blouse with a small bow tie at the throat. She thought it looked demure and at the same time showed off her voluptuous figure. Her heels were high, accentuating her long, shapely legs. Small diamond studs sparkled in her ears. She still wore her engagement and wedding rings, and a gold Rolex watch.

As Elaine twirled this way and that way, a strand of hair slipped out from behind her ear. She loved her hair. It was thick and lustrous and naturally blond. Men loved to run their hands through it. Gus used to love to bury his face in her hair and tell her she smelled like a spring meadow in bloom. Today she wore it artfully piled on her head so that it appeared she was taller than she was. The last thing she did was to spritz a flowery designer perfume into a haze, then stepped under it and twirled around. She sniffed appreciatively.

She was good to go. Such a shame that she had to drive that yellow tin can out in the driveway. She'd be wrinkled and mussed when she arrived at her attorney's office, but it couldn't be helped. Soon, she'd get a new car, one she looked good in. If her attorney was half as good as he said he was, and she was counting on him to be, she just might end up with Gus's Porsche.

In the kitchen, Elaine looked at the clock over the stove—nine forty-five. Fifteen minutes to drive to the lawyer's office, an hour meeting, a ten-minute good-bye, fifteen minutes to get back home, then get her things ready, strip down to a flowing white robe, and head for the attic, where she would set up her altar and cast a new spell precisely at the stroke of noon. It was paramount that she start her spell on time. She shivered at what she needed to do, because it was crucial to her plan to walk away with Gus Hollister's holdings.

Elaine set the new code for the alarm system, scooted out, crossed the deck, and went down the steps to the yellow Beetle. Five minutes later, she was on her way. She didn't look back. If she had, she would have seen a tall man walking a small dog wearing a sparkly colored collar with a matching leash. A man who didn't live in the gated community.

The building that housed the prestigious law firm of Diamond, Diamond, and Diamond in New Town was constructed of old Virginia brick and covered with ivy. The firm itself was as old as the building. The elder Diamond had had it constructed during his last year of law school. It had been completed the day his shingle was handed to him by his father, Sycamore Springs's only doctor at the time. The plaque was brass, and it was polished and buffed every day. The Diamond Building, as it was often called, was more often than not referred to as the oldest building in New Town. Residents were quick to point out, however, that it was not a historic building.

The Diamond family occupied all three floors of the updated, state-of-the-art building, with each attorney, complete with receptionist and two paralegals, having a floor to himself.

Elaine chose the Diamond law firm because of her love of diamonds and the tarot card reading she'd commissioned. One of the cards, she couldn't remember which one, said that precious gems were all around her. Then, when she'd just been in the planning stage of her divorce, she'd cast a spell, which reinforced her decision.

Elaine took a moment to stare at her reflection in the plate-glass door before she opened it. She looked perfect, stunning actually. She settled the Chanel handbag with its gold-braided chain, the bag Gus had surprised her with on New Year's Eve, on her shoulder. She'd been so surprised, because the holidays had been especially grim. She'd shown her gratitude in the only way she knew how. Sex.

Elaine shrugged away the memory as she made her way to the elevator that would take her to the third floor. Like she would even consider the first two floors and the attorneys they housed, regardless of their being named Diamond, too. Only the founder of the firm was good enough for her, so she had held out for Isaac Diamond. Because, Isaac Diamond was old but still sharp as a razor. Not to mention he was a lascivious old man who couldn't disguise the lust in his eyes when he looked at her. Then there was the Diamond money. Piles and piles of money and all controlled by Isaac, who was a widower.

Elaine followed Isaac's secretary to his sumptuous office, which looked to be professionally decorated. It also looked like there wasn't much foot traffic; nor were there any indentations in the comfortable furniture. It was an office that Isaac still inhabited from long years of habit and routine. A place to come to, to prove he still had control of Diamond, Diamond, and Diamond. Which he did. No decisions were made and no new clients were accepted until Isaac voiced his approval. A tightly run ship with billable hours at an all-time high.

Elaine remembered how she had cringed when she was told the firm charged $550 an hour. Paralegals billed at $300. Isaac had assured her she would get it back in spades from Gus when all was said and done. She hated dipping into her local reserve funds, but she had had little choice, so with a shaking hand, she'd written out a check for $25,000 as a retainer. She told herself she had a money spell that she could cast when she returned home that was all but guaranteed to work in four days. Or was it nine? Right now, she couldn't remember. Everything in witchcraft was geared to the numbers four and nine. She loved those numbers and considered them her lucky numbers.

Isaac stood up and came around the desk to greet his newest client, his only client. He put his arm around her shoulders and led her to a chair across from his desk.

Isaac Diamond was a handsome, imposing figure topping the height charts at six foot three inches. According to his doctors, he was still in excellent physical shape at the age of seventy-eight. He played golf three days a week and worked out with a personal trainer twice a week. Today, he wore a custom-made Hugo Boss suit and Bally shoes that were so shiny, he could see his reflection in them. He was tanned and wore blue contact lenses. His hair was white, and there was plenty of it, thanks to hair plugs. Isaac Diamond was vain. Very vain.

"You look like a breath of spring, my dear. How did you weather that horrible storm?"

Elaine smiled. "Thank you. I had a few limbs come down, and my yard looks like a lake right now, but that was the worst of it. Thank you for asking, Isaac."

"The reason I asked you to come in—other than to ask you to lunch—was to tell you that I've heard from your husband's attorney."

Elaine looked across the desk at her attorney. Her eyes were moist and glistening. "Isaac, please, don't refer to Gus as my husband. Just call him Gus."

"Noted, my dear. It won't happen again. Yesterday, late, I think it was around six, and I had left for the day, but I got her voice mail when I got in this morning. Jill Jackson is Gus's lawyer. I'm sorry to say I knew nothing of her; nor did either of my sons. So, I googled her, and I must say, she is going to be a worthy adversary. She's a powerhouse in her own right. She works for Barnaby Beezer. She is his principal attorney. I'm told that in financial circles, the mere mention of her name sends shivers up the spines of opposing counsel."

Elaine leaned back in the comfortable chair and crossed her legs, the skirt she was wearing hiking up an inch too far. She didn't care. What she cared about right now was the prickle of alarm that was making itself known. Gus's friend's—Barney's—top gun. She should have known Gus would get the best. Well, Isaac Diamond wasn't exactly chopped liver.

For the first time in her life, Elaine was unsure what her next move should be. Should she respond? Should she weep and wail? Should she be blasé and say something witty to Isaac?

Elaine tilted her head to the side and made a little moue with her lips. "You aren't telling me some female attorney can out-lawyer the great Isaac Diamond, are you?"

"What I'm telling you, my dear, is this. Gus Hollister has the best of the best going to bat for him by way of Barnaby Beezer. There's not a judge in this town who isn't invested with Beezer. I am myself, just so you know. I sent out queries to some of my peers, and Jackson is going to be a formidable foe. She doesn't like to lose. Actually, she *never* does lose. She takes no prisoners. And she's going to go after you like a dog in heat. I would be remiss if I didn't tell you this. Full disclosure is my motto, it always has been. Now, my dear, I want to ask you two questions.

"One: Is everything you told me in our first meeting true and accurate? I do not like to be blindsided. Now is the time to tell me if you exaggerated about anything or if, out of a desire for vengeance, you might have told a few fibs. People tend to do that in the beginning of divorce proceedings."

Elaine dabbed at her eyes. She shook her head. She didn't trust herself to speak because she thought her heart was going to pound right out of her chest.

"Two: Is there anything in your background that you've neglected to tell me? The reason I ask you this is because Jill Jackson utilizes the Lynus Litton security firm. If there is anything you're hiding, Litton and his people will ferret it out. They don't get any better than Litton. And before you can ask, yes, we have a team of private investigators that we use, but even *I* know that Litton's people are superior. I have my people running checks on Gus, his family, and his friend, Barnaby Beezer. Beezer is going to come up clean, I know that. But we're doing it anyway."

Elaine continued to dab at her eyes and shake her head at the same time. Maybe she'd gone too far this time. Going up against a small-town CPA is one thing. But going against a CPA with a billionaire hedge-fund manager for a best friend was perhaps a bridge too far. *Just my luck to get involved with someone who turned out to have Barney Beezer as his best friend. Maybe this time I should cut my losses and move on. Look for a new mark.*

But the thought of Gus's five-hundred-thousand-dollar mortgage-free house, his Porsche, a percentage of his business, and a possible inheritance down the road won out. She squared her shoulders and gave one last dab at her eyes before she said, "I trust you to handle my affairs, Isaac. I would like to say one thing, however. When I agreed to marry Gus, we both spoke of our pasts. We both agreed whatever came before we met no longer mattered. Gus insisted we sign a paper, just between the two of us, in case things ever got . . . ah . . . sticky. I have that note somewhere, in my jewelry box, I think. I'll look for it and send it on to you or make a copy and fax it to you."

There was no need to tell Isaac that she was the one who had initiated the episode of the little note. Gus had fallen over himself to sign it. In her opinion, at the time, she'd thought it was as good as a prenup, the difference being that this one gave *her* carte blanche to do as she wished, since he could not use her past against her. Now, she could only hope that it wasn't going to come back and bite her on the rear.

"Isaac, if there's nothing else, I have to return home as I have a real-estate appraiser due at two o'clock, and I want to tidy up to make a good impression. I have to get out of that house as soon as possible—too many bad memories. If you're successful in getting the house for me, I want to sell it and, of course, invest the money."

"I had plans to take you to lunch," Isaac said, his tone reflecting his surprise at being turned down.

"I'm sorry, Isaac, I can't do lunch, but if you're free this evening, so am I. I would love to go to dinner with you." *And ply you with liquor and take you to bed. In one hour, I can make all your sexual fantasies come true, you old coot.*

"That's an offer I can't refuse. Shall we meet somewhere, or would you like me to send a car for you?"

"I think I can find my own way if you tell me where you'd like to have dinner."

"I was thinking of La Petite. Shall we say seven-thirty?"

"My absolute favorite restaurant. I'll be there, Isaac. Have a nice afternoon."

Isaac got up, walked around the desk, and escorted Elaine to the elevator. He smiled at her and said, "Don't worry about anything. You're in good hands."

"It's not you I'm worrying about, Isaac. I'm worried about Gus and the way he lies and manipulates situations to suit himself and make himself look good in the process. I didn't find out these traits until after we were married. I put up with it as long as I could. Gus is a control freak. I'm sorry. I said all this before. I'm in no mood to beat a dead horse. I look forward to having dinner with you this evening. Thank you again, Isaac, for taking my case."

Isaac heard the words, but he really wasn't paying attention to them. He was more concerned with the fine-looking woman standing next to him and what he was hoping might follow dinner.

Elaine wiggled her fingers at Isaac as the door to the elevator slid shut. With no one watching her, Elaine leaned against the wall of the elevator and let her shoulders slump. She hadn't pulled it off completely. She was smart enough to know that, and now she had to get to work.

The tall man carrying a black backpack and walking the little dog, a Jack Russell terrier, sauntered up and down the beautiful neighborhood. He seemed not to have a care in the world, being concerned only with his midday stroll on a beautiful April morning. His name was Mickey Yee, Lynus Litton's top investigator. He had an American mother and a Chinese father whom he loved dearly. He didn't speak Chinese, but he more or less understood it. He wasn't married and loved his exciting life as a single man with a dog he adored. Someday he would get married, but not anytime soon.

Lynus Litton had snatched him away from the FBI five years ago with the promise that his offer could top anything the FBI ever had or could pay. The tripled salary and bonuses Lynus paid him, the thirty-day vacations, the company car, and the unlimited expense account made signing on a no-brainer, and he hadn't looked back. Well, sometimes he looked back, when he needed a favor from one of his FBI buddies.

The best part to Mickey was that he was able to take his dog to work with him, something the FBI frowned upon. The dog's name was Booker. Mickey had named him Booker because he'd been working a case, and the scumbag he was chasing owned the dog and had mistreated him—the dog was booking ninety miles an hour to get away from the scumbag. Mickey caught him, cuddled him, and made promises to the dog he'd never broken. Nor would he ever break them.

Mickey did a second lap around the cul-de-sac before he walked to the back of Gus Hollister's house, now occupied solely by his wife Elaine, which was totally screened off from its neighbors by lush foliage. The yellow Beetle was gone. He quickly removed the dog's leash and fished around inside his backpack. Within seconds, he had the back door open and was holding a gizmo in his hand, which he'd paid through the nose for and shouldn't even have to begin with. He watched as the digital display counted down before the gizmo succeeded in turning off the alarm.

"Okay, Booker, we're in. You know the drill. As soon as you hear or see anything, bark twice. You got it?" The dog tilted his head and took a stance beside the back door. "I think I might have an hour at the most."

Mickey prowled the house, looking for anything that might be useful to Lynus and his client. He loved this part of the job—finding things people tried to hide. He corrected the thought—not just *people*, the bad guys, be they women or men. Women, he knew, were devious, more prone to be secretive, where men just blundered through life. At least, that's what he had been taught by his American mother. He'd never disputed her wisdom.

Mickey took the time to appreciate the layout of Gus Hollister's four-thousand-square-foot house and its manly, comfortable furniture. There wasn't a lot of junk or doodads cluttering up the place. He hated the artificial trees, plants, and flowers people tended to decorate with. Nothing but dust collectors. He found it a little strange that there was no rogues' gallery of family pictures. He shrugged—to each his own.

Thirty minutes later, Mickey was finished with the downstairs. Without pulling up the pine floors or knocking out walls, he'd been unable to find anything. He checked the refrigerator, because people were known to hide things in freezers and in bowls of leftover soups and stews. People's refrigerators as a rule were strange yet informative. This one, however, blew his mind.

Mickey poked his head around inside the refrigerator. Four jugs of apple-cider vinegar. Four gallons! Bags of every herb known to man, all neatly labeled, filled the entire second shelf. The vegetable bin held one withered apple and a rock-hard orange. There were no leftovers in containers, no takeout, no eggs, no milk, no juice. Just four gallons of apple-cider vinegar. *What does this woman eat?*

What really blew his mind, though, were the six pure white roses nestled in cellophane, each stem encased in a plastic sleeve that held water. Earlier, he'd checked the cabinets, which held only canned and boxed soup, crackers, and some cereal that had never been opened. The cabinets were essentially bare. He looked over at the counter and saw three overripe bananas. The freezer had an icemaker and a freezer pack for injuries.

"You're doing a good job, Booker. I'm going upstairs. I still have about thirty minutes."

Mickey again marveled at the big house. Five bedrooms for two people. He wondered if the couple had planned on having children, before they'd decided to split up. That's usually the way it worked, before a marriage went south for whatever reason. He was surprised that all five bedrooms were fully furnished. Four guest rooms. He shrugged. People were weird. He went through each room carefully and thoroughly, but there was nothing to be found.

The chests were empty, the closets bare. No one lived in or even visited these rooms. The adjoining bathrooms held one towel each, one bar of soap, and that was it. Everything smelled fresh and unused. New. He didn't like the smell.

The last room in the long hallway had to be the master bedroom, judging by the king-size bed. More like a California king. It was frilly, flowery, and feminine. A room designed for and by Elaine Hollister's taste. Not really for Mr. and Mrs. Hollister.

The walk-in closet, which was almost as big as each of the guest bedrooms, held so many clothes, Mickey found himself overwhelmed. A lot of the outfits still had price tags dangling from the sleeves. Racks and racks of shoes, purses, scarves, and all the things women thought they needed to make a stellar appearance. There wasn't a single thing to indicate that a man had ever been in residence. Either she had completely obliterated any evidence of Gus Hollister's presence or he was like a ghost, leaving no physical traces of his existence. Mickey rather suspected the former and found it very sad, since he knew the story of the house and how it had once belonged solely to Gus Hollister.

Mickey checked every item—the pockets, the insides of the shoes, the handbags—but found nothing to interest him. He kept his eye on his watch as he sifted through the bureau drawers. It was no surprise to him that Elaine Hollister had a passion for lacy, gossamer-thin underwear. Tons of it, everything matching.

His mother always hid things in her sock drawer. But Elaine Hollister did not have a sock drawer, and he could find nothing that would alert him to what she was hiding. Unless you considered six white roses and four gallons of apple-cider vinegar as hidden things. Lynus was going to be upset if he didn't find anything. Hell, *he* was going to be upset. Everyone had secrets and things they hid. Why would this woman be an exception to the rule? Secrets and lies. He thought of the television show *House*, where the lead character said that everyone lies. It was so true. Right now, though, he wasn't interested in lies; he was interested in finding out this woman's secrets. His gut and his long years of snooping told him they were somewhere in the house; he just had to find out where.

The chest at the bottom of the huge bed yielded nothing but extra blankets and pillows. Hands on hips, Mickey looked around. What was he missing? He looked behind the artwork on the walls. Nothing. No safe. Nothing taped to the back of the pictures. He looked behind the plasma TV hanging on the wall. Nothing.

Mickey looked at his watch again. He had fifteen minutes, and he would need every single one of them to put the listening devices into the landline phones. He hustled then and was finished with two minutes to spare. At the last second, his gut instinct kicked in and he decided to put one of the little bugs on top of the doorframe leading into Elaine's bedroom. It was almost directly underneath the trapdoor leading to the attic. From here on in, any phone calls or conversations in or out of the bedroom or in the hallway would be picked up by Lynus and his eavesdropping equipment. The part Mickey didn't like was that he was going to have to sneak back into the house in the middle of the night, find Elaine Hollister's cell phone—which would likely be charging overnight—and bug it, too. He'd done it before, and though it was not his favorite thing to do, you had to take the good with the bad on any job.

Mickey looked at his watch. He'd used up his entire hour, and he still hadn't covered the basement, the garage, or the attic. That meant two more visits. Booker was silent, which meant he was going to be able to get out clean if he left immediately.

Standing in the hallway, he looked up at the ceiling and saw the unpainted wood frame around the attic opening. He knew that if he opened it, there would be a pull-down ladder. The wood looked new. *Why hasn't it been painted? What's up there? And where is the rope that would pull down the ladder?* He was tall enough that he had a good view of the square opening. No pull cord, no handle, no latch. He looked around and saw the switch plate on the wall. He was about to press it when Booker barked twice.

Mickey ran down the steps and whistled for the dog, who came on the run. This time they would exit through the front door. He quickly reset the alarm and walked smartly to the front door, Booker right alongside of him. Outside, they both squatted behind a thick box hedge just as the yellow Beetle roared down the drive to the back of the house.

Man and dog walked rapidly away from the Hollister house as if they had been visitors leaving a meeting. Between the two of them, the only one breathing hard was Booker.

Chapter 13

GUS CHECKED THE HUGE SIDE MIRRORS, SUCKED
in his breath, shoved his foot down on the clutch,
and shifted gears. He cringed at the grinding
gears, but, somehow, he was able to get the big
yellow bus backed up. He shifted again, the
sound as mind-bending as the first time, but
the bus was in first gear, then second, and, finally, the behemoth was moving out of the
parking lot onto the road. His in-drawn breath
was an explosion of sound when he finally re-
leased it. The word *performance* was ringing in
his ears the entire time.

Somehow or other, he made it to the first
assisted-living facility on his list, and there,

right in front, was Elroy Hitchens with three other people, bags and boxes at their feet. Gus pulled to the curb and had a bad moment when he couldn't open the hydraulic door. Cursing under his breath, he finally got it open. His passengers looked at him for permission to board. "Welcome aboard!" he said. His four passengers trooped aboard, introducing themselves as they climbed the steps into the big bus. All of them smiled at him, the men offering their gnarled old hands to be shaken. The little cherub of a lady hugged him and said he must be a blessing to his mama. Her name, she said, was Dolly Madison. Not the real Dolley Madison, she clarified, saying, "I'm not *that* old!"

His passengers safely aboard and buckled in, Gus took his scat behind the wheel. "Where to, Elroy?"

"You got the contracts, Gus? Gotta have contracts."

"They're right here, Elroy. You look them over while we're going to the next place. Okay?"

"Sure. We trust you. Go out to the main road, follow it for half a mile, make a right, then two lefts, and that will be your stop. You will be picking up six passengers."

"This is what I call a real adventure," Dolly bellowed, the excitement in her voice ringing throughout the bus. Gus grinned, listening to the chatter wafting his way as he concentrated on keeping the bus on the road. He had to perform. That was his bottom line.

Gus's second stop made his jaw drop. Huddled on the apron of concrete that led to the double doors of the assisted-living facility were eight people—not six—their fists shooting in the air at the sight of the big yellow bus sliding smoothly to the curb. Then they all clapped their hands in glee, even the four passengers already inside the bus. Introductions were in order. Gus shook hands, always careful not to squeeze too hard. He smiled, he grinned, and he laughed out loud at the seniors' exuberance.

Suddenly, Gus had a surge of feeling as he steered the big yellow bus down the road. Maybe he should initiate a sing-along. Then again, maybe not; his passengers probably weren't up on the latest music. His feeling of power was short-lived when he heard one of the seniors shout out, asking him why a young fella like him had a bus driver's license.

Ooops!

Honesty, his grandmother had taught him and Barney early on, was always the best policy. "I don't have a license, sir. I'm just filling in to help you guys take it on the lam. This is the first time I ever drove a bus! I'll get you where you need to go, that's a promise. And I promise never to drive a bus again until I get a bus driver's license."

More hand clapping, hooting, and hollering followed Gus's declaration.

A robust voice from the middle of the bus shouted out that if they were pulled over by *the fuzz,* they'd all step up to the plate and tell the officer that they'd forced Gus to take them on the lam. Then the voice said, "The police never do anything to old people, so your secret is safe with us, sonny."

Gus believed them implicitly. He thanked them profusely as he struggled not to laugh out loud.

"Your next stop is the mother lode, Gus," Elroy Hitchens bellowed. "You'll be picking up eleven passengers from Pine Crest. That's a satellite facility of Sea Crest. It's a dump. We got everyone who is ambulatory. We all agreed last night to use our first paychecks and sign-on bonuses to relocate those who couldn't come with us from Pine Crest." More hooting and hollering.

"Wheee!" Gus said, his fist shooting in the air as he sailed down the road in the big yellow bus.

Fifteen minutes later, Gus pulled to the curb at Pine Crest. The seniors were huddled, huge smiles on their faces, waiting for him. They piled in and greeted the other seniors as they high-fived one another. While all this was going on, Gus stared at the building where the eleven people had lived for God only knew how long. Elroy was right; Pine Crest was a dump. There was no lawn to speak of and the hedges and straggly bushes were sorely in need of pruning. The windows were unwashed and grimy-looking; the window frames' paint was cracked and peeling. The glass door leading to what he assumed was a lobby had a huge crack running across it. The sign on the building was missing two of its screws and hanging lopsided. He knew in his gut that the inside was probably worse than what he was seeing. A dumping ground for elderly people whose families were too busy to care for them.

Gus knew then that he was doing the right thing, and if he had to do it all over again, he would. He had a new mission in life now, to do whatever he could to give these people a better life, and he now had no doubt that his grandmother and his aunts were on the right track in doing what they were doing.

It was at that moment that Gus Hollister committed himself to doing whatever he could to help his grandmother, his aunts, and all these wonderful people he was transferring to Blossom Farm. Maybe he *should* initiate a sing-along.

The thought flew out of his mind when he realized he was less than a quarter of a mile from the turnoff to Blossom Farm. Should he drop his passengers at the farm, or should he take them to Shady Pines first? No one had said what he was to do. If he dropped them at Shady Pines, how would they get to Blossom Farm, given the flooded grounds? They wouldn't be able to use the golf carts. He seriously doubted the seniors could make the two-mile trek on foot. And yet, his grandmother had said they were up most of the night at Shady Pines, getting it ready for the new residents. How did they get to Shady Pines to do all that? Probably in the van by road instead of across the field. *Performance.* Gus looked at his watch—eleven-thirty. He had to get the bus back to Pastor Evans by noon. The decision was taken out of his hands when he approached the gravel road that would take him to Blossom Farm. He turned right at the sign, which was flapping in the light breeze. A cheer went up from his passengers.

When Gus brought the bus to a full stop, he left the motor running. There was no way in hell he was going to let any of the seniors see him grinding the gears and trying to back up the big yellow bus. It was all about performance.

Gus waited outside the bus until all his passengers were safely on the ground before he turned to his granny. "I have to get the bus back by noon. I'll be back to help as soon as I can." His grandmother smiled at him, a warm smile that made him feel better than he'd felt in days. Even Violet gave him a thumbs-up. Iris wiggled her fingers in his direction, which meant, well done.

The babble of voices with shouted questions jarred Gus. He heard: What time is orientation? Who is doing it? When is lunch? When do we find out more about salary and bonuses?

Gus held up his hand. "Ladies and gentlemen, that will all be taken care of when I get back. I have to return the bus to the church by noon. Just be patient, okay?"

"Okay, sonny. We have nothing but time," someone in the group shouted.

Gus mentally patted himself on the back as

he made his way up the steps to his seat behind the wheel of the big yellow bus. He took a deep breath and wanted to shout his happiness when he shifted gears cleanly and smoothly. He waved as a cheer went up from the group he was leaving behind.

Damn, I feel good!

Gus drove to the closest gas station, topped off the bus's tank, then drove to the church and parked the big yellow bus exactly where he'd found it. He cut the engine, replaced the keys over the visor, then did what all good bus drivers do: he checked the bus to make sure none of his passengers had left anything behind. He found nothing. He left the bus with a light heart and made his way to his vehicle.

Once inside, he pulled out his cell phone to see if anyone had called or sent him a text while he was seeing to the seniors. He had one text and one voice message. The text was from Marsha, his real-estate broker, saying she had found the perfect house for him and had made an appointment to show it to him at four o'clock. Please don't be late was the last line of the text. The voice-mail message was from the fireplug, saying she wanted to see him in her office at four-thirty. She cautioned him not to be late, because she had other late-afternoon appointments scheduled. Gus groaned out loud. He had to make a decision. Before he could think twice, he fired off a text to his broker and said he would meet with her, and he would be on time. He tensed when he called the fireplug and prayed he would get her voice mail. What was it about this lawyer that made him so nuts? He almost let out a whoop when he heard the metallic-sounding voice asking him to leave a message. He quickly left a courteous, polite response, which said he had a prior commitment and couldn't break it, and she needed to give him more notice when she wanted to set up a meeting.

Gus justified the response by telling himself that his divorce case wasn't going anywhere in the next few days, and he might lose the opportunity to view what his broker considered the perfect house to fit his needs. As far as he was concerned, it was a no-brainer. When it came to the fireplug, everything seemed to be a no-brainer.

Not wanting to think about it anymore, Gus turned the key in the ignition and left the parking lot. Why was life always so complicated? Finding no answer to this question, he turned on the radio and listened to Kenny G, who kept him company all the way back to Blossom Farm.

Gus let himself in the kitchen door. A little lady who was one of the original staff was loading the dishwasher. She looked at him, smiled, and asked if she could fix him some lunch. Gus realized he was hungry. "That would be nice, ma'am. I am hungry. Something smells good."

"I'm Aggie," the little lady said, holding out her hand for him to shake. "I work with the feathers." Gus nodded. "We have the U.S. Senate bean soup for lunch with ham-and-cheese sandwiches. Our new guests loved it."

"Well, if it tastes as good as it smells, I can understand why."

Gus sat down and felt guilty when Aggie served him. He said so.

Aggie shook her head. "I love to cook. I grew up on a farm, and my mama taught my sisters and me to cook when we were young. We had to feed the farmhands three times a day. Food is all about the herbs and spices you use. You can take the cheapest, the toughest piece of meat, season or marinate it properly, and you have a gourmet meal. It also helps to serve something sweet afterward." She giggled. "You best hurry, son, the others are chomping at the bit to get going. We seniors say we don't mind waiting, but we really do. We fixate on things. I don't know why that is," she said fretfully.

"You aren't in the minority, Miz Aggie," Gus said as he wolfed down the delicious soup. He gobbled down the sandwich and wished he had a second one. He swigged the last of his sweet tea, wiped his mouth, then carried his dishes to the sink. He thanked Aggie and gave her a hug.

Aggie looked up at him and beamed her pleasure. "That's exactly what a cook wants to hear. Skedaddle now and do what you have to do."

Gus squared his shoulders. *Performance time.*

The talkative seniors were all crowded into the massive dining room. The twelve seats at the table were full. Folding chairs were set up against the wall. Some of the seniors, mostly men, were standing, their backs to the wall. One seat was waiting for him. He swallowed hard. It was his granny's chair at the head of the table. She was turning it over to him. He felt so light-headed at this show of forgiveness, he had to grab hold of the chair. A laptop stood open on the table, along with a yellow legal pad and two pens.

"Okay, everyone, my name is Gus Hollister. I'm a certified public accountant. Rose is my grandmother, and Violet and Iris are my aunts. This," he said, waving his arms about, "is a family affair." He risked a glance at his grandmother and aunts. They were smiling. He was performing.

"We just met your first need: lunch. I hope you all enjoyed it and thanked Miss Aggie, as she is the one who cooked it. Having said that, now that our numbers have increased by twenty-three, Miss Aggie is going to need kitchen help. That means shopping, preparation, and the actual cooking and cleaning up. Three meals a day. I think two volunteers will do it. Now I'm going to go around the room, give you a pen and a sheet of paper. I want you to write your name, and, if you have a cell phone, include the number. I'll input all this into the computer. Next, on the same paper, I want you to tell me about your strengths and what you perceive to be your weaknesses. After we go through all that, with the help of my grandmother and aunts, we'll be assigning you each a job. We are going to work shifts. Four to five hours each, unless you feel you can put more time into your particular task." Gus looked to his grandmother and aunts to see if they approved of his performance so far. They nodded.

A voice from the back shouted out, "I think we all would like you to address our pay, the bonus we were promised, and what we're going to do about the others left behind at that dump, Pine Crest."

"I'm going to let my grandmother address those matters." Gus got up and turned his chair over to his grandmother. He took that time to watch the faces of the people in the room. He didn't think he'd ever seen a happier group. He let his mind drift to his late-afternoon appointment with Marsha to look at the house that might be his and Wilson's new home. He didn't spend too much time thinking about the house, because he trusted Marsha and knew it would work out.

His thoughts took him to the fireplug and how that was going to play out. Well, the ball was in her court now. He checked his phone to see if he had any texts or messages, since he'd turned the ringer off so as not to interfere with his presentation to his grandmother's new staff. He shoved the phone back in his pocket when he saw his grandmother get up and point to the chair. He was suddenly aware that the seniors were clapping. Obviously, they were happy with whatever his grandmother had said about their contracts.

Gus sat down and looked around. "Do any of you have any questions?"

There was only one question, and Elroy

Hitchens was the one who voiced it. "When do we start to work?"

Gus looked at his grandmother, who said, "Tomorrow morning. Breakfast is at seven o'clock. As I explained when you first arrived, we do a shuttle service between here and Shady Pines. So it will be rise and shine early. Sometimes, if business is brisk, we work at least a few hours on the weekends. We'll be posting a schedule, and you'll sign on for weekend duty. Give me a show of hands if you all approve."

Every hand in the room shot upward.

"This is when you show me your papers with your names and phone numbers and what your strengths and weaknesses are, so that I can draw up a schedule for your assignments and your working hours. On your way out of the room, hand me your papers. My grandmother and aunts will now give you a tour and answer any questions you might have," Gus said.

Gus worked industriously for the next several hours. He spread all the papers over the massive dining-room table. He hopped from one end to the other, then from side to side as he made notes on each page and input everything into the laptop. Even in the short period he'd been in the new seniors' company, he felt like he had a handle on their respective personalities. He looked at his watch. Time to leave for his appointment with Marsha. He pulled out his cell phone to check for messages or a possible text. Nothing.

In the kitchen, Aggie was paring vegetables.

He explained that he had to leave for two hours and would be back in time—he sniffed—for dinner. "And, will you tell my grandmother not to touch anything in the dining room?" he added. Aggie agreed and continued to peel carrots.

"What's for dessert?" Gus asked.

Aggie wiped her hands on her apron and opened the huge double oven doors. He saw four chocolate cakes, the aroma tantalizing. He nodded and looked around for Wilson and Winnie but didn't see them.

"They're with the parade. Actually, Wilson was leading the way." Aggie laughed.

Gus shrugged and made his way out to his car. He didn't think he'd ever had a day like this one in his entire life. And yet he felt good, really good. So good in fact that he was going to call Barney to brag and to bust his best friend's chops. He grinned at the thought. But no point in making two calls. He'd wait to see how the real-estate deal went down. That way he could tell Barney he was moving out, thank him for his hospitality, and bring him up to speed at the same time.

Life is looking good.

Chapter 14

Gus typed the address of the property where Marsha was waiting for him into the GPS. If there was no traffic, he should make the meeting right on time. He felt anxious for some reason. Buying a house could certainly account for the feeling. Then he thought about his day with his family and all the seniors he'd been helping. No sense lying to himself— he couldn't wait to get back to Blossom Farm to finish his scheduling. He was sure it was all going to work out. So sure, he started to whistle softly, something he always did when he felt happy.

After the storm, today had been a perfect

spring day. Bright sunshine, and a warm seventy-one degrees. The air was filled with the sound of chain saws, which would have the town back to normal within a few days. Several more days of weather like today, and the ground would dry out. Just a little while ago, he'd heard the weatherman say there was no rain in the forecast for the next few days. Who could ask for anything more?

The monotone voice on the GPS informed Gus that he was less than an eighth of a mile from his destination.

Gus's first thought was that it was a pretty neighborhood, with full-grown trees lining the streets. He noticed that there were sidewalks on which kids could skateboard and roller-skate. He closed his eyes for a second and envisioned himself and Barney when they were ten years old, skating down the sidewalk or riding their bikes. He hoped it was a neighborhood with kids. The houses were all pink brick, with fireplace chimneys jutting upward. Cozy for the cold Virginia winters.

The generic voice on the GPS said he had arrived at his destination. And he had. He pulled his car alongside Marsha's in the two-car driveway. She was waiting for him, leaning against her car, reading a folder in her hands. They hugged each other. "Where's Wilson? Doesn't he get a vote?"

"He's at my grandmother's. Long story. I like this," Gus said, looking around. "The neighborhood is established, and it looks like everyone takes care of their property. No wooden or chain-link fences, no cracks and weeds in the driveway. Looks freshly painted."

"Trust me, Gus, this is the house for you. The owner is abroad; he's a freelance journalist. He lived here for almost fifteen years, then he got reassigned and rented it out. Renters do not take care of property even when they leave a security deposit. We put it on the market to sell. No takers. The economy hit, and now he just wants to unload it. He had the agency contract the work out, so the house is in pristine condition—new carpeting, new appliances, freshly painted, inside and out. If I had the money, I'd buy it myself, but I have two kids in college and an ex who is fighting me in court so he doesn't have to help pay for college. Oh, you said you needed a fence in the back. Well, you got two of them. When the owner first moved in, he put up a chain-link in the back because he had two springer spaniels. Then he decided he didn't like the way the fence looked, so he planted a boxwood hedge in front and back so now, over the years, the chain-link monstrosity can't even be seen. Wilson will be perfectly safe in the backyard."

"Sounds good; let's take a look."

Fifteen minutes later, Gus said, "I love it. I'll take it."

"I knew you would. Listen, Gus, with what you told me about your impending divorce, I've been thinking about something. Maybe we need to do a little creative, for want of a better word, *accounting* here. I spoke to the owner earlier this afternoon, and he's okay with it as

long as you are. When your wife's attorney runs
your financials, this house is going to show up as
an asset, and she'll want her share. Instead, you
rent for now, the monthly rent going toward your
mortgage payment when the divorce is final.
The owner is willing to wait on the closing, he
just wants the mortgage payment and the util-
ity payments off his back. What you pay in rent
will alleviate that. You following me here?"

"I am, and I like it. So, I pay out first, current, and last month's rent on the books and
this is mine, right?"

"Yes."

"When can I move in?"

"If you had your toothbrush with you and a
sleeping bag, you could move in right now.
Give me a check for the rent, and I'll give you
the keys, and the place is yours the minute you
sign all these papers. We'll hold your check for
the down payment at the agency until you tell
us it's okay to cash it. You don't want that showing up in your financials, either."

"This is working out just perfectly, Marsha. I
don't know how to thank you. I have to get
some furniture. Any ideas?"

"Gus, you saved me a boatload of money on
my taxes over the past few years. It's I who
should be thanking you. Stonehill's can deliver
tomorrow. The store is open till six-thirty today.
In this economy, store owners are bending over
backward for customers. By tomorrow night,
you and Wilson can be snug as two bugs in
your own digs."

Gus felt embarrassed for some reason. "That was business. It's what I do."

Marsha laughed. "Well, this is what I do, so we're even. Sign your name, then we can shake hands. I'd like to take you out to dinner the way I always do when I finish up a deal, but I have another appointment, and I don't want to be late."

Gus handed over two checks and signed his name to the real-estate documents. Instead of a handshake, he hugged the Realtor. And then they went their separate ways.

It was almost six-thirty when Gus walked out of the furniture store in New Town, clutching his bill of sale. Delivery tomorrow would be between eight and nine a.m., the first delivery of the day. He'd spent more than he intended but consoled himself with the fact that he planned to stay in the pink brick house for the long haul. If he was lucky enough to get back his old house after the divorce, he'd sell it and give his grandmother the money. He would have a yard sale and get rid of all the furniture and all the memories of Elaine.

On the drive back to Blossom Farm, Gus thought about what he'd bought. Two deep chocolate–colored chairs, a big, deep wheat-colored sofa, a seventy-six-inch plasma TV on which to watch ball games with Wilson, a complete bedroom set, and a set of stools for the kitchen so he could eat at the counter. He'd furnish the dining room and living room at some point when he had more money. For now, he had the basics. All he needed was a trip to Target for towels, bedding, dishes, pots and pans, and stuff for everyday living. One grocery-shopping trip, and he would indeed be a resident at 11 Bombadile Court. He wondered if his neighbors would bake him a welcome cake or bring over a covered dish. He hoped the neighbors were nice. Maybe they'd invite him to backyard barbecues. Or maybe he could barbecue and invite them. Whatever, he'd make it work.

Gus stopped at the last traffic light before he had to turn down the service road that would take him to Blossom Farm. The car stopped on the opposite side of the road was a bright yellow Volkswagen Beetle. Not many of those in Sycamore Springs. In fact, he didn't think there was another one, which meant Elaine was sitting at the light. The urge to step on the gas pedal and cross traffic to smash head-on into the little car was so strong, Gus had to clutch the wheel to make sure he didn't do it. If he'd been driving his own car, he thought he might, just might, have done it, but he was driving Barney's Jeep Commander. He sat still—even though the car behind him honked its horn— as Elaine whizzed past him without so much as a glance. In the quick glance he got of her, he saw that his wife was what he called dressed to the nines. She used to do that for him when she wanted something. He moved forward when a second, then a third angry honk of a horn forced him to go.

Now he felt depressed. He pressed buttons

on the stereo system and stopped when he heard music that felt soothing to his tortured soul. To further torment himself, Gus drove past the turnoff for his grandmother's house, and instead drove all the way to his old house, where he used to live with Elaine. He stopped at the guardhouse and said hello to Eddie, the guard who had worked there from the day he'd moved in.

"Evening, sir. You just missed your wife. New car?"

"Evening, Eddie. Just a loaner for now. I know, I passed Elaine on the way. I'll be coming right back out. Good to see you. Have a nice evening."

The cell phone in his pocket vibrated, but he ignored it. When you were doing something stupid, you needed to concentrate on the stupid part to make sure you got it right. Sitting in the driveway of the house his grandmother had bought him caused him to choke up. His eyes burned. Once upon a time, he had loved this house. Now he hated it with a passion. Sitting here was worse than stupid. He lost track of time as his memories attacked him, one after the other. Finally, as dusk was settling, Gus backed up the car, turned, and headed back the way he came.

When he came to the guardhouse, he waited until Eddie got around to opening the gate for him to leave. He didn't pay one bit of attention to the Asian man walking a Jack Russell terrier on the other side of the guardhouse.

* * *

When Gus cut the engine and crawled out of the car, he knew his grandmother and the aunts were going to look at him as undependable, as he had said he'd be back in two hours. It was now about four hours later. Performance be damned. He squared his shoulders and entered the house. For the most part, it was silent, his grandmother sitting alone in the kitchen working at one of her ledgers. She looked tired.

Gus poured himself a glass of sweet tea, perched on the end of a chair, and rattled off what he'd done since he left the house to keep his appointment with Marsha. "I had to take care of things, Granny. I'm all set to go. Did anything happen? Is there anything I need to know before I get started?"

Rose smiled. Her grandson looked more tired than she felt. "Life sometimes has a way of interfering with one's plans. We did okay today. Tomorrow will be better than today, that's for sure. Everyone is tired, the excitement and all. Old people"—she laughed—"can take just so much excitement in one day. Go along and do what you have to do. Did you have dinner?"

"No, but that's okay. I kind of lost my appetite somewhere along the way." It was a lie, he was starved, but he wanted to get to work; the seniors were depending on him. He could always eat. "Where are Wilson and Winnie?"

"With Vi and Iris in the storage room. They're fine, Augustus. Run along now so I can finish this. There's a plate warming in the oven for you if you get hungry later."

Gus worked through the evening, stopping just once for a bathroom break and to refill his glass of ice tea. He barely noticed that at some point Wilson had come into the dining room and settled himself at his feet. He felt comforted.

It was five minutes past midnight when Gus carried the work schedule out to the kitchen and laid it on the kitchen table for his grandmother to see first thing in the morning. Every person was accounted for; every shift of work for whatever endeavor they would work on was accounted for. He'd even made suggestions for increasing inventory, and mapped out a more efficient means of storing supplies and product. He knew he'd whittled down hours, possibly days, of futile work for the seniors if they followed his advice. Tomorrow, after his furniture arrived, and he made his trip to Target and the grocery store, he'd come back and pitch in again.

The house was so silent, Gus felt like an intruder. Wilson waited at the door, but there was no sign of Winnie. "Just me and you, huh? Well, let's head for home. I have a lot to tell you. I think we found our niche. Finally."

Wilson beelined toward the stove and nosed the oven door. "Oh, yeah, dinner. You know what? I'm too tired to eat, Wilson. Let's just go home." Wilson was having none of it. He growled softly until Gus opened the oven door. When he saw the dinner plate loaded with sliced chicken, stuffing, cranberries, mashed potatoes and gravy, string beans, and a dinner roll, he changed his mind. He sat down on the floor and started to eat, sharing with Wilson. "Kind of like old times, huh, big guy?" Wilson woofed softly.

It was eleven o'clock the next morning when Gus unlocked the side door of his new house. The furniture people had delivered on time and even hooked up the new TV for him. He'd tipped them accordingly. He'd made his run to Target and gotten everything he needed. He'd washed the sheets, and the towels were just waiting to go in the dryer. His new dishes, glasses, silverware, and pots and pans had gone through the dishwasher. The supermarket trip had taken a little longer than expected, as he picked up just about one of everything, careful to stock up on Pop-Tarts for Wilson.

He was exhausted, but it was still a good feeling. That's when it hit him that he hadn't called Barney. Just as he was about to hit his speed dial, a neighbor about his age walked over and held out his hand. "Jeff Lucas. I live next door. Welcome to the neighborhood. Your Realtor left a short bio of you and your dog in everyone's mailbox yesterday by way of introduction. I'd stay and talk more, but I just came home to check on my sprinkler system; it's out of whack. Don't want my yard to flood. Guess the storm fouled things up. My wife, Sara, said she's going to bake you a cake to welcome you to the neighborhood. See ya," he said as he headed toward his own house.

Gus grinned. "Hop in, Wilson. Seems like a nice guy. I think this is going to turn out just fine." Barney would just have to wait till he got to Blossom Farm, because Gus didn't like driving and talking on his cell phone at the same time.

The minute he parked the car at Blossom Farm, Gus pulled out his cell phone and noticed for the first time that there were four messages from the fireplug. He groaned. Instead of listening to them, he hit the speed dial for Barney, who sounded like he was asleep when he answered. "What now?"

"What now, indeed! I have news to share and thought you would want to know. I can hang up and call you back later if you like."

"I'm awake now. Let's hear it." Gus relayed yesterday's events and what had transpired so far today.

"So what you're saying is you're back in the fold and working your ass off to show everyone that you know how to perform. You bought a house but actually you're renting it and are doing some creative accounting for the time being. You sat outside your old house and had an attack of déjà vu because it was a stupid thing to do. How am I doing so far?"

"You're doing good. Wilson loves me again. Granny and the aunts are feeding me. I'm a happy camper."

"That's good to hear. I was worried about that guilt by association thing where you and your granny were concerned. I don't understand why you were in such a hurry to buy a house. Isn't mine good enough for you?"

"Aren't you listening, Barney? It's not about the money or your big house. It's about me and Wilson picking up the pieces and starting over in our own place. Yeah, it's going to be tough, and I'm going to have to watch my pennies, but I can do it. If I have to, I can moonlight on the weekends for extra money. I appreciate everything you've done for me, you know that. I'm not a taker, Barney. You of all people should know that. Just tell me you're okay with all of it, and you'll make my day."

"Of course I'm okay with it. I'm just jealous that you're having all the fun, and I'm stuck here in Hong Kong. I'm thinking of retiring, Gus. What do you think of that?"

Gus started to laugh and couldn't stop. "I think I know someone who might hire you. Part time. No pay, no benefits, just oodles and oodles of goodwill, smiles—and you'll go to sleep at night with a smile on your face." Barney laughed because he knew Gus expected him to laugh.

"Well, I gotta go. Any news from Phil Ross?" asked Gus.

"Damn, didn't I tell you? Phil retired last year. He just gathered all that information as a personal favor. Jill Jackson hired someone else. Don't worry about it. By the way, how is all that working out for you?"

"Gotta go now, Barney. Granny's at the door,

and they need me," Gus said, and let Wilson out of the car.

"How'd you like that, Wilson? I got out of answering him. Pretty slick if I do say so myself. Come on, let's see what the seniors have in store for us today."

Woof.

Chapter 15

MICKEY YEE AND HIS DOG BOOKER STROLLED along the bike and walking path in the gated community where Elaine Hollister lived. He spotted a bench that would allow him to sit as dusk settled. This was the time of evening when dog walkers were out and about. He didn't think anyone would pay attention to him if he sat for a while without drawing attention to himself and his dog. He leaned back on the wooden bench, threw his arm over the back, then handed Booker a rawhide chew to keep him busy. Just a man and his dog out for an evening stroll.

In the pocket of his T-shirt, Mickey had a minirecorder. He turned it on and listened to Lynus Litton's voice relaying the information from the report that the detective assigned to follow Elaine Hollister had submitted. He'd listened to the tape at least six times since arriving at the gated community. He had already committed it to memory. He understood all that he heard, but something puzzled him. Something Lynus Litton didn't have the answer to.

The investigator, Don Parker, said Elaine Hollister had had no visitors once she arrived home, until the time she left to go to her dinner engagement with her attorney, Isaac Diamond, which was verified by the audio tape from the bug Mickey himself had planted on Hollister's landline. The conversation confirmed the dinner date and renewed the offer of a car to pick her up, an offer Hollister again declined. What Mickey didn't understand was the two hours of muffled conversation or dialogue that Lynus said could be heard on the audio. He had orders to check his bugs to see that they were in working order. Always thorough, Mickey had, as usual, checked the bugs several times before he'd installed them. So, did Elaine Hollister talk to herself? Did she read aloud just to hear her own voice?

Lynus had left instructions for Mickey to stay in touch with Don Parker over open cell phone connections. Don was to call him the minute Elaine left the restaurant in case he was still in the house and needed time to get out clean. His last conversation with Don led him to believe that after dinner, the couple would head for someplace a little more intimate. Probably to discuss Elaine's case, Don had said, tongue in cheek.

Mickey looked at his watch, and saw that it was already seven thirty. By the time he and Booker got to the Hollister house, night would have descended, making his job easier. He got up, settled his backpack more firmly on his shoulders, and picked up Booker's leash. "Time to go, Booker."

Twenty minutes later, Mickey Yee was standing inside the Hollister kitchen. A night-light low on the floor gave the state-of-the-art kitchen a dim, pale glow but gave off just enough light for him to make his way through the dining room, also lit by a low night-light on the baseboard. "You know what to do, Booker. I'll be on the second floor."

He sniffed, wondering what it was he was smelling. *Perfume? A room air freshener? Women like those things for some reason. Some kind of aerosol spray like Lysol? No, that isn't it.* It was something he'd smelled before, but he couldn't put a name to what it was. Whatever it was, he didn't like it.

Mickey galloped up the steps and ran down the hallway to Elaine Hollister's bedroom. He blinked. It looked like a tornado had swept through the room. Clothes and shoes of every description littered the bed and floor. Obviously, the lady couldn't make up her mind

THE BLOSSOM SISTERS 187

what she should wear to the dinner engagement with her attorney. The bathroom looked worse. Makeup was everywhere, and wet towels littered the floor. What really interested him, though, was the cell phone charging on the vanity. Quicker than lightning, he had the phone bugged. He plugged it back in, careful to place it exactly where it had been. Talk about luck. Now he didn't have to worry about breaking into the house in the dead of night, with Elaine Hollister sleeping upstairs.

Mickey moved to the landline on the night table. He checked it, tested it, and was satisfied there was nothing wrong with the bug. He moved out to the hall, pressed the button that would lower the ladder that led to the attic. The ladder dropped, then unfolded. It looked like a dark pit overhead. The strange scent seemed to sweep through the opening and engulf him. He didn't see a light switch anywhere, so that meant he'd need a flashlight. He rummaged in his backpack and withdrew a small Maglite that, when turned on, would illuminate an entire room.

Mickey stuck the end of the powerful light between his teeth, grabbed the arms of the flimsy ladder, and climbed, the Maglite lighting the way. The fine hairs on the back of Mickey's neck moved. He crawled across the floor as soon as his feet left the ladder. He squatted and looked around, the Maglite showing him something he had never expected to see.

Mickey gaped at the makeshift altar, complete with a crisp white altar cloth. The altar was filled with vases of white flowers, colored beads, black candles, and incense holders. A vial sat in the middle of the altar, clearly labeled, in fine script, HOLY WATER. Next to the holy water was a dish of salt.

That's what the smell was; Elaine Hollister had been burning incense since his last visit. Here in the attic, the smell was overpowering. Mickey was absolutely, positively certain that by the time he left this place, he'd have a really bad headache.

Still squatting on his haunches, Mickey didn't like what he was seeing at all. He felt creeped out at the strange altar. Then he spotted the Bible, with a pair of reading glasses sitting on top of it. The hair on the back of his neck moved once more. He moved the light to see what was beyond the makeshift altar. He saw cardboard cartons and empty mailers. A furrow built itself between his brows as he tried to comprehend what he was seeing.

Witchcraft? Voodoo? Mickey shivered. He moved the Maglite and saw a sheaf of what looked like heavy yellow parchment with all kinds of symbols and signs that he wasn't familiar with. He could clearly see the words, SPELLS and RITUALS, in heavy black-and-gold lettering. Then he thought about the four jugs of vinegar and the full shelf of herbs in the refrigerator in the kitchen downstairs.

Mickey fumbled with the cell phone in his pocket, on which he had an open line to Don

Parker. He whistled softly and told him what he was seeing.

"Sounds to me like you got a high-priestess thing going on. I'd say from what you're telling me that Hollister practices either witchcraft or voodoo. I'm not an authority on the subject. I'm just saying. I think you need to talk with Lynus, but I think that explains the conversation that was on the tapes. She was probably casting spells or chanting. I saw a movie once, and something like that was in it. I gotta say, Mick, looking at that woman, I never would have thought she'd be into something like that."

Mickey cleared his throat. "Me, either. This is creeping me out. What's going on there?"

"Looks like they're having brandy and coffee. They look like any other couple out to dinner. No kitschy-coo, no hand-holding, nothing like that. They each had two glasses of wine. They'll be leaving in about twenty minutes is my best guess. Keep the line open and get ready to leave in case she heads home. Call Lynus and tell him what you're seeing. You bring a camera with you?"

"Yeah."

"Take pictures of everything. Even if you think it doesn't apply."

"Okay. I'll get back to you." Mickey shoved the cell phone back into his pocket. He pulled out a second one and called his boss. He rattled off his findings. When he heard Lynus whistle, he knew he was really onto something.

"Take pictures, and I want to see you and them in my office first thing in the morning. Don't forget to take a picture of the inside of the refrigerator."

"Okay, no problem." Mickey broke the connection, then dug out his digital camera. He positioned the Maglite to give him the best light. He snapped the altar from all angles. He took a picture of the Bible and the reading glasses. Then he took a shot of the cardboard cartons and the empty mailers. He could see the words INITIAL B ENTERPRISES on one of the mailing labels. When he stretched his arm across the altar to get the boxes and mailers into better position, he knocked over one of the vases holding the white roses. "Oh, crap!" he groaned as he watched the water spread across the altar.

There was no way he could cover that up. Always confident, he decided that the best-case scenario would be Elaine Hollister would think that a rat or a mouse had toppled the vase. He snapped the pictures he wanted, then backed his way to the opening and the ladder that would take him down to the second floor. He looked around to make sure he wasn't leaving any signs that would indicate there had been an intruder. Once he'd reset the alarm and locked the door, Mrs. Hollister wouldn't know the difference.

Mickey put the Maglite back in his backpack and made his way down to the kitchen, where he took pictures of the vinegar jugs and the shelf of herbs. The lighting was perfect for the shot. He closed the refrigerator door and returned the camera to his backpack. He set the alarm, whistled for Booker, and they left the house. Outside, he drew a deep breath. He'd screwed up. He needed to call Lynus.

Mickey and Booker jogged all the way to the security gate and left the area as quickly as they could. The minute he was settled in his car, he called Lynus to report his screwup. He listened as his boss reamed him out about sloppy work, then he listened to his apology, saying mistakes happen. He didn't feel one bit better. The kind of mistake he'd just made could mean the success or failure of the investigation.

"Okay, Booker, let's call it a night. I know you're hungry, and so am I. Tomorrow is another day." That's when he remembered the stack of black-and-white notebooks, the kind they sold in drugstores a long time ago. He wasn't sure, but he thought he'd had one for one of his English classes. *Crap. Did I take a picture of the notebooks? Not specifically,* he decided, *but maybe they'll show up on one of the other shots. You're getting sloppy, Mickey,* he warned himself.

Gus woke with Wilson's nose nudging his chin. Time to get up. "Okay, okay! I'm up. Hey, buddy, how'd you do the first night in our new digs?" Wilson let loose with a loud bark. "That good, huh?"

Gus staggered out to the kitchen and opened

the door for the shepherd. He stood there watching his dog search out the perfect bush, scratched his head, felt the bristles on his cheeks, and decided coffee was what he needed. His big decision was whether to make breakfast or wait to eat at the farm. Or, he could pick up a breakfast burrito on his way to the fireplug's office. Coffee and juice, he decided, and he'd grab something else later. Wilson wouldn't see it that way, he knew, so he filled a bowl with canned dog food and kibble, then set down a fresh bowl of water. The time was six-ten.

As Gus waited for the coffee to drip into the pot, he looked around his new kitchen. He liked that the sun would come in the kitchen window in the morning, and he could look out into the yard while he sipped his morning coffee. He made a mental note to find out if there was a morning newspaper delivery in the neighborhood. There was nothing like a morning cup of coffee and the day's news, in his opinion. He knew there were millions of people who would rather read the news online. He was definitely not one of those people.

Gus poured his coffee and let his mind wander. He'd slept well, felt rested. He felt like he was ahead of the game, because he'd slept in a brand-new bed. Then again, he'd been exhausted when his head hit the pillow.

His thoughts next took him to the day he'd planned out for himself. First and foremost, he was going to see the fireplug to see what she wanted to do where he was concerned. From there, he'd stop by the office to check on things. After that, it was out to the farm and the seniors. He wondered what his grandmother had thought of the schedule he'd left behind and what she'd made of the suggestions he'd like to implement.

Gus finished his coffee, checked Wilson's bowl, then rinsed it and put it into the dishwasher. He refilled his cup and carried it upstairs. He showered and shaved, then dressed in a pair of crisp khakis that Maggie had ironed for him while he was staying at Barney's house. He checked his polo shirts but ended up wearing a pale blue button-down oxford shirt. He rolled it up to his elbows, slipped his feet into Docksiders, and was ready to go.

"Okay, Wilson, time to put a move on. Get whatever you want to bring with you because it's going to be late when we get back. Just *ONE* thing, Wilson, not an armful. You can play with Winnie's things when we get to the farm." Gus watched, amused at Wilson's attempt to pick one thing to bring to the farm. He picked up a tattered-looking stuffed rabbit with only one ear and half a tail. It was his favorite toy, the one he slept with at night. He picked it up twice, and twice put it back on his bed. He finally chose a ball with a hole in the middle and a ring through it. He looked up at Gus, his signal that he'd made his decision.

"I suppose someone will want to play tug of war with you. Time to get our show on the road."

Gus's plan was to arrive at Barney's offices as

close to seven-thirty as he could. He'd had a key to the building ever since Barney opened his offices. He would wait in the lobby to greet the fireplug on her arrival. Whatever was going to happen would then happen.

He had the building to himself when he arrived, and took a seat in one of the buttery-soft chairs scattered throughout the medium-size lobby. Wilson lay at his feet. Gus sat quietly, his thoughts of the farm and what lay ahead of him.

He knew that the fireplug was approaching when Wilson rose to his feet and walked over to the door. If the attorney was surprised to see a dog greet her, she didn't show it. Nor did she show any surprise when she saw Gus getting up off the chair he'd been sitting in. *She'd make a good poker player,* Gus thought. He watched as she scratched Wilson behind the ears for a few moments.

"Good morning, Mr. Hollister. How nice to see you so early in the morning."

Gus knew that she was thinking, how nice of you to ruin my day so early. "I know we didn't have an appointment, and that we've been playing telephone tag. I'm sorry about that. So, can we discuss whatever it is you want to talk to me about? I also wanted to give you my new address and the phone number at my new house in case you can't reach me on my cell phone."

"Follow me, Mr. Hollister. I can give you exactly thirty minutes, then I have to leave for court on another matter."

Gus looked around the fireplug's office. It

surprised him, and he wasn't sure why. He liked it, though. He took a seat across from the polished desk and waited for her to take her seat of power. That's how he thought of it, a seat of power. If he compared his office to this one, his would fall into the pigsty category. Not that it was dirty, just messy.

Jill folded her hands and leaned forward. She adjusted her granny glasses more firmly and stared across at him with unblinking intensity. "Do you have anything you want to ask me before we discuss your wife's petition for divorce, Mr. Hollister?"

"No. My wife is divorcing me. I am not contesting it. If this were a perfect world, I'd tell you to fight till hell freezes over not to give her anything, but I know this is not a perfect world, so I'm probably going to have to make some kind of settlement. You already know the deal on the house. I was a fool, I admit that. So I guess what I'm saying here is do the best you can on my behalf."

Jill's cell phone took that moment to chime to life. Gus watched as she fished it out of the pocket of her jacket. She identified herself, then listened. All Gus could hear were the words, "I'll ask him. He's here right now. Yes, that is strange. Thanks for the heads-up.

"Now, where were we, Mr. Hollister?"

"I was telling you to do the best you can do on my behalf. I'm not naive enough to think I'm going to skate on this. Is there anything you need me to do on my own behalf?"

"I wanted to discuss what you're willing to part with. I'll be calling Isaac Diamond, your wife's attorney, for a face-to-face. I've engaged the services of a private detective agency. We have ongoing surveillance on your wife. Right now, that's all I'm comfortable telling you. And I want to caution you about talking to your wife. I don't want you to be surprised if she calls you. If you're like most people, I'm sure you have caller ID on your new landline at home and, of course, it will show up on your cell phone. If she calls, let it go to voice mail and call me right away."

"Okay, I don't have a problem with that. She's the last person I want to talk to. What is it you hope to find out with surveillance?"

"After I find out, I'll ask you what is normal and not normal where your wife is concerned. Then I'll make a call on it. We do have time before I'm going to schedule a meeting with Mr. Diamond. Again, I'll let you know when that is going to happen. You and your wife might or might not be at that meeting."

"I understand. I hope you got my message where I apologized to you."

Yessireee, this lady would make a great poker player.

"I did. I accept your apology." The expression on the lawyer's face was that of someone who had bitten into a lemon. Jill reached into a drawer and withdrew a yellow legal pad. "Now, give me that new address and phone number. You moved out of Barney's house?!

Living in a mansion with live-in maid service, cooked meals, someone to do your laundry, six cars at your disposal, everything free. What's not to like? Why did you move?"

Gus wanted to reach across the desk and grab Jill Jackson's lovely throat. *Lovely throat.* The words left him confused for a moment. He might have dropped it right there, but Jill started to tap her fingers on the desk as she waited for his reply. "Because I'm not a person who needs a fancy house with maid service and six cars. I can cook and do laundry and take care of myself. My grandmother taught me early on how to be self-sufficient. The only reason I moved into Barney's house was because of Wilson, and because I had to get my head on straight. I'm renting a house with an option to buy if it's a good fit for Wilson and me."

"Is that the same grandmother you turned your back on in favor of Elaine Hollister?"

"You damned well know it is. When are you going to stop jamming that down my throat, Miss Fireplug?" *Oh, shit, did I just say that?* Obviously, from the look on the lawyer's face, he did just say that, and he'd struck a nerve.

"What did you just call me?"

Gus knew his face was flaming red as he tried to weasel his way out of his comment. "Sorry, I was thinking of something else. I didn't mean . . . I wouldn't . . . I meant to say Miss *Jackson.*"

"Now, why don't I believe you? You know what, Mr. Hollister, I think we've had enough for one day. I'll call you when I need to talk to you again." Gus noticed that her face was as pink as his felt, and her lovely throat was also pink.

"I do need to ask you one question, however. What do you and your wife do with all the vinegar in your refrigerator? Four gallons to be exact. And what do you use all those herbs for?"

Gus thought those were the stupidest questions he'd ever heard in his life. "Vinegar! What herbs? When were you in my house? I don't know what you're talking about."

"Need to know, Mr. Hollister. Okay, so the vinegar wasn't there when you left a few days ago, is that what you're saying?"

"That's what I'm saying, Miss Jackson. I guess Elaine uses it for something."

"And the attic?"

Gus threw his hands in the air. "What about the attic?" There's nothing much up there but my skis and an old toboggan. In the spring, I pack up my winter clothes and put them up there and bring down the spring and summer clothes. I suppose Elaine put some of her stuff up there. She pitched a fit a few months back and wanted a ladder put in so she could go up and down. It's electric. I personally never used it. Why?"

"I'm not sure, Mr. Hollister. I really have to go now. I'll call you when I need you or to apprise you of new developments."

Gus knew when he was being dismissed. He got up just as Wilson did. He almost tripped over his dog, who was hell bent on going around the desk to check out the fireplug. Gus was stunned to see how the lawyer's face softened as she bent over to scratch Wilson behind the ears and rub the sweet spot between his eyes. Wilson was a goner the moment she did that. He licked her hand and whimpered softly as Jill continued to stroke the big dog's head.

"One last thing, Mr. Hollister. I don't want to hear that you're feeling remorseful and need comfort by sitting in the driveway at your old house. Yes, I know about that. Your wife took out a restraining order on you. She could have had you arrested. Do not do that again. Do you hear me?"

"How the hell——? Never mind. Yes, I hear you, and it won't happen again. I knew that Elaine wasn't home; I had passed her on the road going the other way, so I felt safe doing it."

"Like I said, don't do it again."

Gus hung his head. Caught again like a schoolboy. "Let's go, Wilson. Thanks for seeing me without an appointment. I appreciate it." He didn't mean to stare, but he couldn't help but gaze at that lovely throat. He'd hurt her feelings, and she was having a hard time with what he'd called her. He wanted to apologize again but knew he'd just make matters worse.

Outside, he mentally kicked himself as he opened the door of Barney's Jeep. If they were giving out awards for stupidity today, he'd take one hands down.

Gus drove to his office and spent ten minutes hearing that everything was running smoothly. He trooped back outside and headed for Blossom Farm, all the while thinking about the young lawyer. He realized he knew virtually nothing about her other than that she was a capable attorney. What was her personal life like? Obviously, she liked animals in general and dogs in particular. He recalled the fish tank and how restful it was watching the fish swimming in lazy circles. The clean lines of the office and the lack of clutter and the comfortable furniture should have given him some clues. He wondered if Barney had any insights on her personal life. And if he did, would he share what he knew? Doubtful, knowing Barney.

On a whim, Gus made a left turn, then a right turn, and stopped at The Flower Shop. The perfect name for a florist. He parked in the tiny lot and told Wilson to wait and guard the car. He ran into the store and ordered two dozen white roses to be sent to Jill Jackson. "Put lots of green stuff in the arrangement," he added. He scribbled his and Wilson's names on the card. Corny for sure, but he did it anyway. He paid cash and asked for the delivery to be made that day.

Gus felt a little better when he climbed back in the car. "I sent roses, Wilson, and I did that because I have a big mouth and don't stop to think before I talk. I hurt her feelings. Granny taught me better than that. She liked you, though. That's a good thing, Wilson. You might have to run interference for me from here on in where she's concerned.

"Now, we have to get to work, and I have a feeling it's going to be a really long day."

Wilson pawed Gus's arm, his signal that things were okay, before he settled down for the ride to Blossom Farm.

Chapter 16

AFTER COURT, JILL JACKSON ENTERED THE BEEZER building, a scowl on her face. She swept past the security guard with a flash of her ID pass without even looking at him. Normally, she had a smile for the guard, oftentimes inquiring about his grandchildren and his dog, Molly. Not today, though. Today, the young lawyer sprinted forward like she had a life-or-death destination in mind.

When the elevator stopped at her floor, she sailed past the receptionist and walked down the hall to her suite of offices. Her secretary, an early fiftyish woman, held up her hand and said, "Whoa! Whoa there, Jill. Slow down. What? Did someone rain on your parade? Step on your toes? I know you didn't lose in court, so what's with the attitude I'm seeing here?" Louise Atkins had been with Jill since her first day at Beezer. Familiarity was an okay thing where the two women were concerned. Not only were they boss and employee, they were personal friends. Had anyone else been within hearing distance, Louise would never have allowed personalities to show, because she was too professional to permit that to happen. She waited to see what Jill would say.

"Court was a waste of time; the judge granted a continuance. I knew that would happen going in. Like I said, a waste of time. No one rained on my parade, and no one stepped on my toes. Were there any calls?"

"Mr. Beezer and Lynus Litton called. Mr. Beezer wants you to call him back. Nothing urgent, he said. Mr. Litton said he needs you to return his call ASAP. So, what happened? Why do you look like a thundercloud? Don't tell me there is nothing wrong, Jill. I know you too well. Let me help; that's why I'm here."

Jill took a moment to stare up at her friend and secretary and only saw concern for her. She struggled with herself as she tried to decide if she wanted to respond. "If I ask you a question and tell you all I want is a yes-or-no response, can you do that?"

"Absolutely. What is it, Jill? I've never seen you

look like this. Plus, you're agitated, and you're always cool as a cucumber, even when you're losing. Mr. Beezer told me once he'd hate to play poker with you." Louise had said this before to Jill, and it always garnered a smile of sorts. Not this time.

"Okay." Jill took a deep breath. "Do I look like a fireplug to you?"

"Yes!" Louise said smartly without missing a beat.

"I do? Are you just trying to rile me up?"

"Why would I do that? You asked me a question, and I answered it. Don't you tell me time and again that a lawyer should never ask a question he or she doesn't already know the answer to?"

"I do say that. It's true, and it's the first thing you learn in law school."

"Then why did you ask me if you knew what my answer would be?" Louise drew herself up to her full height, adjusted the trim jacket she was wearing, then went back to her desk. She sat down with a hard thump, but her gaze stayed on Jill, who seemed to be having a hard time with her answer. "I assume someone hurt your feelings at some point this morning, and you're having a hard time dealing with it."

Jill crossed her arms against her chest. She nodded, her face miserable.

"Jill, you don't have to look like a fireplug. All you have to do is change your mode of dress. You wear so many layers, it's hard to tell there's even a body under them."

"What's wrong with what I'm wearing? Tell me one thing that's wrong."

"Are you sure you want to ask me that? Do you even look in the mirror before you leave the house in the morning?"

"I wouldn't ask if I didn't want to hear your answer, and of course I look in the mirror before I leave the house. Well?"

"No one wears brindle or drindle skirts or whatever they're called anymore. There must be ten yards of material in that skirt. Minis are in, and so is spandex. A blouse, a vest, and a jacket are way too much apparel for a small person like yourself. Put all that on top of ten yards of material, and you look like a walking tent. And let's not forget those combat boots you wear. And your color choice is drab. All you wear is beige, brown, or gray. It makes you look washed-out. You don't even wear makeup. You need color."

"Well, thank you for your opinion. I think. My shoes are not combat boots, Louise. They are Ferragamo ankle boots."

"Yeah, well try telling that to the fashionistas. The characters on that old TV show *Little House on the Prairie* used to wear the kind of shoes you wear."

Jill lifted up the hem of her long skirt and looked at her shoes. She liked them; they were comfortable, and she'd paid a lot of money for them. She liked comfortable shoes because she liked to walk back and forth to the courthouse. Taking care of her feet was important.

"So what are you going to do about your mode of dress?"

Jill whirled around. "What makes you think I'm going to do anything about my mode of dress?" Jill looked so shocked at her secretary's question, Louise had to hide her smile.

"That's a trick question, right?" Louise sniffed. "There's also the pickup truck you drive back and forth to work. Ladies, like some lawyers I know, do not drive pickup trucks. At least not the ones I know."

"Yep. I have a Jaguar. I drive it to church on Sunday. How about some fresh coffee?"

"Coming right up. Be sure to return Barney's call. Lynus Litton said he really needed to talk to you, so you might want to call him first. Is that the same six-year-old car that has four thousand miles on it?"

"*GO!*" Jill roared.

Settled in her office, Jill removed her jacket and hung it on the coat tree. She looked at the sleeves of her striped cotton shirt. What was wrong with the beige-and-white-striped shirt? She'd washed it, starched it, then ironed it. She was meticulous when she ironed her shirts. The camel-colored leather vest with the three toggle buttons was a favorite of hers. It was worn, soft, and comfortable. Maybe she didn't need to wear a vest. She thought about rolling up the sleeves of her blouse, and removing the vest, but if she did that, Louise would be right. Well, maybe she could open the buttons on the vest and roll the sleeves of the blouse to her elbow. She didn't do either one.

Fireplug. She would never imply to anyone that they looked like a fireplug. Never. Whether or not Jill wanted to admit it, Gus Hollister had hurt her feelings. She thought about her client then and how embarrassed he had been after he'd called her Miss Fireplug. She hated thinking about him and his case. If there were a way to pass him off to someone else, she'd do it in a heartbeat, but Barney would never allow that to happen. Maybe if Gus wasn't so handsome, she wouldn't feel like this. She'd been hard on him, and she wasn't sure why. Maybe because of his beautiful wife. A female thing. She argued with herself then. Gus Hollister was human. His case wasn't unique. Men did stupid things when they were married and the marriage ended. But, in most cases, at least the ones she'd handled, there hadn't been a grandmother and elderly aunts involved.

Gus had further confused her when he said he had moved out of Barney's luxurious house. Most people would love being waited on hand and foot and living in the lap of luxury, and all for free. She had to give him points for that. Maybe there was something there, but she wasn't seeing it. Barney said Gus Hollister was the salt of the earth. He said Gus was kind, generous, caring, a good friend, and that he loved him more than if he were a flesh-and-blood brother. So, yes, there was something there. Maybe she had preconceived ideas about

Gus, and he hadn't measured up to those preconceived ideas, and she didn't want to admit
that she was wrong about the kind of person
he was. Everyone made mistakes. People de-
served second chances when they screwed up,
providing they admitted the mistakes and corrected them.

Jill was so deep in thought, she didn't see
Louise come in until she set a mug of coffee
on the desk. "Thanks," Jill said.

Jill waited until Louise closed the door behind her before she picked up the phone and
dialed Lynus Litton's personal number. The
greetings over, Jill said, "What do you have
for me?"

"I just wanted to give you a heads-up. When
I hang up, I'm going to upload a bunch of pictures one of my investigators sent me. I think
they're going to surprise you. It appears that
Elaine Hollister is into voodoo, witchcraft, casting spells, and performing rituals. I have to
admit this is something I am not familiar with.
I did an Internet search and found it all very
interesting. I have to say, I got a little spooked.
And there's one other thing. Mickey Yee, the
investigator who got the pictures, had a bit of
an accident while he was in the attic where
Hollister does her . . . whatever it is she does.
Trying to position some empty boxes and mailers for a photo, he knocked over a vase of flowers
on the altar. That means Elaine Hollister is going
to know someone was in her attic. Mickey wore
gloves, but he was there. He reset the alarm, but

if Mrs. Hollister is as smart and crafty as I think she is, she might call the alarm company and they'll be able to tell her the times the alarm was turned off and on, and she'll know for certain. But, there is also a possibility she might think a rat or a mouse, possibly even a squirrel, got into the attic and knocked over the vase. I just don't know, Jill. But you need to know everything I know. If she goes the route of the alarm company, someone might have seen Gus Hollister sitting in the driveway last night. She'll accuse him in a nanosecond. And he'll have no comeback."

Jill felt like pulling her hair out. "Okay, got it. Anything else?"

"I'll be sending you the report on Gus Hollister. He's clean, Jill. He's who he says he is. He did what hundreds of guys do, got mixed up with the wrong woman, compounded that mistake, and ended up marrying the mistake. Other than that, there's nothing there where he's concerned to throw up any red flags. We're still working on the grandmother and the two aunts."

"Okay, Lynus. Thanks. I'll be in touch." She was just about ready to turn on her computer when Louise opened the door and whistled sharply.

"Ta da! Look at this, Jill," she said, thrusting a vase of white roses forward so Jill could get a better look. "Someone actually sent you flowers! And they smell wonderful. Bet these cost a small fortune." She carefully set the vase on the corner of Jill's desk and stepped back. "Well! Aren't you going to look at the card? It's not every day a woman gets flowers sent to her workplace. C'mon, Jill, open the card. When was the last time you got flowers, here or at home?"

"Never! No one ever sends me flowers. I got a corsage for my senior prom, but that's it. Okay, okay, I'm opening it." Jill's eyes popped wide. "They're from Gus Hollister. He signed it with his name and his dog's name."

Louise thought her boss looked shocked. "Now, that's sweet. You need to have more of an open mind where your client is concerned, Jill. They're just beautiful. Enjoy them," Louise said, turning to leave.

Jill waited until the door was closed before she leaned over to smell the huge arrangement of roses. Was Hollister sucking up or was he genuinely sorry for his crass remark, and this was his apology? She sniffed the flowers again, and propped the little card up next to the vase. The flowers were almost in her line of vision, and she'd be able to see them all day long as she worked. Her first flowers. How amazing was that? She felt almost giddy at the thought. A man, a client actually, had taken the time to send her flowers. Later, when she wasn't so busy, she was going to give some serious thought to the white roses. She was glad they weren't red roses. She hated red roses.

Jill clicked on her computer, brought up Lynus's e-mail, and looked at the attached pictures. She studied them for close to an hour before she printed them out. Then she reached for a magnifying glass and studied the printouts. Lynus was right. It looked like Elaine Hollister was into voodoo and witchcraft. She cringed when she saw the toppled vase on the altar. But the mailers and boxes were clearly visible. Initial B Enterprises. She frowned as she tried to recall if she'd ever heard of the company. Nothing came to mind. "Hmmmnn." Jill pressed a button on the console. "Can you come in here, Louise?"

"Yeah, boss. What's up?" Louise asked from the doorway.

"I want you to go to the main library and get me some books on voodoo and witchcraft. Try to get older books. I want everything you can get on rituals and spells. I could order them from Amazon, but that will take about a week. I'm going to search the Net, but I still want to have some books on hand."

Louise raised her eyebrows.

"Take a look at these pictures," Jill said.

Louise picked up the pictures and looked at them one at a time. "Oooh, this is not good. Okay, I'm on my way. Do you want me to bring back some lunch?"

"Sure, a ham and cheese on rye, and don't forget the pickles."

Jill was already clicking away even before Louise was out of the room.

While Jill Jackson was surfing the Internet, Gus Hollister was sitting down to a very late breakfast at Blossom Farm. His grandmother sat across from him, watching him eat. She smiled. Augustus had always had such a healthy appetite. She was complimenting him now on how hard he'd worked on creating a schedule for the seniors.

Gus carried his dishes to the sink, topped off his coffee cup, then sat down across from his grandmother. "Listen, Granny, you need to stop with the trips to the post office; it takes too much time and costs too much. Let's open an account with UPS, and they'll give us the shipping supplies, they pick up, and you save labor. You guys have been chasing back and forth to three different post offices. That's a lot of hours that are being wasted. Now, having said that, do you all understand that you need to tell me which . . . I don't know how you define it . . . but which *thing* right now is earning you the most money? I'm not talking about the steady bread-and-butter money that keeps you going, like your newsletters."

"That's easy. The fascinators. We have so many orders we can't fill because the feathers are so hard to work with. I'm thinking this is a bit of a fad, so we want to cash in now while they're so popular. I forgot to tell you yesterday that one of our new staff had a great idea. A freebie. A good-luck charm, a talisman, if you will. A faux-jade four-leaf clover. Sonia even knew where we could order them in bulk. Violet placed the order last night for overnight delivery today. We plan to mail them to all past and current customers. A goodwill gesture you can call it. Personally, I jumped at the idea."

"There you go again, massive mailing. All the more reason to use UPS, as they will pick up the packages. You also need a postage meter."

"Okay, I'll put that on my list," Rose said. "I'm glad you're on board, Augustus."

"Me, too, Granny. Me, too."

"Okay, then, let's get down to the nitty-gritty and concentrate our efforts on what we have to do to bring things up to date, where you can make the most money in the shortest period of time. We figure out how to capitalize on our people resources and make it happen. How long does it take to make one of those fascinators—those feather things? One other thing, Granny. Once the members of your staff become familiar with their jobs, I want you to rotate them. Each member of your staff needs to know every other job in case of any kind of setback—and there will be setbacks of one kind or another, you can count on it. If everyone knows everyone else's job, you won't lose momentum. Do you agree or not?"

"I totally agree. We can't keep operating by the seat of our pants. We all know we need structure and discipline of a sort. But to answer your question on the fascinators, it takes a half-hour to make them. Depends on who is working on them. Our fingers are not as nimble as they used to be. It's not an easy task, to attach the thin wires to the feathers. The wires have to be cut just right, so the feathers aren't bouncing all over the place. But we precut them, so we conquered that problem. The main problem, Augustus, is the coloring for the feathers. We've only had a few orders for white ones. Without a doubt, we could make a lot of money but . . ."

"How is your feather supply?"

"We have enough to fill our current orders. We have a long wait list simply because we didn't know if we could fill the demand. Like I said, Augustus, it's coloring the feathers that's our problem. It's dye versus spray and where to do it. We need ideal conditions because feathers are virtually weightless. If you so much as breathe on them, they move. Do you have any suggestions?"

"Actually, I do. Pastor Evans still has bingo nights, doesn't he?" At his grandmother's nod, Gus continued, "You know that big drum they use to turn the numbers before they call them? Do you think he'd let us use it if we made a donation to the church? I remember when Barney and I were kids, you used to take us with you at night when it was your turn to work bingo. We could use the drum to contain the feathers after we dip them in whatever coloring you decide to use. If the feather hats are a lasting sale item, you might think about ordering a new drum for Pastor Evans because the color is going to come off on the wire mesh of the drum. Fans will blow at slow speed to dry the feathers as they tumble. What do you think, Granny?"

"I think you're onto something, Augustus. You go over to the church, and I'll have everyone ready to go to work as soon as you get back. Do you want me to call UPS or will you do that and set up an account for us?"

"I'll make the call when I get to the church. Huddle together and figure out which will work best—dye in tubs or sprays."

Rose rummaged in one of the kitchen drawers for a whistle. She gave it three sharp blasts, which meant, meeting in the kitchen ASAP.

Chapter 17

G<small>US DUSTED HIS HANDS DRAMATICALLY BEFORE</small> shaking hands with Pastor Evans. "Appreciate your help, Pastor." He eyed the oversize drum that was resting in the back of the Blossom Farm van. He wasn't sure he could count on help getting it back out of the van when he got to the farm. Out of the corner of his eye, he noticed a man with a backpack walking away from his car, toward the entrance to the day-care and preschool center. He'd seen him somewhere recently but couldn't remember where. Probably the guy's kid forgot his lunch or his gear, and he was dropping it off on his way to work. Gus shrugged. In the scheme of things, it hardly seemed important. He put it out of his mind as he climbed behind the wheel of the van. He had made it as far as the parking-lot exit when his cell phone rang. He looked down at the number and grinned. Barney! He backed up away from the exit and parked while he took the call.

"How are things in Hong Kong, Barney?"

"Nothing much ever changes here. What's going on? Fill me in, Gus."

"Are you calling me because my attorney called you to complain about me?"

"No. Why? C'mon, Gus, what did you do now to ruffle her feathers?"

"I fouled up, okay? I apologized, and I even sent flowers. I guess I hurt her feelings, and there's no excuse for that. I'm trying to screw up the courage to invite her out to dinner. A truce of sorts. What—she didn't call you?"

"She did not. You might as well tell me what it was you did. Guilt is a terrible thing. You know that. And . . . pal, that's another reason why you're in the position you're in now. Tell me, you'll feel better. It's called clearing your conscience."

"I addressed her as Miss Fireplug. Jesus, Barney, it just slipped out. I didn't mean to say it out loud. It's how I think of her. I know I hurt her feelings, and I'm going to do my best to correct my comment. It's all those clothes, and, for crying out loud, she has *layers* of them. She drives a pickup truck. I try not to be judg-mental, but it's what I see, okay?" The silence on the other end of the line bothered Gus. "I know you're pissed, Barney, and you're disappointed in me. I'm sorry."

"Gus, she's a top-notch attorney. If she weren't, I would never have hired her. Did you ever stop to think there might be a reason she dresses like she does and a reason why she drives a pickup truck? And what does her mode of transportation have to do with anything, anyway?"

"You're right, Barney, I'm not arguing with you. I'm not even defending myself. She's my lawyer. I think I'd like to know she's . . . that she has a personality. She's like a goddamned robot. And she hates me. It's hard to be nice to someone you know hates your guts."

"I'm coming home. I should be there sometime tomorrow night. No, I'm not coming back because of you and your problems."

"Then why are you coming back? When you left, you said you were going to be gone *six months*."

"I'm tired of making money. You seem to be having all the fun. I want to be part of it. All work and no play makes for a dull boy. I believe that. I want to be there to see you take your bus driving test. Tell Granny and the aunts I'll be bringing home some jade and some beautiful silk for them."

"Come off it, Barney. You love money. You worship money. You eat, sleep, and dream about money. You'd rather cut off your left foot than give up money."

"I didn't say I was giving up on money. I still

love money, but everyone gets to take a hiatus at some point in their life. I want to take my hiatus now."

Suddenly, alarm crept into Gus's voice. "You aren't sick, are you, Barney?"

"No, I'm not sick, Gus. I'm fine."

Gus wasn't sure he believed his friend, but he let it go. "What are you bringing home for the fire . . . Miss Jackson?"

"None of your business."

"What are you bringing me?"

"A whole new attitude, pal."

Gus felt his blood pressure rising. He tried to shake off what he was feeling. "If you're saying in a roundabout way that you're coming back because you think I'm screwing up, just say it, Barney."

"I told you. I'm coming back because I'm tired of just making money. I want to stop and smell the roses for a little while. And I want to help with Granny and the aunts, if you all want me. Listen, I gotta go. See you tomorrow night."

Gus didn't bother saying good-bye. He just clicked off and took a deep breath. He shifted gears and drove to the EXIT sign. Out of the corner of his eye, he saw the man with the back-pack coming out the door of the preschool, when he looked in his side-view mirror to see if anyone was behind him.

As Gus drove along, his thoughts went to Barney and his return Stateside. Without think-ing, he made a left turn and followed a service road that would take him to the DMV so he could pick up a bus driver's manual. And then, when he got back to the farm, he was going to talk to Granny and ask her opinion as to what he should do next where Jill Jackson was concerned. Barney's words rang in his ears. *Did you ever stop to think there might be a reason she dresses like she does?* Well, hell, yes, he'd thought about it, and the only answer he could come up with was his lawyer liked dressing like a bag lady. End of story. And it wasn't any of his business to begin with. As to her mode of transportation, that wasn't his business, either. As long as a vehicle got you where you had to go, that was all that mattered. So why was it bothering him?

Gus shrugged off his thoughts as he parked, ran into the DMV, and asked for a bus driver's manual. He looked at it and shoved it into his back pocket. He'd read it tonight while he and Wilson watched TV. He wondered then if he was putting the cart before the horse. Where was he going to get a bus to practice on? Pastor Evans? Maybe he could practice in the parking lot. He'd ask Granny to intercede. There was no way he wanted to break a promise to Elroy Hitchens and the other seniors.

Gus pulled to a stop at a traffic light. Tapping on the steering wheel, impatient to get moving, he looked into the rearview mirror and frowned. Two cars back was a silver car. The guy with the backpack had been driving a silvery-colored car. His heart fluttered in his chest. *Am I being followed? If I am, is it because of Elaine?*

The light changed and Gus moved forward. He didn't have time just then to try to lose his tail, assuming that it was a tail. *Watching too much* Law & Order, *or am I getting paranoid?*

Jittery with his thoughts, Gus drove carefully, his gaze going to his rearview mirror when he felt it was safe to take his eyes off the road. If he was being followed, he hated leading his tail to Blossom Farm, but it couldn't be helped.

An hour later, Gus, with the help of several of the seniors, managed to get the huge drum up on the back porch. Seniors swarmed through the doors. They looked like they knew what they were doing, so he entered the house and sought out his grandmother. "I need to talk to you, Granny. I need some advice, and if you can spare Violet and Iris, I'd like to include them, too."

"This sounds serious, Augustus. Are you okay?"

"If you mean am I sick, no, I'm not. I just need some advice. Female advice. I think we should go outside to talk."

Wilson came on the run and waited for Gus to give him a good scratch behind the ears. Gus obliged. Wilson was the first one out the door when Rose, Violet, and Iris appeared.

Outside, Gus let loose with his problem. "Obviously, I know nothing about women, so I'm asking for your help. I don't know what to do. By the way, Barney is coming home. He said he's tired of making money. I don't believe that for one minute. He's bringing jade and silk for you ladies. And I think someone is following me. Probably someone Elaine has hired to keep tabs on me. You need to know that. If you want me to stay away, I can do that. I don't want to cause any problems for any of you. Private detectives dig and dig and dig. That's why they get paid the big bucks. This could mean trouble."

Violet squared her shoulders. "I think we can handle interference, Augustus. I also agree with you about Barney. Now, as to the young attorney who is handling your divorce . . . you said she accepted your apology. You sent her flowers. You are thinking of asking her to dinner. I say, do it." Iris and Rose agreed.

Gus felt dizzy as he tried to absorb all the advice they were throwing at him. What he walked away with was that he needed to be humble, complimentary. "And, Augustus, you need to listen and pay attention to what the young lady says. If you get stuck, go to the men's room and call us; we'll talk you through it."

Gus felt like he was sixteen and going out on his first date. He'd been married, had relationships in the past, for crying out loud. If Barney were here, he'd laugh his head off.

"Where are you going now, Augustus?" Rose asked.

"To the post office to pick up your mail. I can do that every morning to save you guys time. Traveling to three different post offices takes time. I'm sort of surprised that you get orders by way of the postal service as opposed to the Internet."

"There are people who do not have computers, Augustus, or even access to computers. People still write letters and put stamps on the envelopes. I know in your eyes those people are Neanderthals, but it is what it is. When you get to the post office, just say you're there to pick up Initial B Enterprises' mail, and they'll give it to you in a sack. Those sacks have to be brought back here. What is on your agenda for the rest of the day?"

"If you don't need me, I thought I would try to get myself settled in my new digs. I need to pick up a few more things and some additional groceries. I also need to pick up my own mail at the office and pay some bills. I'm just a phone call away if you need me to do anything."

Violet sniffed. Of the three sisters, Violet was the most unforgiving. "I think we can manage, nephew. But, we do appreciate all you've done for us."

"Thanks for your advice. I'll be back with the mail." Gus waved as he exited with Wilson on his heels.

On his way to the Jeep, Gus noticed movement in the front yard; Mr. Younger and his sons working on the old sycamore. Gus walked over and looked down at the monster logs, which were being split into firewood. He asked about the part of the tree where he and Barney had carved their names. "It's right there on the steps, Mr. Gus. Your grandmother told us to save it for you. You can take it now if you want. Shame this old tree had to go like that, but Mother Nature is a strange lady."

Gus was surprised at how heavy the slab of bark was. He felt his eyes start to burn. His index finger traced the deep carvings he and Barney had done what seemed like a lifetime ago. He nodded, picked it up, and carried it out to the driveway. He opened the back of the Jeep and settled it in the corner on top of an old blanket. He walked back to where Alex Younger was standing and shook his hand. He whistled for Wilson, who was sniffing the fresh-cut wood.

Ninety minutes later, Gus had returned to the farm and was unloading the sacks of mail on the back porch. As if by magic, three seniors appeared, scooped up the sacks, and disappeared. Talk about a well-oiled working machine.

Gus was back on the road and headed toward his office. He constantly checked his rearview mirror to see if the silver car was following him. He thought it was there, three cars back. He was certain of it when he pulled into the Target parking lot. "Well, have at it," he mumbled under his breath as he bolted into the store and was back out in thirty minutes. "What'd you see, Wilson?"

Woof!

"Yeah, that's what I thought. Okay, let's take this guy for a ride. Buckle up, Wilson."

* * *

Elaine Hollister finished her coffee and headed back upstairs to shower and get ready for the day. She felt irritable and out of sorts. She'd spent a miserable night once she got home from Isaac Diamond's house in the wee hours of the morning. The intimate evening had not gone according to *her* plan. Isaac Diamond, even in his seventies, was no pushover, and he hadn't bought into her act. In her opinion, he was nothing more than a dirty old man who chewed up the little blue pills like they were M&Ms. She'd never worked so hard for nothing in her entire life, and only to lose.

She needed to get cleansed. Even though she'd scrubbed herself raw when she'd returned home hours earlier, it was imperative that her body be purified before she climbed the ladder to her altar so that she could perform her daily ritual.

The white linen gown felt good when she dropped it over her aching body. She shook her shoulders so that the gown settled more comfortably on her body before she pressed the switch that would lower the ladder to the attic. As the hydraulics kicked in, Elaine did her best to clear her mind so that it was as pure as her cleansed body. She took several deep breaths before making her way up to where her altar waited for her. At the last rung, her arm stretched out and hit the switch in the floor that turned on the lights in the attic.

She saw everything all at once, the boxes and empty mailers behind her altar, the over-turned vase of white flowers, the roses wilted and already starting to turn brown. Panic rippled through her as she let her gaze rake all the tools that she used to perform her spells and rituals. Her hands trembled as she set the vase upright. She picked up the wilted roses, turned around, and threw them down the ladder. The petals scattered all over the floor, which meant that when she descended, she'd be stepping all over them. The thought bothered her.

Elaine turned and eyed her altar, her heart beating like a trip-hammer. *The cloth is soaking wet. Defiled. And I don't have a backup cloth.* She cursed under her breath. She'd had plans to perform two rituals today. Three, now, since she'd spent the better part of the night with Isaac Diamond. Bastard. How could she have been so wrong?

But all that was the least of her problems. *Did someone break into the house last night while I was out? How else could the vase have toppled over? A rat? A mouse? Possibly a squirrel. No. Gus had an exterminator come by once a month. If a rodent had taken up residence in the attic, I would have seen droppings when I originally set up the altar. No, someone was in the house, someone who obviously knew how to pick a lock and bypass the alarm system. Gus? No, not Gus. Then who?*

Elaine tried to calm her racing heart, her nerves twanging all over the place as she backed up and descended the ladder. She raced into the bedroom and dialed the alarm company and blurted out her questions. When she hung up the phone, she had to sit down on the side of the bed, she felt so light-headed. Someone who was smart enough to know their way around an alarm system had broken into her house not once, but twice. The first time whoever it was had broken in, they spent an hour in the house before turning the alarm back on. The second time, they stayed in the house exactly forty-eight minutes before reconnecting the alarm.

The house looked the same as far as she could tell. Nothing looked out of place. She knew that her jewelry, what there was of it, was still in her jewelry box, because she'd put her earrings in it when she got home, along with her watch with the diamond bezel and the special medallion she'd worn around her neck last night. So, then, why would someone break into her house? Obviously a professional of some sort, looking for . . . what, she didn't know. It had to concern the divorce proceedings. Maybe it even concerned Isaac Diamond, with plans to blackmail her. Although she thought that the latter might be a stretch.

Her head swimming with all manner of possibilities, Elaine raced back up the ladder to carry her materials down to the dining room, where she was going to set up an emergency altar. It took eight trips before she had everything ready. Then she looked around in a panic.

Dammit. I don't have a spare altar cloth. Wait. Maybe I do. She ran over to the buffet and yanked at a drawer. There was a brand-new, white linen tablecloth, complete with a sticky label that said the dimensions were 108 by 96 inches. Just big enough to cover the dining-room table, which had three additional leaves. She peeled off the sticky label, shook the tablecloth out, and spread it across the table. She quickly replaced everything the way she'd had it in the attic, minus one vase of flowers.

Elaine ran into the living room, where there was an elaborate silk flower arrangement. She yanked at several white silk orchids and carried them back to the dining room, where she placed them in the empty vase. She looked at everything with a careful eye.

I'm good to go. She was about to sit down when she looked down at the smudges on her priestess gown and felt like crying. She wasn't pure. She had to take another shower and change into a fresh gown.

Elaine mumbled and muttered all the while she soaped and showered and dried herself off. She ran to the closet, ripped a clean white linen gown off the hanger, pulled it on, and ran back down the stairs.

Like the high priestess she perceived herself to be, Elaine took a seat in front of her altar. She sat quietly, her hands on her knees, as she took deep breaths, holding her breath to the count of seven, then expelling it in a soft *swoosh* of sound. When she felt sufficiently calm, she reached for a long match, struck it on the side of the special box, and lit the black candle and the two slender incense spears. She waited till the aroma from the incense permeated the room. In her hand, she held a small black bag of herbs to ward off evil. She sprinkled salt over it, then picked up the small bottle of holy water and dripped some on the bag. Then she waved the bag through the vapors of the incense sticks. Back and forth, back and forth.

Finally, Elaine closed her eyes and started to chant words she knew by heart from long months of repeating them daily. The words flowed evenly and with passion. She ended her chant with, "All my enemies to leave my life. I cite the number nine and the number four. Four enemies, Augustus Hollister, Rose Blossom, Violet Blossom, and Iris Blossom. Remove these enemies from my life. I offer up everything on my altar. I want no harm to come to the four because I know if I wish such a thing, that wish will come back to me fourfold. I cite the number nine for this to take place. Nine minutes, nine hours, nine days, nine weeks."

Elaine stared into the flame of the black candle as she envisioned Gus Hollister and the Blossom sisters walking away, their pockets inside out as they left all their worldly possessions behind. For her. Only her.

With spots in front of her eyes from staring into the flame of the candle, Elaine blinked as she reached behind her to the sideboard, where she had placed her Bible and her glasses. She opened the Bible and started to read the Psalms that pertained to her ritual. She read aloud, passion ringing in her voice.

When she was finished, she closed the Bible, set it back on the sideboard, and removed her glasses from the tip of her nose, where they rested. She stood up, opened her arms wide, and intoned, "The portals to the universe are now closed. Thank you for hearing my pleas."

Elaine sat back down and repeated the earlier procedure. She placed her hands on her knees and did her deep breathing exercises. After she leaned over and blew out the black candle, she carried the container with the incense to the kitchen and set it in the sink.

Elaine felt buoyant as she practically flew back to the dining room, where she prepared her altar for a second ritual. To be sure, she had everything ready for what she called a *twofer.* She ripped through her ritual manual until she found the page she wanted. Her index finger raced across the words as she committed them to memory.

This second ritual was a money ritual, one she performed weekly, but today was the first time she would add a second part to it. Isaac Diamond was the second part of the ritual.

Elaine placed new sticks of frankincense in a crystal cylinder. She set up four green candles, not the squat black kind she'd used earlier. These candles were more like short, thin tapers, which would burn out by the time the ritual was finished. Green symbolized money. Next to the candles were a small green change purse and a small box covered in green felt. She reached for a green velvet drawstring bag, which, according to the ritual instructions, was called a prosperity bag. From the sideboard she picked up a handful of loose change—four pennies, four nickels, four dimes, four quarters—and placed them in the coin purse. She deposited four one-dollar bills in the green felt money box.

Elaine reached for the special gold medallion. It was old, something she'd found in a pawnshop years before. She'd had it modified several days after purchasing it, into a miniature recording device capable of recording for two full hours before the tiny tape had to be replaced, which in the end had cost more than to purchase it. The medallion had proved to be invaluable over the years.

Elaine walked over to the sideboard and picked up a large green crystal and a small container of cinnamon oil. She would use the oil to anoint her candle, the felt-covered box, and the change purse. The last thing she had to do was place jasmine flowers in the middle of the altar. She rummaged in one of the drawers in the sideboard for the pressed jasmine that she'd preserved last summer when they bloomed at the side of the house. The salt to be used this time was sea salt, as opposed to the table salt she'd used in the first ritual.

Elaine looked at her altar, staring at each article to make sure she had it placed properly. Satisfied, she sat down and did her deep breathing preparations.

Calm now, Elaine stared into the flames of

the flickering tapers as the vapors from the incense wafted about the dining room. Her hand stretched out to pick up the medallion. She clutched it in her hand as she started to chant, the number four taking precedence in everything she asked for. Four minutes, four hours, four days, four weeks. Her voice was as passionate as before, her arms waving upward as she pled for help. When she was finished with her chanting, she reached for the green crystal and rubbed it over her forehead, her cheeks, her chin, then up and down her arms. Then she rolled the crystal in the sea salt. The crystal went into the green velvet drawstring bag. The rest of the sea salt was sprinkled over her head. Then she counted the coins and placed each one into the same bag as the crystal. The four one-dollar bills followed. Once again, Elaine anointed the bag, the change purse, and the green money box with the cinnamon oil. Using the same oil, she dabbed her forehead, her neck at her pulse points, and her wrists.

Elaine sat down, took deep breaths, closed her eyes, and chanted her money ritual. "In *hours* of four, my money worries will be no more. In *days* of four, my money worries will be no more. In *weeks* of four, my money worries will be no more. In *months* of four, my money worries will be no more." She repeated the chant four times before she let out a long sigh of completion.

Elaine squared her shoulders. She picked up the medallion again and pressed a little button on the back. Isaac Diamond's mellifluous courtroom voice filled the dining room. Elaine grimaced as she stared into the flickering flames of the tapers sitting on the dining-room table. She repeated Isaac Diamond's name four times as she wrote his name four times on a piece of paper. She folded the paper into a little square and reached behind her for a small glass jar. She slipped the folded square into the jar and turned the lid.

"Four, four, four, four." Now she had to wait four minutes before she could fill the jar with the special boiled vinegar mix in the refrigerator, along with the herbs that she'd poured into the vinegar when she returned home in the early hours of the morning.

Elaine watched the minute hand on her watch. When the big hand reached eleven, Elaine ran to the kitchen and opened the door of the refrigerator. When the big hand reached the twelve, she poured the vinegar mixture into the glass jar in her hand. All the while, she chanted, "Four, four, four, four!"

In a flash, she was back at her altar, the small jar still in her hands. She passed it over the flames of the four candles. Then she waved the jar over and through the vapor from the incense sticks. Finally, she anointed the jar with the cinnamon oil.

Done.

But there was one thing she still had to do. She had four hours to take the little jar with the vinegar mixture to a body of water and throw it in.

Elaine leaned her head back against the chair and closed her eyes. Her ritual was complete. She felt drained, but cleansed.

As Elaine set about cleaning up her altar, she kept chanting, "Four, four, four, four."

Chapter 18

Gus felt jittery for some reason as he put his groceries away. He looked at Wilson, who was watching him like a hawk; he smelled meat. "I'm going to make it all up to you, Wilson. You and I are going to barbecue two nice, big, thick tenderloins. We'll eat out on the deck and spend the night together. We're home, big guy; this is it for us. We are home." Wilson tilted his head to the side and stared up at his master. At some point, the dog must have made up his mind that things were indeed okay, because he let loose with a soft growling sound that made Gus laugh out loud.

Gus spent the next half-hour marinating the steak, preparing a salad, and scrubbing a potato that he would bake and then top with sour cream and chives. He was as much at home in the kitchen as he was in the laundry room, thanks to his granny, who had taught him to cook and clean and do his own laundry at an early age. He considered himself truly self-sufficient.

Satisfied with his preparations, he reached for a chew bone for Wilson and a beer for himself and went out to his deck. He looked around and decided he needed some flowers or some kind of greenery to take away the starkness from the deck. He liked that the Realtor had chosen bright-colored cushions for the deck furniture, and he really liked the bright, lemon-colored table umbrella. At some point, he might think about ordering a retractable awning, since the deck got sun for the better part of the day. He thought about all those ads he kept seeing on TV each year when winter came to an end.

Gus leaned on the railing as he gulped at his frosty beer. He liked the pruned bushes and shrubs. He thought he could keep up with everything once he got the right equipment. Saturdays would be lawn days and cleaning days—unless one of the trees in the yard turned out to be a money tree that showered him with coins and bills so he could afford to hire a gardener and a part-time housekeeper. The vision of a money tree with the coins and bills raining down was so funny, Gus burst out laughing. Wilson raised his head long enough to look around to see what was so funny. He went back to his chew bone.

Gus let his thoughts wander then. He skimmed over thoughts of Elaine. How weird was that? How was it possible he could skim over someone he'd loved with all his being a little more than a week ago? His thoughts took him to Granny and the aunts and their newly recovered relationship. He smiled with feeling. He so loved those old gals. Barney invaded his thoughts at that point. He loved his best friend as much as he loved his granny and his two zany aunts. It bothered him that Barney was suddenly coming back to the States when he had said he was going to be gone for months. He didn't believe for one minute that Barney was tired of making money. Barney, the protector. Barney wanted to make sure nothing happened to him, since he was going it alone with too many things on his plate. Gus smiled at that thought.

His beer finished, Gus walked over to a bright yellow trash receptacle with a large white daisy painted on the side. Women. He could actually see Marsha painting the daisy on the can. She'd think the colored trash can would perk up the deck. And it did. He made a mental note to send Marsha a gift or, at the very least, some flowers for all her help.

Back in the house, Gus looked at the old-fashioned phone hanging on the wall. He didn't know why, but he felt compelled to call his grandmother. He didn't stop to think, just punched in the numbers. Violet answered the phone. To Gus's ear, his aunt sounded frazzled. "What's wrong, Aunt Vi?"

"Technically, nothing is wrong. We just can't cope with the fortune cookies. We're trying, but we aren't meeting the demand. We have roughly twelve restaurants we supply cookies for—fifteen hundred each a week. That's eighteen thousand cookies each and every week. We have to bake the cookies, insert the fortunes, wrap the cookies, then deliver them. We just don't have enough ovens. We might have to cancel this service, and that would be a shame, because we make some serious money with fortune cookies. We've tried to streamline our operation, but it's hard. If you have any ideas, we'd like to hear them, Augustus. We have to make a delivery in two days and are seriously behind."

Gus didn't think he'd ever heard Violet talk so much at one time. And she had actually asked him for help. His chest puffed out. "I can be there in fifteen minutes, Aunt Vi. I need to see the operation with my own eyes."

"Thank you, Augustus. We'll be expecting you."

Gus set the marinating steak back into the refrigerator and whistled for Wilson. "Wanna go for a ride, big guy?"

Wilson ran to the door as Gus slid the sliding doors shut and locked them. He checked everything the way he always did: lights off, stove off, doors locked. He was good to go.

Seven minutes into his drive to Blossom Farm, Gus knew he was being followed by the silver-colored car. He bit down on his lip, looked over at Wilson who was riding shotgun, and said, "Hold on, bud, we're going to catch this guy." Wilson's ears went straight up as he anticipated action. "When I catch him, you bite him on the ass. You hear me, Wilson?"

Woof.

Gus careened around a corner, downshifted, and pulled to the curb just as the silver car barreled behind him and screeched to a stop. In one swift motion, Gus had his Louisville Slugger bat, which he had transferred from his Porsche to Barney's Jeep, in his hands and was in the middle of the road. He raised the bat and got ready to swing. Straight at the silver car's windshield. A black Mustang swung around Gus as its driver leaned on his horn. Gus ignored it when the silver car's window slid down.

"Get out of the damned car, or your windshield is confetti. Wilson! He makes one wrong move, you bite him on the ass. You hear me, Wilson?"

Unmindful of moving traffic, which was light, Gus approached the man getting out of the car, his hands up in the air.

"I'm not a cop, so put your arms down. Who the hell are you, and why the hell are you following me? And don't lie. You've been following me for days now."

Mickey Yee eyed the menacing shepherd, who was showing him his teeth. He saw the fur on the back of the dog's neck moving in the light afternoon breeze. He put his arms down but froze in position as he wondered what it would be like to get bitten on the ass by the monster dog standing in front of him. The visual was not one that appealed to him. He remained statue still, one eye on the man swinging the bat, his other eye on the ferocious-looking dog.

Gus swung the bat back and forth. "Talk to me and make it good, mister."

"My name is Mickey Yee. I'm a private investigator. I work for Lynus Litton, who is working for your attorney, Jill Jackson. Yeah, I have been following you. Someone else is following your wife. I'm not the one you should be worried about. That black Mustang that went around you when you cut in front of me is who you should be worried about. He's been following you also. It's been like a damned parade for days now. I even know the skank's name: Bill Donovan. He'll do any job, break the law for a buck. I'm thinking he's working for your wife or her attorney, but that's just my guess."

Gus lowered the Louisville Slugger and called Wilson to his side as he digested what the man standing in front of him had just said. "Are you telling me I have a tail on me?"

"For several days now, yes, that's what I'm telling you. The guy's a sleazeball, so when and if you ever see his report, most of it will be lies."

"Why are you following *me?*"

"Orders. By the way, you're boring as hell. I thought I'd go out of my mind when you were shopping at Target. What, you can't make up your mind when it comes to towels and sheets?"

"Thread count is important. Towel thickness is just as important, for absorbency. Didn't your mother teach you that? Boring! I'm a hell of an interesting guy."

"I guess I missed that lesson. Okay, so you made me, now what?"

"Stop following me."

"You sure you want me to stop? If I keep following you, then I can keep tabs on Bill Donovan. Would that dog really have bitten my ass?" Yee asked anxiously.

"Yeah, and loved every minute of it. Stop following me. I'll deal with Donovan on my own. Go on, get out of here."

"Hollister, hold on a minute. Listen, it's not just Donovan. I saw someone else out at your grandmother's farm yesterday. No clue who he was, but he was snooping around. Mud on his license plate, so I couldn't run the number. I have a soft spot for old people, and I wouldn't want to see anything happen to your grandmother and the people who come and go. I have to admit, they have me wondering what's going on there, and don't try to tell me they're playing bingo or some such shit."

"What did the guy you saw look like? And, they *are* bingo addicts. They live for bingo. They eat, sleep, and drink bingo."

Mickey Yee looked disgusted. "Hey, the guy's probably a dick, okay? What he looked like yesterday doesn't mean he's going to look the same today. And while he was driving a beat-to-shit Honda yesterday, today he might look like a movie star and be driving a high-end car. Old people are prey. I just gave you a heads-up. So, you want me off this or on it? Or are you still going to go this alone? Makes me no never mind."

Gus realized everything the detective said was true. "No, okay, stay on it. But . . . I don't want you to tell anyone I made you. Will you agree to that?"

"Hell yes, man."

Gus swung the Louisville Slugger. "You go back on your word, you're going to find out what a bite on the ass will feel like."

"You got it. Can I go now?"

"Yeah. I'm going to the farm. If you see anyone at the farm watching my grandmother, call me, okay?" Gus rattled off his cell-phone number, and Yee punched the numbers into his own cell phone.

Wilson whined all the way to the farm. "Get over it, big guy. One of these days you're going to get the chance to bite some bad guy's ass, trust me on that."

Wilson dropped his head onto his paws as if to say, *promises, promises, promises.* Gus reached over to scratch the dog behind the ears. He grinned. God, how he loved this dog.

The kitchen at the farmhouse smelled wonderful. Chili, if his nose was on the money. He also smelled the sweet scent of vanilla, and something baking. While the kitchen was huge, with two double ovens and two stove tops, every burner seemed to have something cooking and bubbling on it. He could see the trays of something baking in the double ovens.

Iris appeared out of nowhere and said, "Chili and rice pudding for dessert. We can send you home with some of each. We're baking the fortune cookies. With all our new staff's meals to prepare, this kitchen is getting a workout, and we're stumbling over each other. The summer kitchen looks the same as this one does. We simply do not have enough room, Augustus. Something has to give."

"I see that. Tell me how the cookie operation works," Gus said as he headed for the steps that would take him down one level to the old summer kitchen. It didn't look old now—everything was new and modern. In the old days, before air conditioning, the summer kitchen was used for all the cooking so the rest of the house didn't get too hot.

The contents of pots were simmering, and the same vanilla-sugar-cinnamon scent was present. On the long counter, he saw trays and trays of baked fortune cookies ready to be packaged.

"We can bake two trays of cookies every twenty-five minutes. Each tray holds thirty-six cookies. We have two double ovens, so that means we're baking one hundred and forty-four cookies in these two ovens every twenty-five minutes. We need an extra five minutes to slide the cookies off the trays and get the next batch ready, so actually it's thirty to thirty-five minutes. The same goes for the two double ovens upstairs, for a total of two hundred and eighty-eight cookies. We bake from seven in the morning until eight at night. We are not meeting our goal of eighteen thousand cookies for the Chinese restaurants we service, although we did meet it last month. Prep time includes mixing and inserting the fortune into each cookie. Two hours to do all this as we try to mix enough dough to carry us through the whole day. Out of every nine hours the ovens are going, we're only utilizing six of those hours for actual baking. That's a total of 3,456 cookies a day. Having said that, it's not *actually* 3,456 sellable cookies. Some break, some burn, and we have a lot of throwaways, making the count more like thirty-two hundred on a good day. Sometimes even less than that. Last week, our actual count of cookies that were delivered was fifteen thousand. Having said that, there are seven days in a week and with each restaurant giving out an average of two hundred fifteen cookies a day for lunch and dinner, we're short. We've had to cut back on the number of restaurants we service."

"Just Chinese restaurants?" Gus asked.

"In the beginning, it was just Chinese, then some of the Japanese takeout places wanted to place orders. We also have four Vietnamese locations who want our cookies. Most of the restaurants have takeout orders, so you have to factor that in the numbering, too. People sometimes ask for two cookies; children want them. We don't have a good bead on that end of things. I remember Rose saying that last month when she was doing the final tally for the month."

"How much do you make on, say, fifteen hundred cookies?"

"Rose has all those numbers. We are making a profit, but according to Rose, not enough to justify the work that's entailed. We pay two Asian students at the university to come up with the fortunes. They send them via a download from the Internet. We print them out, cut them to fit the cookie; then there's the cost of the ingredients, the cost of the wrappers, the labor to wrap them, and, of course, to mix the dough and do the actual baking. Then there's the cleanup and getting them ready for delivery on each restaurant's delivery day. Even though our staff does not take a salary per se, our expenses are quite high."

Gus could feel his head start to spin at what he was hearing. "Correct me if I'm wrong here, Aunt Iris. Right now, you can meet demand, but it's taking too much time for the amount of money you're making. Is that what you're saying? You need to ask yourself, is the money worth all the aggravation of trying to make more? Don't take this the wrong way, but you guys are not youngsters anymore, and stress and pressure is not good for anyone, especially the elderly. I give all of you kudos for going at it full bore, but there have to be limits to what you all can do. That's why I made up a work schedule and insisted that each of you and your staff learn each other's jobs, so it doesn't come down to a few pulling the whole wagon. Are you following me here, Aunt Iris?"

Gus watched as Iris's shoulders drooped. "I am, Augustus, and I think you need to speak with your grandmother. We all love the fortune cookie operation, especially the fortune part. We stress to our two Asian students who make them up that they be upbeat and positive fortunes."

"Can you blow that whistle for Granny and Aunt Vi?"

"I can do better than that. They're up in the voodoo and witchcraft room. Seems we have a client who lives in the vicinity and is one of our best customers. Her testimonials will blow off your socks. It's all about cleansing the mind and *believing*. Vi told me about an hour ago that an e-mail came in from that client relaying a more than positive outcome to a special ritual that was performed today. When we get those, we post them. And then we get a real spike in orders."

All Gus could do was shake his head. *Voodoo and witchcraft! Who knew?*

Even though he was a CPA, Gus couldn't compute the numbers in his head.

Chapter 19

ELAINE HOLLISTER REMOVED THE SMALL JAR OF vinegar from her bag and looked around to see if anyone was watching her. As far as she could tell, the few people lakeside were packing up their blankets and picnic baskets to go home. She palmed the little jar, drew her arm back, and pitched it with such force that she would have been the envy of an all-star baseball pitcher had one been watching. She chanted under her breath, then took a long, deep breath, holding it for a count of ten before she expelled it. She felt so light-headed, she thought for a moment that she was going to black out, but she squeezed her eyes shut and waited for the wave of dizziness to pass.

Elaine smiled as she turned and walked back to the picnic area where she'd parked her car. She looked at her watch. Three minutes to four. She'd made her offering to the depths of the lake right on time. Now all she had to do was wait to see what happened to Isaac Diamond. There was no doubt in her mind that *something* would happen to the lawyer. She just wasn't sure what it would be.

Elaine slid into the little yellow car, settled herself, turned over the engine, flipped in a CD, and drove out of a lot that was now almost deserted.

Overhead, dark clouds were gathering. It would rain shortly, she thought. Just another late afternoon April shower. She hoped it wasn't as ferocious as the one a day or so ago: she'd cowered in the bathroom while Mother Nature had wreaked havoc on the state of Virginia. She hated storms. She didn't like rain, either, when it came right down to it. Who cared if the grass needed watering? Who cared if the leaves on the trees and bushes were wilted? She had more important things to worry about. Gus used to fret about the water bill and about Wilson when it thundered. She had been thinking too much about Gus over the past several days, and that was not a good thing. Gus was out of her life, and she was moving forward. She did think it a tad strange, though, that he hadn't come whining and crying about how much he loved her and he hadn't come to ask her to give him another chance. Why hadn't he done that? Even though she'd put a restraining order in place, he could have called or sent her a text, but he hadn't done either of those things.

Maybe she was slipping, and she'd miscalculated his feelings for her. No, she'd had him, as the saying goes, wrapped around her little finger. His lawyer probably told him the same thing hers had told her—no communication.

Elaine rolled down the window to look upward. The clouds were moving faster, and they looked darker than they had just minutes ago. She stopped for a red light and let her eyes wander to the side of the highway. The Jade Pagoda. She could get takeout. And right next to the Jade Pagoda was the Fine Wine and Spirits Shop. She could pick up a few bottles of wine and have a party all by herself to celebrate what she hoped would be the demise of Isaac Diamond. Ooops, she had to stop thinking like that. She didn't want Isaac Diamond's demise; she just wanted him out of her life and her retainer paid back and maybe something for that obscene performance she'd had the night before. Blackmail was such a sweet thing when you held all the cards. Maybe the right word should be *restitution*. *Blackmail* was an ugly word, but sweet at the same time.

The light changed. Elaine turned on her blinker and made a left turn. She parked in the Jade Pagoda's parking lot and was not surprised to see it nearly empty. Too late for lunch, too early for the dinner crowd. That had to mean she'd be in and out in record time. She could go next door, pick up the wine she wanted while they prepared her food, and, if she was lucky, she'd be home before the rain came.

The wind was brisk—the temperature had been falling steadily since she'd started out around three-thirty. Fireplace weather. No sense in turning on the heat for just a few hours.

Elaine loved it when things worked in her favor. She did indeed make it home just as the first raindrops fell on the back deck. The drops were big and splattered in all directions, which told her it would be a brief shower at best, but it was more than chilly.

Safely inside with the door locked and bolted, and the alarm set, Elaine first made a fire, then carried a small folding table into the den. She liked to eat watching television and with a fire at the same time. The truth was, she loved her own company and her own thoughts. She only had one rule in her life—not to get attached to anything but money. Money could buy whatever she needed. Attachments were baggage, and, more often than not, she moved on in the middle of the night. It was so much easier to leave with just a bankbook and an overnight bag, which she kept in the trunk of her car, than to carry cumbersome items she wouldn't need in her new life. A new life meant new things. Always new things, new people, new surroundings, new everything.

Elaine devoured the food until there wasn't a crumb left. She was on her third glass of wine when she pulled out the four fortune cookies she'd insisted the manager at the restaurant give her. Today, four was her magic number. All compliments of Initial B Enterprises.

She read the first one. *You are almost there.*

Fortune cookie number two: *Success is right around the corner.*

Fortune cookie number three: *Your lucky number is four.*

Elaine danced with excitement when she read the third fortune. She bounced up and off her chair as she twirled and whirled, her fists shooting in the air. She was trembling so much she could barely open the last one.

Fortune cookie number four: *A windfall is about to drop in your lap.*

Elaine slumped back in her chair, her thoughts all over the map as she stared blankly at the television screen. This was when she had to be patient. Sit and wait for whatever was going to happen. She stared into the flickering flames as they danced in the fireplace until her eyes closed, and she fell asleep.

The landline on the table next to the sofa rang at seven-thirty, waking her from a sound sleep. She managed a garbled "Yes" to the person on the other end of the line.

"Mrs. Hollister, this is Wendy Manning, from Isaac Diamond's office. I'm sorry to be calling you at this hour of the day, but the partners asked me to call all of Isaac's clients to inform them that he suffered a serious accident late this afternoon. I saw in his appointment book that he had a meeting scheduled for tomorrow with you. Nick or Lee can see you, or you can wait till we have more news on Isaac's condition."

It wasn't often that Elaine was at a loss for words, but this time she was, as she tried to figure out what to say. The best she could come up with was, "How terrible. Can you tell me what happened and the time it happened?"

"The time?"

"Well, yes, the time, because, you see, I was speaking with him earlier," Elaine lied.

"All I know is that Nick said they, and by *they* I mean EMS, transported him to the hospital at four-thirty this afternoon. They did say it wasn't life-threatening, but that it was serious. Isaac isn't a youngster, as you know. I'm sorry, but I'm not at liberty to say any more. What do you want me to tell Nick and Lee?"

Elaine had her wits about her now. She hoped her elation wasn't showing. "Just tell them I'll get back to them, and, of course, cancel my appointment for tomorrow. I'd like to send flowers if that's okay."

"Let me get back to you on that," Wendy said.

"That's fine. Thank you for giving me the courtesy of a call." Elaine replaced the phone in its cradle and let out a sigh so loud she startled herself. Talk about instant gratification.

Elaine was so giddy with the news she'd just heard, that she picked up the wine bottle and brought it to her lips. She gulped until the bottle was empty. In a wild, crazy moment, she threw the bottle at the fireplace and watched it shatter. She fell back into the chair and closed her eyes. Overcome by the wine, she once again fell into a deep sleep.

As Elaine was drifting off to sleep, Gus Hollister was firing up his new grill on the deck. The rain, what there was of it, had come and gone, but it was too cool to eat outdoors. Wilson was panting at the scent of the marinating meat sitting on the counter.

"You're doing the dishes, Wilson. I'm cooking, so that means you do the cleanup. We really should talk about the division of chores." Gus had always talked to Wilson like this and hadn't the slightest reason why. Wilson listened, then ignored him. Maybe it had something to do with living alone, or maybe it had something to do with Wilson's being his best friend and a stand-in for Barney. He tried to remember if he'd talked to the dog like this when he lived with Elaine. Scratch that thought. He didn't want to think about Elaine now or ever again.

Gus let his thoughts go to his grandmother and the aunts and the massive project they were involved in. He had to do something, come up with a working plan, before things collapsed on top of them. He was convinced in his own mind that it was just a matter of time before that happened. What was going on now was temporary and could not be sustained for any length of time. His thoughts were coming lightning fast as idea after idea popped into his head, only to be rejected. He wished Barney were here, with his analytical mind.

Gus checked his baking potatoes. Not done yet. Wilson wouldn't care, but Gus cared; he liked his potatoes mushy and soft. Wilson just scarfed his down, along with the imitation bacon bits Gus sprinkled on his. He set the table and got Wilson's plate ready. Man and dog. For now, he loved it.

The scent of the sizzling steak on the grill had Wilson dancing in circles. Steak night, his favorite night of the week.

Gus talked to the shepherd nonstop as he poured himself a beer, mixed his salad dressing, and checked the potatoes again. He was always chatty with his dog, but today he rather thought he was going overboard. Wilson must have thought so, too, because he kept looking up at him, wondering what was going on.

Gus knew what was bothering him even if he wouldn't give voice to his thoughts—and it wasn't his grandmother, his aunts, or Initial B Enterprises. He had to call Jill Jackson and invite her out to dinner. He had to make amends, and he had to do it as soon as possible, preferably before Barney returned tomorrow night. "It is what it is. You know that, Wilson." Wilson barked to show he was in the game even though he didn't understand what game, as he waited for his dinner.

An hour later, the kitchen tidy, Wilson out romping in the wet grass, Gus pulled out all his schedules and got to work at the kitchen table. He was going to get this right or die trying. He pushed all thoughts of Jill Jackson, Mickey Yee, and some scummy bastard spying on the seniors out of his mind as he set to work.

At eleven o'clock, his eyes heavy with grit, Gus called it a night. He let Wilson out one last time before trudging upstairs to his new bed. He was about to slip under the sheets when he looked down at Wilson's bed. "You better find it *now*, Wilson, before I get in bed, because I'm not looking for your baby. Go get it! I'll wait to turn off the light."

He was, of course, referring to Wilson's one-eared rabbit, which he'd had since puppyhood and which was the security blanket that he slept with curled under his chin. Wilson was back in a flash, the bedraggled one-eared rabbit clutched in his teeth.

" 'Night, Wilson."

Woof.

Gus grinned as he squirmed and wiggled until he found just the right spot in his brand-new bed. He was asleep within seconds. Not Wilson, who lay quietly in the dark, his ears tuned to any new or strange sound in the house. Ninety minutes later, satisfied that his and his master's world was safe, he lowered his big head on his beloved rabbit and fell asleep.

Gus woke late the following morning and could hardly believe it was eight o'clock. He didn't exactly have a fire burning in his belly, but it was close. He stomped his way downstairs, let Wilson out, then made coffee. He removed his cell phone from the charger and, before he could change his mind, dialed Jill Jackson's personal cell number as opposed to going through the main number to the Beezer building. He sucked in his breath, wishing he'd rehearsed a speech of some sort. She answered in the same flat business tone she always seemed to use when it came to him.

Be witty, be charming, Violet had said. *Be yourself,* Iris had said. His grandmother had just looked at him with pitying eyes and said, *Do your best, Augustus.*

"Jill, this is Gus Hollister. I'm calling to invite you to dinner this evening." He rather thought he'd give up his left hand to see the expression on her face at that moment.

Almost at a loss for words, Jill ran her fingers through her hair at this unexpected turn of events. "You don't have to invite me to dinner, Gus. If you want to stop by the office later to discuss the case, we can do that."

"No, no, I don't want to discuss the case. I just want to take you to dinner. You can pick the restaurant if you like. It can be fancy or it could be that hot dog joint in New Town that everyone raves about. I'm thinking, seven o'clock."

Jill tried to suck on her tongue to work up some saliva. "You mean, like a *date?*"

"Well, yeah. I drive up to where you live, once you tell me where that is, I ring your bell, hand you some flowers, you put them in water, then we get in my car. And I hold the door for you, the way my granny taught me, and off we go. Yeah, yeah, a date."

Jill Jackson laughed. Gus was so startled at the musical sound of her laughter, he felt his face turning beet red. He'd never heard such a pleasing, beautiful laugh. He felt tongue-tied.

"Okay, I accept. I live around the corner from you, on Morningstar Court. I'm the only brick house on the court, you can't miss it. Seven, you said?"

"I did say seven. Yes, ma'am, seven o'clock. Seven is a good time for dinner. I usually eat at seven." *Jesus, what the hell is wrong with me?* He was babbling like some lovesick teenager. And she lived around the corner from him. How weird was that?

Jill laughed again, and this time Gus felt goose bumps running up and down his arms. "Where would you like to go?"

"How about Bandoliers in New Town? They serve all kinds of food."

"Bandoliers it is. Do you really live around the corner from me?"

"I really do." Jill didn't laugh this time, but there was laughter in her voice.

"Well, that's . . . great. I guess. I'm just renting. I could move if you think I shouldn't live there." *Well, damn, did I just say that?*

"New neighbors are nice. I don't even know mine. We could probably holler to each other across the fence. My backyard backs up to yours."

Now, how did she know that? Stupid. Stupid. Stupid. He'd told her the other day that he had moved. She'd probably checked it out or was familiar with his address. "Well, let me know when you're going to holler, so I'll know to answer."

Shit, shit, shit. That didn't even make sense. Quit while you're ahead and get the hell off the phone before she thinks you're certifiable. "I'll see you at seven, then."

"Okay."

Done. I have a date. Well, hot damn!

Jill was all thumbs as she tried to press in the number to Lynus Litton's office. Jill said when he answered, "I want those four hours you talked to me about. Three and a half would be better, but I'll take the whole four, and I need them today. Did you hear me, Lynus? Today."

"Whoa! What's got your panties in a knot?"

"You said I need four hours. Okay, I'm calling you on it. It has to be today; I have a date tonight. Seven o'clock."

"You mean a *date*, where the guy knocks on your door and brings flowers and candy, that kind of date?"

"Yes, dammit. What? You think no one would ever ask me out on a date? Well, someone did, and I need those four hours. Well?"

Lynus turned cagey. "Sounds important. You smitten? You realize when you sign up for those four hours, you turn yourself over to Sam and Mandy, and you have to let them have free rein. You can't back out. You go with it all the way. The works. If you give them any trouble, I'll hear about it. I have a reputation to uphold. I never send them clients unless I think both parties can handle it. You still game?"

Jill thought about it. "Yes," she said curtly.

"Okay, give me ten minutes, and I'll get back to you. This is going to be pricey. You need to know that going in."

"Okay, okay. Will I be happy with the results?"

"Knowing you, probably not, but you'll blow the guy's socks off. You still game?"

Jill didn't even think about her response. "Yes, I'm game."

"Okay, I'll get back to you."

"Louise!"

"My God, what?" Jill's secretary bellowed on the run. "What's wrong?"

"I have a date tonight! Lynus is . . . well, I have a four-hour—I guess you'd call it *overhaul* of my person. He's calling me back."

"A real date, a knock-on-the-door kind of date?"

"Yeah, yeah. Why does everyone keep saying a knock-on-the-door date? We're going to Bandoliers. It's with Gus Hollister."

"Your client? He's a stud! I thought you hated him! He actually asked you out on a date when you've been so hateful to him? Are lawyers allowed to date their clients?"

Jill squirmed in her chair. "I don't know if they are or not, and I don't care. I think it's up to the individuals. I never dated a client before. I don't hate Gus Hollister. I hate what he did to his grandmother and his aunts by choosing that *person* he married over them—and look what that got him. There are different kinds of hate, you know. Besides, you know as well as I do that a lawyer cannot pick and choose clients by the way they look and act. And, yes, it's a *real* date. You sound like Lynus. And, no, he's not a stud. Studs are farm animals. He's just a good-looking guy who looks buffed. *Puffed?* Whatever the word is these days."

Hands on her hips, Louise looked at her boss over the top of her reading glasses. "So, you are finally going to get rid of that gypsy attire you've been wearing since the big flood a hundred years ago."

"Looks that way. Don't get carried away. It's just a dinner date. Gus Hollister is trying to make amends to me for hurting my feelings. I accepted his apology, but he is obviously still feeling guilty, so I am just trying to . . . help things along. Anger gets you nowhere, as you have pointed out to me time and again. Now, are you happy?"

Louise leaned up against the doorframe and crossed her arms over her chest. "Well," she drawled, "if that was all true, why are you going for that four-hour makeover or whatever it's called? You could go in that same outfit you're sporting right now. Sounds to me like this is more than a thank-you date. I rest my case."

"And you find this all so very amusing? I should fire you."

"Ha-ha!" Louise said as she backed out of the door to return to her desk.

Jill drummed her fingers on her desk as she waited for the phone to ring. She looked at her blunt-cut nails and winced. Everyone wore acrylic nails these days, even Louise. Maintenance. She hated anything she had to keep up with. Although she had thought more than once about getting a French manicure. *Thought* about it. She thought about a lot of things. Well, now it was time to put up or shut up.

The phone rang. Jill let it ring four times before she picked it up, because she didn't want Lynus to suspect how anxious she was. Her greeting was casual and bored sounding. At least that's how she hoped she came across to Lynus.

"How does eleven o'clock sound?"

"Doable, Lynus, doable. Let's be clear, four hours or three and a half?"

"Might run to five. It's out of my hands. I'm not the expert. Just go with the flow, Jill, and try to enjoy it all."

"Five hours! You could clone someone in five hours! Are you putting me on?"

"No, I'm not. When I explained your . . . situation, they said possibly five hours. Don't shoot the messenger. Let's face it, Jill, you need a lot of work."

Jill was near to tears. "My God, do I really look that bad?"

"Honey, we all let ourselves go at some point, and I'm sure you had your reasons. And I do not want to know what those reasons are. It's going to take some time to . . . to repair all the . . . imperfections you let get out of hand. Just for the record, women kill to get any kind of appointment with Sam and Mandy. That's how good they are. You have a pen handy?" When Jill said she did, Lynus rattled off the address of the salon where Jill was to go for her makeover.

"I can't believe I'm doing this. I can't believe I'm doing this. I can't believe I'm doing this," Jill muttered over and over as she packed up her briefcase. Even though she had hours until her appointment time and what she'd agreed to do, she wanted to go somewhere quiet to think. Her intention was to buy a bagel and some coffee and go to the park and find a quiet bench.

Jill waved to her secretary as she sailed through the office and out the door. She couldn't help but wonder what she'd look like when she walked back through that door the next time.

Chapter 20

JILL JACKSON STOPPED AT THE HUGE YELLOW arrow at the signpost for the turnoff to the Sunset Spa. As she made her way down a winding road lined by old sycamore trees that were just starting to green up, she thought it a beautiful, serene setting. In her opinion, it was the perfect location for a spa. The building surprised her because she had had no idea it even existed, nestled as it was behind the lush shrubbery. How many times had she driven this road with no thought that this magnificent building was hiding behind the luxurious plantings? She winced when she recalled Lynus's words, *Bring your checkbook, as this place is pricey.*

Jill parked in the minuscule lot, slid out of her truck, and looked in awe at the building. Mediterranean style, perhaps. Or something out of Babylon. Whatever it was, it was gorgeous. The word *pricey* ricocheted around and around inside her head. Up close, the building and the landscaping were even more awesome. The shrubbery looked like it had been pruned with manicure scissors. Not a leaf was out of place, every stem in perfect alignment. A rainbow of flowers bordered the colored flagstone walkway. At the door, a discreet sign said to ring the bell for admittance. Jill rang the bell. A pleasant-looking woman in what she thought was like a pale yellow doctor's coat opened the door to her with a wide smile. She introduced herself as Mona and said she would be her guide for her stay at Sunset Spa.

"Let's get you settled, then I'll introduce you to Mandy and Sam."

Five minutes later, Jill was in a small, luxurious, restful-looking room. She struggled to define the scent permeating the room but had to give up when she couldn't identify it. From somewhere, the sounds of water trickling over stones could be heard, along with a tinkling sound from a wind chime somewhere in the building. Jill could feel her eyelids start to droop. Mona smiled.

"Hang your things in the closet and put on the robe and slippers. They're new, and you'll take them with you when you leave. Do you have any questions?" Jill shook her head. "I'll be back in a few minutes to take you to Sam and Mandy."

Jill bit down on her lower lip as she stared at the yawning interior of the closet in which she was to hang her clothing. She looked around as a feeling of panic overwhelmed her. She moved then to the door; her hand was on the knob to open it so she could bolt. She wasn't a prisoner, she could leave anytime she wanted. All she had to do was say that she had changed her mind, that she wasn't in the mood for a makeover, and that she'd come back some other time. But that would mean she was a coward. Lynus would look at her in a different light. She'd be forced to look at herself in a different light.

Her cell phone took that moment to ring. She debated if she should answer it, but the debate didn't last long. She was one of those people who could not ignore a ringing phone. She clicked on to hear her secretary tell her that Isaac Diamond's office had just called to say that Isaac was in the hospital as a result of an accident. She went on to say the other two Diamond partners didn't know if their office would continue to represent Elaine Hollister or if she would engage another law firm. Jill made a face, muttered something that sounded like she'd get back to Louise later. She turned her phone off when she remembered a sign at the entrance that said that all cell phones must be turned off, and they were to be left in the client's locker. Jill always obeyed the rules.

Jill looked around for a mirror. She almost blacked out in relief when she didn't see one. She wondered exactly what a few minutes meant. Five?—ten?—before Mona came back to take her to Sam and Mandy. She licked at her lips and started to remove her clothing. She kicked off her ankle-high boots, placing them neatly on the floor of the closet. Off came the jacket, the vest, the long-sleeved blouse, the skirt, the half-slip. She squeezed her eyes shut as she removed her bra and panties.

She could feel the raised scars that covered the right side of her body. She thought then about the eleven skin grafts she'd undergone to repair the burns before she had called a halt and had said no more. "Suck it up, Jill, and get on with it," she muttered under her breath. She slipped her arms into the fluffy white robe, tied the belt, then slid her feet into the matching slippers, just as a knock sounded at the door. "Are you ready, Miss Jackson?"

"I am." Jill opened the door and stepped into the hallway.

Mona chatted as she pointed out different statues nestled into little nests of greenery along with small fountains with trickling water that lined the hallway. She knocked softly on a door, opening it at the same time.

Jill didn't know what she was expecting, but Sam and Mandy Dressler's appearance surprised her. She had formed a mental picture in her mind of two movie star look-alikes, impeccably dressed and coiffed and made up to look like the beautiful people they catered to.

Mandy Dressler was small and round with gray hair, pink cheeks, and granny glasses. She wore pale green scrubs, the kind technicians wore in hospitals. She had a beautiful smile. Sam Dressler was just as small and round. He, too, was pink cheeked and he had snow-white hair and a matching Vandyke beard. He also wore wire-rimmed glasses. His smile was just as beautiful and warm as his wife's. It was hard for Jill not to bask in their warm, welcoming greeting.

"Welcome to Sunset Spa," the Dresslers said in unison. Mandy motioned to a soft, buttery-looking beige chair. "We need to ask a few questions. First, do you have any medical issues, and are you on any medication we should know about?" Jill shook her head as she was handed a clipboard to check off the questions she was being asked verbally. She did it all in record time and signed her name, along with the date. She handed the paper over.

Mandy scanned the printed form, satisfied that it matched Jill's verbal answers. "Question and answer time. You don't seem . . . excited or relaxed to me, Miss Jackson. Why do I have the feeling you'd rather be somewhere else right now instead of preparing to be pampered for a few hours? Am I wrong?" she asked gently.

Jill chewed on her lower lip, something she always did when she was nervous. "The answer is yes and no. Lately . . . lately people have been . . . commenting on the way I dress and saying . . . things that are far from flattering. Lynus . . . Lynus suggested I come here. At first,

I said no. And then . . . well, I changed my mind earlier this morning, and I do appreciate your fitting me in on such short notice."

"Is there a reason, in your opinion, why suddenly you've decided to come here? I ask only because we want you to have an enjoyable experience at Sunset Spa," Sam said, his blue eyes twinkling.

Her moment of truth. "Yes, I guess so. I'm tired of evading and explaining, and I was asked out on a date for this evening. The person . . . the man who asked me for . . . for the date . . . is someone who . . . who called me a fireplug. I guess I do look like that sometimes."

"And . . . ," Mandy prompted gently.

Jill felt like she was on the witness stand. She squared her shoulders. "When I was eight years old, I was in a house fire. A new gas hot-water heater had just been installed at our house. It exploded somehow, and my parents and brother died in the fire. I was the only survivor. I was in the hospital off and on for several years. The right side of my body was burned pretty badly. I had many, many skin grafts until I just couldn't do it anymore. I tried to hide it, and I'm still hiding it. I thought . . . the more layers I put on myself, the less noticeable it would be. I've been to shrinks—the aunt who took me in after the fire insisted on it—but it was something I just couldn't overcome. I withdrew from treatment but managed to go to college and law school, and still work. Money was never an issue—my parents had excellent insurance. The people who installed the hot-water heater paid handsomely, and my aunt invested the money for me. Then I turned it all over to my boss, who invested it again with still higher returns. I never have to work another day in my life unless I want to. And, I want to. I never used the money because . . . to me it was . . . death money. Now you have my whole life story."

The Dresslers smiled. "Then let's get you started. We'd like to see a smile, though. How about this, when you leave here, you're going to look and feel like a million dollars. Can you accept that?"

Could she accept that? She was here, wasn't she? She'd just confessed her life story to two strangers. All because some guy called her a fireplug. Was it the word *fire* that pushed her to come here, or was it guilt and shame? Vanity was probably the answer. She shrugged. "Yes, of course," she responded.

Mandy pressed a button on the desk. Mona appeared as if by magic to lead Jill out of the room. Jill turned in the doorway, and said "Woohoo!" Then she laughed.

Sam and Mandy looked at each other and joined in the laughter. "I think that little confession opened a door that's been locked for a long time. I'll see you later, Sam. I have some shopping to do," Mandy said.

"Have fun, my dear. I know how you love to shop. Just remember our promise to Miss Jackson that she's going to look and feel like a million dollars when she leaves here."

"I'll remember, dear. I so hope that young man is worth all this. I'm thinking, Sam, even if for some reason tonight doesn't end with a promise for the future, Miss Jackson will be able to walk through that door she opened with more confidence than when she walked in here."

"I hope we find out the answer at some point in time," Sam said.

"I'll see you when I see you, my dear," Mandy said as she reached for her purse. This was the part that she liked best, the transformation of the client. She smiled.

The hours passed in a blur. Twice, Jill dozed off because she was so relaxed. She had a deep hour-long body massage and a wonderful facial, which allowed her to fall asleep. She loved the whirlpool, with the jets pummeling her entire body. She dozed off again during her pedicure, while a technician applied acrylic nails to her fingers and finished it off with a French manicure. She slept for thirty minutes before she was transferred to a bare room, where she got spray-tanned.

"It will look just like the sun kissed your entire body. The plus to spray-tanning is it will downplay the pinkness of your scars."

While she stood with her arms and legs spread to dry, Jill decided this was a day she'd never forget, and she wasn't even finished yet.

When the technician announced that the spray-on tan was dry, Jill was taken to still another room, with no mirrors but wonderful lighting. The beautician twirled the chair Jill was sitting on, as she ran her fingers through Jill's long, curly hair. "Do you have something in mind, or are you willing to leave it up to me? First things first, your hair is way too long. Long hair is not in fashion, and is best worn by young girls. Are you ready for a new look to go with the new you?"

Jill drew in a deep breath. "I am. I'm not a fancy kind of person, so can you give me an easy-to-care-for, casual kind of look?"

The stylist, who said his name was Brandon, said, "I think it's time to get rid of the Shirley Temple curls. How will you feel if I straighten your hair and give it some highlights? I'd also like to thin it out a little."

Giddy with what she was going through, Jill could hardly believe her own words when she said, "Go for it, Brandon."

Another ninety minutes passed before Brandon turned down the lighting and pressed a button to reveal a mirror behind a wooden panel. Jill gasped as she leaned forward to view her new hairdo. Who was this person? In her wildest dreams, she never thought she could look as good as she did at that moment.

"You like?" Brandon asked.

"I love it, Brandon. I really do."

Brandon grinned. "Okay, now it's time for your makeup session. Ready?"

"Oh, yeah." Jill grinned in return. Suddenly, she was loving this whole new experience.

While Jill was being pummeled, scrubbed, rubbed, caressed, sprayed, and painted, Gus Hollister was banging his head on the wall for the fourth time. He had gone to Barney's to exchange the Jeep for his Porsche, having decided that he was not going to pick up his date in a Jeep. Now, he was exhausted with the effort he was expending to get through to the Blossom sisters.

Gus threw his hands in the air. "Let's go through this one more time. I know you're tired, and so am I. We've been at this for hours, and I really have to leave, because I have a dinner engagement, which you all endorsed, by the way."

They were on the back porch, with the door to the kitchen closed for privacy. The coffeepot had been filled, then refilled. Everyone's nerves were twanging from too much caffeine.

Violet, more hostile toward Gus than her sisters, looked at her nephew. "Nephew, we made a commitment to our staff. What you're suggesting to the three of us can't possibly work. If we do what you say, there won't be enough work for everyone. We just can't go back on our word. We cannot break a promise; surely you can understand that."

"Yes, Aunt Vi. But there will be work for everyone, just less work. I do understand. Will you just stop, close your eyes, and envision the inside of this farmhouse? It's total chaos, it's overcrowded, you're all meeting yourselves coming and going, plus the kitchen as well as the summer kitchen is being used twenty-four/ seven, with all the cooking for so many people three times a day. And don't get me started again on your storage arrangements for supplies. There is not one inch of space available. You need to relocate. Granny, there is all of Shady Pines. Why aren't you all working out of there? There is an industrial kitchen at Shady Pines, and that's what you need. Read my lips, a fully equipped industrial kitchen."

"Because we live here, that's why. We started here, and it just naturally followed that we would continue working here," Rose said defensively.

"What that says to me is you three took the easy way out. Everyone else has to shuttle back and forth while you three call the shots. I'm not trying to demean you, it just doesn't make sense from a productivity standpoint. Shady Pines has to be around fifty thousand square feet and is virtually empty except for the one wing that's occupied. At one time it was a thriving operation, now with just caretakers watching over the property. I know, I know, all the rules and licenses are in effect. Will you all just think about the space, about having everything in one place? It makes more sense for the three of you to take the golf cart over in the morning and back again at the end of the day. You need to scale back and just do an eight-hour shift instead of this round-the-clock nonsense.

"As much as you all don't want to admit it, you aren't getting any younger. Believe it or not, you're actually getting older. Just like everyone else on God's green earth. Why in the name of everything that is holy do you want to work everyone to an early death? You're a family, all of you, so that means you need to enjoy each other's company, make all the things you haven't been able to do—either for health reasons, lack of money, or whatever else—work for you. This is the time when you should be enjoying your lives and still be productive, but not to the point of obsession."

Iris looked up at her nephew. "But you said you wanted us to do away with some of our projects. We need all those projects to keep earning the money we've been earning. More so now that we've added to our staff."

"I looked at your books, ladies. They are robust. You paid out outrageous bonuses none of you need or even want for that matter. I can see a salary of some sort, absolutely. I can see vacations twice a year for as many days as you all decide on. You can take bus trips. Hell, I'll even drive the bus for you, and I'm sure Barney will agree to do it, too. I'm going to get my bus driver's license. You're obsessed with making tons of money and forgetting to live your lives. I'm tired, and I'm sorry if I'm not coming across to your satisfaction."

"I understand everything you're saying, Augustus. You are making some valid points. Perhaps we could arrange a meeting with everyone, and you could give a PowerPoint presentation. Would that work?"

"It would, but I want you to close up shop for a week or ten days. We can hire people to help us move Initial B Enterprises to Shady Pines. What we're doing now, what I set up for you all, was just supposed to be temporary. I told you that at the time, and you agreed. You said you all wanted the new staff to feel like they belonged right off the bat. We assigned jobs, but it's around the clock, with no real routine. People, especially elderly people, and I mean no offense, need to sleep at night; they don't need to work shifts. It's unsettling. They don't need pressure and deadlines. The bottom line is that you have too many irons in the fire. We need to whittle back and go with just your moneymakers. As an example, the fortune cookies. You could corner the entire market here in Sycamore Springs and even the outlying towns. You can hire delivery boys from the college. Think about how much easier it will make your lives."

The sisters looked at one another as Gus droned on and on. Finally, Rose said, "You need to go home now; it's getting late, Augustus. You certainly don't want to keep the young lady waiting. We will talk about all of this tonight, and, by tomorrow, we'll have an answer for you, one way or the other. We appreciate your concern for our well-being, and we know your heart is in the right place. Will that work for you?"

Gus sighed. "It will work if you talk and discuss it all with an open mind. I just want you to remember one thing: Money can't buy happiness. You all found happiness and fulfillment. And made a lot of money in the bargain. You don't need more sacks full of money to continue. Being more than comfortable financially, being happy, and having the companionship of each other should be your top priorities from here on in."

"You're forgetting our overhead, nephew," Violet snapped.

"No, Aunt Vi, I am not forgetting it. If you operate out of Shady Pines, you can take many tax deductions. It has to be a legitimate operation from the get-go. That's what I'm trying to drive home to you all. You can do this. You really can. But you're going to have to make concessions for the well-being of all of you, not just you three.

"Okay, I'm leaving now; you have a lot to think about. I'm here for you and will do whatever I can to get you all on the right road, because I love you and care about you."

Rose stretched out her arms to her grandson. She hugged Gus, and he hugged her back. He turned to see if Violet and Iris would do the same. He was thrilled when both his aunts smiled and held out their arms.

Gus whistled for Wilson, who came on the run.

"Call us," Rose said. "Go to the men's room and call so we know how it's going. Good luck tonight."

Gus laughed. "Didn't you say the exact same thing to me when I went off to my first prom?" The sisters laughed.

It was five-thirty when Gus climbed into his reclaimed Porsche for the trip home. An hour and a half to stop for flowers, get home, feed Wilson, shower, shave, dress, then drive around the corner to pick up his date for the evening.

He couldn't decide if he was dreading or anticipating the evening. He started to whistle. *Whistling is a good sign,* he thought. Maybe the dinner would go well, and he and Jill Jackson would actually become friends of a sort.

Hope springs eternal. That's what his grandmother always used to say. She probably still said it, for all he knew.

Gus felt so good, he continued to whistle. He had a feeling that he had finally gotten through to his grandmother and aunts with the last round of discussions. But he was no fool. He knew things could change on the turn of a dime.

Chapter 21

GUS TOOK SO LONG TO SHOWER, SHAVE, AND dress that Wilson started prancing around thinking he was going for a ride again, his favorite thing to do. "What do you think, Wilson? Too much gel in my hair? My aftershave too strong?"

Wilson pawed the tiled floor and let loose with a short bark that meant, let's move already.

Gus stretched his lips in front of the mirror to make sure nothing was stuck in his teeth. *What the hell is wrong with me?* He was acting like he had just marched into puberty. *Teeth okay, not too much gel, aftershave minty but faint.* His khakis held a sharp crease, his loafers had a nice shine, and his pale yellow shirt was perfectly ironed. By himself. His tie matched the shirt perfectly. His khaki jacket was fairly new and finished off his attire. He was good to go.

Gus checked his back pocket to make sure his wallet was where it belonged. His keys were on the kitchen counter, as were his cell phone and the flowers he'd bought on the way home. Gus hung up his wet towel, exited the bathroom, and headed downstairs, Wilson bounding ahead of him. The time was six-fifty. It would only take him two minutes to drive around the corner, park, walk up to Jill Jackson's door, and ring the bell.

After picking up his keys and cell phone from the kitchen counter, Gus checked the front door to make sure it was locked; it was. He turned the two lamps on in the living room. He made sure there were two night-lights in the kitchen that would start to glow as soon as dusk fell so that Wilson could find his water bowl and the bowl of dry dog food he always left when he went out and left Wilson at home.

"Okay, big guy, I'm outta here. Answer the phone, fold the laundry, and, if you have time, make my bed. Get your rabbit and settle in. I won't be more than a few hours. I'll leave *Wheel of Fortune* on for you. Here's a Pop-Tart—make it last—and a chew bone. You got all that, Wilson?"

Woof.

Gus couldn't believe the butterflies jumping around in his stomach when he got into his car and turned on the engine. He looked over at the bunch of spring flowers wrapped in layers of green tissue paper. He shrugged. He remembered the horror of his first date, when he was a teenager and he'd taken his date to a fast-food joint. He'd been so nervous he couldn't eat, even though he was starved. His grandmother had warned him to check his teeth to make sure nothing was stuck in them. To this day, nothing had ever been stuck in his teeth. She'd told him to chew slowly and not wolf his food the way he always did at home. The horror was he'd obeyed all his granny's advice, and the girl whose name he couldn't even remember had gobbled her food, then ate his.

He hadn't been this nervous with other dates, or with Elaine. What was there about Jill Jackson that had him in such a tizzy? Guilt. That's what his Aunt Vi would say.

Gus pulled into Jill Jackson's driveway. It was a pretty little house, with flower beds and a flower-lined walkway. In the center of the front yard, there was a huge sycamore tree that he knew would shade the entire front of the house when it was in full leaf. He looked down but couldn't see even one weed. The bushes were pruned, the lawn mowed. He didn't know how he knew, but he suspected that the backyard held flowers and shade trees. She probably had a terrace or a deck with nice outdoor furniture, where she would sit going over her legal stuff.

Gus sucked in his breath and rang the doorbell. He stepped back and waited, the flowers moving back and forth in the early evening breeze.

The door opened and Gus said, "I'm here to see Jill Jackson."

He heard the musical laugh, then his face turned beet red. He blinked, then blinked again. He couldn't think of a thing to say, so he thrust the flowers forward. *Who is this person standing in front of me? Fireplug, my ass.* He could feel the heat on his face and neck. He thought he was going to strangle himself.

"I guess this is where I'm supposed to say, I clean up good. Come in, Gus, and I'll put these flowers in water. They're so pretty. Thank you. I love flowers."

"Yeah, me, too. I mean, I like flowers outside. I don't pick them, I just like to look at them. You look different!" Gus blurted out.

Jill laughed again. "Listen, I need to tell you something. Isaac Diamond's office called this morning. It seems he had some kind of accident and is in the hospital. The firm doesn't know if your wife is going to stay with them, or if she'll go with another firm. That means things are at a standstill. Do you have any questions? Because, if you do, I'd like to get them out of the way now and not discuss business over dinner."

Gus shook his head as he listened to the words, but they really didn't signify anything to him. He didn't want to think about Elaine or her lawyer. He was concentrating on this beautiful creature standing in front of him. And to think, he'd called her a fireplug. His face and neck started to heat up again.

"You look great!" Gus blurted out.

"Yeah, I know." Jill laughed. She twirled around in her high heels and the bright yellow dress that flirted with her knees. "I'm vain." She giggled again. "You look nice yourself."

Gus Hollister fell in love at that moment. He risked a glance at his watch. At 7:04, he, Gus Hollister, fell in love with Jill Jackson. The date and the time were now engraved in his mind forever and ever. He could hardly wait to tell his grandmother and the aunts. He watched as Jill positioned the vase of flowers on the kitchen counter. He wasn't sure, but he thought she probably sat on the stool on the other side of the counter to eat or have coffee. The flowers would be directly in her line of vision. The thought pleased him.

"You ready?" he asked, his voice husky at what he was feeling.

"I am. All I have to do is lock the door and walk out."

"Turn on a night-light and the outside light. It will be dark when we get home."

"Good point," Jill said lightly as she fit the key in the lock.

Gus held the car door for her, watching how gracefully she got into the bucket seat. He also admired a generous slice of leg when her dress hiked up. He saw the puckered skin on her upper thigh, but it wasn't registering. She showed no embarrassment, but the moment she was settled, she tugged at the dress.

Gus couldn't believe it when he ground the gears. He'd been driving a stick shift for years and years and never let the gears grind. *What the hell is wrong with me?* He had never felt so inadequate. He had never been good at small talk about trivia, but he struggled to appear manly and nonchalant. He risked a glance at her and saw that she looked amused. Crap. She probably thought he was being sophomoric.

"Do you like Bandoliers?"

"I do. I've only been there a few times, though. I like the tablecloths and cloth napkins. The lighting is good, too. And the tables are generously spaced so you don't hear other people's conversations." She laughed then, and Gus almost melted into the seat. "How's that for casual conversation?"

Gus grinned. "Better than I could have come up with. Dates are . . ."

"Stressful?"

"Yeah."

"But we know each other," Jill said. "Unfortunately for both of us, we got off on the wrong foot. I allowed you to see only the business side of me. And you reacted to that and let me see your unflattering side. Let's just start over and just be Jill and Gus who are going out to dinner at a nice restaurant."

"Whew! That works for me."

"Well, there you go. What would you like to talk about, Gus?"

"I used to be a Boy Scout. Barney was, too. We actually made Eagle Scout. If there was a catastrophe, I could probably save you in some fashion, by building a fire without matches and finding roots and berries for you that are safe to eat."

Jill laughed so hard tears rolled down her cheeks. "That sure does make me feel good, Gus."

In spite of himself, Gus laughed along with her. "Your turn."

"After you save me, I could give you a recital. I took ballet lessons when I was little. I can still stand on my toes. I don't have a tutu, though."

"I have a vivid imagination. What color?"

"Pink and white."

"I have the vision in my mind now. We're here," Gus said, swerving into the first parking place he saw.

Gus bustled out of the sports car, rushed around to the passenger side, and opened the door for Jill. He got another glimpse of her thigh and the long scar, and felt light-headed. He reached for her arm and pulled her forward. She smelled so good, he wanted to bury his face in her hair.

The next thirty minutes passed in a pleasant blur after they were seated in a dim, candlelit corner. They ordered white wine and smiled at each other across the table as they each contemplated the menu.

Gus ordered prawns stuffed with crab meat and Jill ordered pecan potato–crusted salmon.

They both chose the house dressing for their salads, then ordered a second glass of wine. They made small talk, mostly about Barney and his anticipated return later that evening.

Gus was now relaxed and enjoying the conversation he was having with his dinner companion, the woman he'd just fallen in love with.

The waiter served dinner, and suddenly Gus fell back into teenage mode. He couldn't eat the delectable food sitting in front of him. He made a pretense of cutting and moving the food around on his plate. It took him forever to chew a piece of the shrimp.

Jill stopped chewing long enough to ask, "Is something wrong? You're not eating. Aren't you hungry?"

Gus was tempted to make up a story about his grandmother making him eat something earlier, but in the end decided to go with full disclosure. He confessed to the teenage episode with his first dining-out date at a fast-food joint.

Jill smiled. "I promise not to watch you eat, and I can guarantee that shrimp or crab won't stick in your teeth."

"I like your sense of humor. I just told you a secret. Your turn," Gus said, popping half a shrimp into his mouth.

"I got burned in a house fire when I was eight years old, and the right side of my body is scarred pretty badly, that's why I dress the way I do. This salmon is really good. Do you think they'd give me the recipe if I asked for it?"

Whoa.

"Secrets aren't good. I'm all for full disclosure. I'm sure they'll give you the recipe minus one of the ingredients. At least, that's what my grandmother told me. 'Recipes,' she said, 'especially family recipes, are meant to stay in the family.' I'm not sure, but I would think chefs probably feel the same way."

Jill stopped eating and stared at Gus across the table in the candlelight. "Aren't you going to ask me any questions?"

"No. I won't share your secret with anyone. I'm not a kiss-and-tell kind of guy. Not that I kissed you. Oh, hell, you know what I mean. Please don't tell anyone about my secret."

"Deal," Jill said, holding her hand out across the table. Gus reached for it. He thought it felt like soft silk. He held her hand an extra few seconds. Jill drew away first.

Gus finally felt comfortable enough to relax when he realized he was enjoying the give and take with his dinner companion. Being honest with himself, he thought he had never had such an enjoyable dinner. He liked this new Jill Jackson. It appeared she liked him, too. Just after the waiter arrived to remove their dinner plates and take their dessert order, Gus excused himself to go to the men's room, where he called his grandmother. His conversation was bullet fast and ended with his confession of telling Jill about his teenage dinner date. Obviously, his grandmother had him on speakerphone, because he could hear his aunts laugh. He ended with, "She was burned in a fire, and she said she's scarred. It happened when she was a kid."

There was no embarrassment when Gus returned to his seat and said, "I had to check in with my grandmother and aunts."

"That's nice. You're lucky, Gus, that someone cares enough about you to want you to check in. I don't have anyone; the aunt who took care of me after the fire passed away a few years ago."

Jill leaned across the table. Gus thought she looked beautiful in the soft candlelight. "I need to apologize, Gus, for my . . . attitude when we first met. I thought you were throwing away a lifetime of love and caring, for someone who treated you like dirt. I'm sorry, I really am."

"I wasn't exactly a peach myself. But that's behind us. In the end, it will all work out the way it's supposed to. I'm just glad you stuck with me."

The waiter was back with two plates of red velvet cake and coffee.

"I love sweets," Gus confessed.

"Me, too. When I have time, I bake raisin-filled cookies."

"I'm addicted to Pop-Tarts, and so is my dog. That's our sweet and treat every day."

Jill laughed.

God, how I love the sound.

And then dinner was over, and it was time to leave. Gus paid the bill and acted like the gentleman he was and got up to hold the back of her chair.

It was a beautiful April evening. The dark sky sparkled like diamonds. Gus didn't want the evening to end. He wished he knew how Jill felt.

"I really enjoyed dinner, Gus. It's been a long time since I had a night out like this. Thank you." Gus felt his chest puff out. She, too, had enjoyed dinner.

There was very little traffic, and Gus made every green light. He was parking in Jill's driveway in less than fifteen minutes.

"Don't get out, Gus. I can make it to the doorway on my own." She leaned over, gave him a quick kiss on the cheek. The next thing Gus knew, she was sprinting up the walkway. It all happened so quick, he didn't know what to do. He lowered the window and shouted, "Can I call you again?"

Gus heard her laughter. "If you don't, I'll call you!"

The grin stayed on Gus's face on the drive around the corner to his house. He let himself in. Wilson raced to him and barked. Gus gave him a good scratch behind the ears. "Did you fold the laundry?"

Woof.

"Any calls?"

Woof, woof, woof.

"Three calls. Wow! Did you make the bed? I hope you tucked the corners in. I hate it when my bed is wrinkled."

Woof, woof, woof, woof.

Gus laughed. He loved this game he played

with Wilson. He listened to the three messages on his phone. Nothing he had to deal with now. He ran upstairs and checked the bed for Wilson's benefit. He laughed. "You're getting better, buddy. You need to work on the other side a little."

Back downstairs, he made a pretense of checking the dryer, then said, "Okay, you couldn't get the door open. Wanna go for a walk?" Wilson ran for his leash and off they went. Down to the corner and around the block, not once but twice, so Wilson could mark his territory. Their evening walk took forty-five minutes, until Wilson tugged on the leash, meaning it was time to head for home and the treat that was always forthcoming after a long evening walk.

"Okay, buddy, let's go home, so I can tell you about my evening before I bust. We can sit on the deck and enjoy each other's company." As they rounded the corner to their street, Wilson jerked free and raced for home, the leash dragging behind him. Gus gaped at the figure sitting on his front steps, a huge duffel bag at his feet.

"Barney!"

"Yeah, it's me." He was tussling with Wilson but stopped to hug Gus. "So, how's it going? How did dinner go?"

"Come on in, we'll have a beer on the deck. I was going to sit out there and tell Wilson how it went. This way, I'll only have to tell it once. You just get in?" Gus said, looking at the huge duffel bag.

"Yeah, came straight here from the airport. I'm moving in with you."

"Huh?"

"Yeah, I'm moving in with you. I like this house. I walked around and peeped in the windows while I waited. I think I can be comfortable here."

"What's wrong with that mausoleum you live in? I only have one bed."

"You just said it, it's a mausoleum. I can sleep on the floor. I'll buy a bed tomorrow unless you don't want me moving in."

Gus shrugged. "Me casa, you casa." He uncapped two bottles of beer, reached for a Pop-Tart, and headed out to the deck.

"Talk to me, buddy," Barney said.

Gus talked and talked until his beer was finished. He walked into the house for two more and returned. "So, what do you think? I want to know more about your return and the decision you made to give up making money."

The two old friends talked into the wee hours of the morning. A parade of beer bottles lined the table, yet neither man was drunk. "Why didn't you tell me about the fire and her scars? It doesn't make a difference, but I wish you had told me. Maybe if you had, I wouldn't feel like such an ass."

"It wasn't my place to tell you. Just so you know, Jill never even told me. It was in her background check. You need to give some thought, now, to perhaps hiring a new lawyer if you plan on seeing her on a social basis. I'm sure she's already working on that herself, but it won't look good, especially if Elaine gets wind of it." Gus nodded.

Gus told Barney about Jill's phone call from the Diamond law firm. "I guess that puts things on hold, at least for the moment. What do you think, Barney?"

"Big white-shoe firm. Big retainers, all about billing. I think they charge something like five hundred dollars an hour. At least that's what I heard, but it was awhile back. I guess my question is, where did Elaine get that kind of money to sign on with them?"

"I don't know, Barney. Elaine always kept her finances separate from mine. We shared *my* income, though. Don't say it. That's the way marriage is supposed to be, it's all about sharing. You're one, so to speak."

Barney snorted. "Too bad Elaine didn't think the same way you did."

"Yeah. Come on, let's go to bed. We need to be at the farm early in the morning."

Upstairs in the bedroom, Barney looked at the bed and the covers.

"Wilson's job is to make the bed. He's getting better at it. He thinks he just has to do my side. If you sweet-talk him, he might let you sleep with him in his bed."

Barney started to laugh and couldn't stop. "See, this is why I didn't want to go back to my house; it's no fun there."

Gus snapped his fingers. Wilson was on the bed in a heartbeat.

Barney eyed the dog bed. Dog hairs by the boatload. What the hell. "Does Wilson have fleas?"

Wilson reared up and let loose with a yowl of outrage.

"Guess that answers your question," Gus said as he punched his pillow to fluff it up, then turned off the light.

Gus's last conscious thought before he fell asleep was that he would dream about Jill Jackson.

Chapter 22

THE SUN WAS JUST STARTING TO CREEP FROM the horizon when the black candle on Elaine Hollister's altar flickered for the final time. The green candle was just a pool of melted wax in the little dish. She'd been sitting at her altar in her high-priestess robe for twelve hours, chanting, slipping in and out of what she thought of as a trance. She folded her hands into a steeple, bowed her head, and rose to her feet. She uttered one last chant before she ended her night-long vigil. She didn't move as she waited to see if any thoughts or visions would come to her. She wasn't sure in her own mind if she should pack up her altar or leave it as it was until she returned from her visit to the hospital to see Isaac Diamond. She needed a sign. She'd come too far and didn't want to make a rash mistake for lack of patience.

Elaine stood statue still until the sun's early morning rays crept through the slats of the plantation shutters covering the dining-room windows, straight across to her altar in thin stripes. Seeing the stripes of sun on the altar was all Elaine needed. She had her answer.

Slowly and methodically, Elaine packed up everything on her altar. She removed the linen tablecloth, carried it to the washer, and turned the machine on. Later, when the cloth was in the dryer, she would wash her linen gown. She returned to the dining room and replaced the silk flower arrangement that was the centerpiece. Next, she opened all the shutters. The room was instantly flooded with early morning sunshine.

It was after eight when Elaine entered the kitchen to make coffee. While she waited for it to drip into the pot, she smoked two cigarettes. She wasn't a smoker by any stretch of the imagination, but she'd found that smoking after an intense ritual calmed her to the point where she thought she was almost having an out-of-body experience. She loved the feeling.

Two cups of coffee later, Elaine made her way upstairs to get ready for the day.

Showered, powdered, and perfumed, Elaine took exceptional pains with her makeup, hair, and her outfit. She decided that her makeup was flawless, and she looked dewy and healthy.

Her luxurious, honey-colored hair was swirled with stray tendrils curling by her ears. She reached for a can of sparkle and sprayed her hair. Just one quick press of the pressurized button and her hair glistened. The outfit she had chosen was a designer suit that was so severe, one knew it had cost a fortune. And it had. It was the color of oyster shells. The blouse that she chose to go under the suit had a demure string bow at the throat. It was the color of a morning dove. She looked at herself from every angle in the mirror. She was satisfied that there was nothing more to do. In her mind, she looked perfect. Simply because she *was* perfect. And how could one improve on perfection? One could not, that was her bottom line.

Elaine slipped her feet into sling-back spike heels that showed off her legs and gave her a regal look. She was a head turner, and she knew it full well. A smile played around the corners of her mouth as she made her way downstairs. It was a shame that she had to drive that shitty little yellow Volkswagen. She belonged in a Mercedes convertible. Soon, she'd be driving one, she was certain of it.

Elaine had a bad moment when she reached the door. She was about to set the alarm when a thought occurred to her. She quickly rummaged in one of the kitchen drawers for a roll of duct tape. She picked up a pair of shears and a ballpoint pen. Outside, she set the alarm and closed the door behind her. She made a mark on the doorframe and cut off a strip of duct tape and stretched it across the door. She smoothed out the tape so there were no creases or wrinkles. If anyone broke into her house, she'd know it when she returned because the mark she'd made on the doorframe would come off on the sticky side of the duct tape. Plus, no matter how hard you tried to reuse duct tape, you could tell once it had been pulled free of whatever it was sticking to. Gus had told her that, but she couldn't remember why. On a whim, she scribbled a note on the duct tape: *the police are watching this house.* She ran around to the front door and did the same thing. There wasn't anything else she could do, so she left the house and drove to the hospital where Isaac Diamond was a patient.

Elaine had called precisely at six o'clock last evening when the new shift came on duty, to ask if Isaac could have visitors and was told he could and that no real visiting hours were in effect. The news fit in perfectly with the rituals she had performed all night long. As far as she was concerned, Isaac Diamond was toast. He just didn't know it yet.

Gus stopped the car with a wide sweep in front of Barney's garage. Barney hopped out and opened the garage door. "I'm going inside to fetch some more knock-around clothes, and I'll meet you at Shady Pines in thirty minutes. Listen, pal. You sure it's okay for me to bunk in with you? You sure you don't mind?"

"If I did, you'd know it. Get your stuff and

make it snappy. I told Granny we'd be ready by eleven for our sit-down orientation. The seniors get antsy when things don't go off on time."

"No problem," Barney said, sprinting through the garage.

Gus backed up and swung his car around. Ten minutes later, he parked in what was once the Shady Pines assisted-living facility. He reached for his briefcase, which contained all his notes and schedules.

Inside, Gus headed straight for the industrial kitchen. The kitchen was huge, as was a room that was probably a pantry of sorts, with extra refrigerators and cabinets for staples. Gus eyed the industrial ovens and the two stoves with sixteen burners in total. The two industrial ovens had six shelves each for baking trays. The microwave ovens lining a side wall were huge as well. He closed his eyes as he tried to imagine how many people could be served meals from this kitchen. What he didn't know was whether the food had been prepared from scratch, or had come from a food-service company and simply been reheated. He made notes on the yellow legal pad in his hand.

He looked at the page in his notes with the heading, FORTUNE COOKIES. He opened the oven doors, bent over to look inside. He scribbled more notes. He moved on to the stoves. His gut told him his grandmother would never okay prepared and heated food. Sixteen burners going three times a day. It would work for now, since occupancy was a little over thirty, more if you counted Granny and the aunts. Food service versus local vendors. Granny would want local, that much he knew. Which then opened another can of worms. Who was going to do the shopping? Maybe they could cut deals with the locals for delivery if they bought everything in bulk. Gus made more scribbles in his notepad.

Gus eyed the industrial dishwashers and the huge sinks. Hospitals used throwaways. He made more notes on his pad. Labor hours in the kitchen versus throwaway plastic. Maybe they could get rid of one of the sinks and put in another oven if they could justify the use of plastic plates and plastic utensils. More notes. He was so engrossed in his scribbling and his thoughts, he didn't see Barney until his buddy clapped him on the back.

Gus explained what he was doing. Barney absorbed it all as he walked around, then peered at Gus's notes. "I agree, we take out one sink and put in another oven. Right now, there are going to be thirty-some people, not counting Granny and the aunts. When and how will you decide if you're going to take in more people?"

"I don't know, Barney. Let's check out the rest of this place. The good news is it's sound and in excellent condition. Four wings. Right now, only the east wing is being used, with rooms to spare. The seniors are gung ho, and we're going to have to rein them in. I believe they think that they can fill this place and just keep doing what they're doing. They can't do it financially. I need to tell you something, Barney. They do not take kindly to the word *no!*"

"What you're saying is, they're stubborn?"

"Try *fixated.* And they want it all done yesterday. We have to convince them that whatever we come up with is beneficial to all of them."

Barney groaned. "Are they more or less stubborn than Granny, Vi, and Iris?"

Gus grinned. "They're running neck and neck. Granny will listen, but that doesn't mean she'll agree. See, they were doing fine, according to Granny, before I came along."

"What about the legal end of things? Do any of these people receive Social Security? Where does that money go? Who controls all of that?" Barney asked.

"Granny has a lawyer and an accountant, but from what I can tell, the lawyer, at least, isn't topnotch. They need hands-on twenty-four/seven help, at least for now."

"Are you thinking what I'm thinking?" Barney asked.

"If you're thinking about asking Jill to take over the legal end, then yeah, and if you mean me and my firm doing the accounting, then yeah again. I'll do it for free, but I guess Jill will need to be paid."

Barney laughed out loud and slapped his knees. "That just goes to show how much you know about that young woman. First things first, she does not need the money. This is something she'd love to do simply because she'd have a whole passel of grandmothers and grandfathers. She is so good with elderly people, you have no idea. I'll hate to lose her, but she's a perfect fit for this operation. Do you want to ask her, or shall I?"

"You sure about that, Barney?"

"Oh, I'm sure," Barney drawled.

"Then, I'll do it. Or we can do it together. We can walk over to her house this evening and broach the subject."

"That'll work. What's next on the agenda?"

"Let's walk this place. I was thinking we could use the entire west wing to store all the supplies. We won't need all the rooms for storage and can use the other rooms for the computers for their newsletters—that voodoo and magic stuff they do. I wish they'd get out of that, but they're digging in on that. They say it's entertainment, not for real. Jesus, Barney, they have Web sites, blogs, they tweet, they have it going on. They just need to be organized. Then there's the sex hotlines, the sex newsletters. Don't go getting excited here. I've seen them, and about all they say is just because there's snow on the roof doesn't mean there isn't a fire in the chimney, that kind of thing. Nothing outlandish. Oh, and they advertise in AARP. Barney, they have thousands and thousands of members. What the hell they're members of, I still don't know."

Barney leaned against the wall so he wouldn't fall over laughing. "Hey, don't get me wrong here. I am not laughing at the seniors; I am laughing *with* them. I think this whole thing is great. Damn, I'm glad I came home. I can't wait to get started."

Gus looked at his watch. "We should head to the community room, so we can get this show on the road. I have to tell you, none of the seniors are keen on the idea of shutting down for ten days till we get this ball rolling smoothly. They like being productive and contributing. They're going to fight us tooth and nail. We're going to have to be at our most persuasive. I gotta warn you about Oscar; he's pretty vocal. He's the one who wanted to take me out to the barn to kill me."

"What?" The word exploded out of Barney's mouth faster than a bullet.

"I *think* he was joshing me. But he looked serious."

"I got your back, big guy."

"Thanks, Barney."

Gus led the way down one hall, around the corner, down another hall, and finally they came to what Shady Pines back in the day called the community room. The seniors had set up chairs in neat rows. It looked like everyone was present, including his grandmother and the aunts.

Elroy Hitchens shouted out so that everyone could hear, "The bus driving test is next week, young fella." All the seniors clapped.

"I'm on it, Elroy," Gus shouted back. The seniors clapped again. Barney clapped the loudest.

And then the meeting got under way. It went from curiosity to anger to belligerence, then back to anger, with shouted comments that hurt

Gus's ears. Barney marched up front to take his place next to Gus. He put his fingers to his lips and whistled. As one, the seniors clamped their lips shut. They sat quietly like chastised children, which had not been Gus's intent.

"Okay, ladies and gentlemen, I'm here to suggest a solution to Initial B Enterprises' problems. I repeat, it's just a suggestion, and I'd like all of you to consider it, then vote on it. So, here we go."

Gus talked for a full hour, outlining a plan that he thought would work for all concerned. When he wound down, the thirty-or-so seniors stared at him like inquisitive squirrels waiting to see if there would be anything else for them to consider.

Albert Givens stood up and posed the first question. "What are we going to do for the ten days you say we are not operational?"

Barney stepped forward and introduced himself. "You'll be working with me. We need to do a lot of paperwork where you all are concerned. We need to square away your Social Security payments. That money was going toward your room and board where you lived prior to moving here. Staying here is free. So we need to make your money work for you, and that's where I come in. You'll be paid a salary, but it won't be a lot of money at the end of the week. But by the same token, you will only be working a few hours a day. Weekends will be free for socializing. We're going to run this operation like the business it is.

"We want each of you to write down every-

thing you think we need to know. What you
like to do, if you excel in anything in particular, your food preferences, your current health
status, and anything else you want us to know
so we can provide the best of the best for you."

A little lady named Anna Bristow stood up
and asked about the gardens that she and several of the others had planted that would provide fresh produce for the whole summer.

"I don't see this as a problem, Anna. We have
the golf carts, and there's enough room on the
back of each cart to transport the produce in
baskets. Put that down on your sheet when you
write what you're good at or want to do."

Rose took the floor. "How do you want me
to discharge the legal firm and the accounting
firm when we've been doing business with
them since we started?"

"Barney and I can do that. You have both
firms on a retainer, and you really haven't utilized all the money you paid out. I'm working
for free. The lawyer we plan to bring on board
will probably donate her services. It's win-win.
People change firms all the time, and no one
takes offense; that's just part of doing business.
I feel confident when I tell you I think we can
have all the legalities and accounting up to
snuff inside of a month. You won't have to do
the ledgers anymore, Granny. Everything will
be computerized and will serve as valid records
should you ever have to produce them to any
agency making inquiries into your business."

"When do the ten days start?" Violet asked.

"Today. We're going to start carting all your

inventories over here and use the west wing to store them. You will also work in designated rooms in the west wing for each project. It will be a day or two of chaos, but we'll get it all worked out. We're up for volunteers to help us cart all your supplies and inventory. We can call Pastor Evans to see if he has any high school kids who want to work a few hours after school.

"Barney and I are going to leave you for a bit. Talk about this among yourselves, and if you're all in agreement, fill out the sheets about your likes, dislikes, and goals. We'll be back in an hour for your decision."

A short round man in the back stood up, introduced himself, and asked for confirmation as to the two weeks' vacation and how it would be arranged.

"With a travel agent," Barney said, heading for the door.

"What about holidays?" Elroy Hitchens called out.

"All holidays are paid and you have Christmas week off, too," Barney shot back.

"Well, I want to go to Las Vegas. They give seniors a free lunch and twenty-five dollars to gamble. Can we do that?"

Gus thought Barney was going to pull his hair out. "You can go wherever you want on your vacation."

"It has to be a senior trip, or you don't get the free lunch and the twenty-five dollars. A bus trip. B-U-S!" Elroy bellowed, his eyes on Gus. "A special trip, not a vacation."

"I'll work on it, Elroy," Gus said, shoving Barney ahead of him.

"Damn! I'd rather go up against a bunch of Wall Street sharks than those people. You sure we can make this work, Gus?"

"Yeah. I'm sure."

"You gonna drive a bus all the way to Vegas, Gus?" Barney laughed so hard, tears rolled down his cheeks.

"Only if you're my copilot." It was Gus's turn to laugh. "I think you need to buy these guys a bus, Barney. I mean, you're rich, it won't make a dent in your bottom line, and I'm sure you can write it off."

"A big yellow bus?"

"Well, yeah. You'll need to call Detroit and order it. Get all the bells and whistles and make sure there are seat belts. Elroy is going to want TV for the long trip."

Barney gaped at his friend.

"Isn't this fun, Barney?" Gus asked.

"I gave up making bushels of money to do this and to buy a bus. Already I'm losing money. And yeah, I'm having a hell of a good time."

"Sure you are. Wait, it's going to get better. I'm feeling the love, I really am. Listen, Barney," Gus said, turning serious, "you're *getting* this, aren't you? It's not about money with the seniors. It's about being a family, belonging, your peers watching over you, helping you. They just want to be productive, to count for something at their age. Before they came here, according to Granny, they were the forgotten ones. Barney, if I live to be a hundred, I will never forget the looks on the seniors' faces when I rolled up in that yellow bus. They couldn't wait to get on that bus, to get as far away from the facilities where they'd been living. I was the guy who made that happen. At least, the getaway part. We both know *that* feeling from when we were kids."

"What? You think I'm not getting it? Of course I'm getting it. What the hell do you think I'm here for? Sometimes you're a jerk, Augustus Hollister."

"Takes one to know one." Gus grinned. They were back to being kids again. He loved every minute of it, and he knew Barney did, too.

Chapter 23

ELAINE HOLLISTER SASHAYED INTO SYCAMORE Memorial Hospital and walked straight to the information counter, where she asked for Isaac Diamond's room number. "I'm his grand-daughter," she explained. She waited, looking around to see who, if anyone, was watching her. Visitors, nurses in white uniforms and rubber-soled shoes, and technicians moved from area to area. She didn't see anyone who might be paying attention to her. She'd never been here before, so she asked where the gift shop was, then she asked, "By any chance, do you know if Grandpa has any visitors? I don't want to intrude if other members of the family are visiting. I can wait my turn."

The sweet young candy striper offered to call the nurses' station to ask. A moment later, she said, "The head nurse told me that Mr. Diamond has no visitors, and you can go straight up. His room number is E444. The gift shop is around the corner."

Elaine almost fainted when she heard the room number—444. How perfect was that? She forced herself to take several deep breaths before she was ready to walk on jittery legs to the gift shop, where she bought a single white rose with some mixed greenery nestled in a slender glass vase. She hoped she would remember to wipe her fingerprints off it before she left. The gift shop attendant wrapped several napkins around the sweating vase she'd taken out of the cooler. "So it doesn't slip out of your hands," the volunteer said. Problem solved.

Elaine's thoughts were all over the place as she walked to the elevator and pressed the button for the fourth floor. A good-looking young intern stepped into the elevator and stood next to Elaine. Any other time, she would have gone into full flirt mode, but she barely noticed the young man.

Elaine got off the elevator on the fourth floor, and checked the painted arrows on the wall with the room numbers. She didn't bother going to the nurses' station but went directly down the hall to Room E444. The door was closed but not completely. Elaine knocked softly and opened the door at the same time. She made sure she closed it all the way behind her. She didn't step forward until she heard the clack of the heavy-duty door snap shut. "Good morning, Isaac!" She loved it that the old man looked pasty and gray, as well as shocked to see her standing in his hospital room. "How are you? Your office called me the other day to tell me about your accident."

Isaac did his best to cover his surprise at seeing her standing there. His eyes were wary. "Everyone is trying to make my accident more than it is. I'm being discharged tomorrow and will have some physical therapy at home for a few weeks. I told them I was driving myself home tomorrow. I'm so sure of it, I had my son drop off my car last evening. This is just a blip on my hip. Get it—blip hip?"

"I guess what you're trying to say is you're the same seventy-eight-year-old superstud you were the night you manhandled me. With the aid of four little blue pills." Elaine made a sound of disgust in her throat before she said, "I just came here to tell you that I want a refund of my retainer."

"Elaine, as much as I appreciate your coming here, I really am not up to doing business of any kind. I'm sure my partners offered their services. Make an appointment to talk with them. I can tell you this, though. We did quite a bit of work on your case. We hired private detectives, I had meetings about your case, there were e-mails and phone calls and, of course, our hourly rate all gets deducted from that retainer."

"Isaac, Isaac, you aren't listening to me. I didn't *ask* you to return it. I *told* you to return my retainer. I won't take no for an answer." Before Isaac could respond, Elaine moved to the bed and reached for the CALL button, which was twined around the bars of the bed. "Don't even think about calling out, because if you do, I'll give you a chop to your throat that will crush your larynx. Tell me you understand what I just said."

Isaac nodded.

"Okay, now, this is what we're going to do. Ooops, I meant to say what *you're* going to do. I'm just going to listen. Oh, Isaac, you look . . . scared. What's wrong? Are you not feeling well? Not that I care. Try and get comfortable because I'm going to make your day, you son of a bitch!"

"What's wrong with you, Elaine? Why are you threatening me like this? And you are threatening me."

"Why? You have the nerve to lie there and ask me why? All those disgusting, degrading things you made me do the other night, that's why. You're a pervert. You're a dirty old man."

"You could have left anytime you wanted. You went along with it because you wanted me to lie and cheat for you. I'm a lawyer, and I don't do things like that. I take my profession seriously."

"You took advantage of my greed. I admit it.

You said you would make it come out right in the end if I had sex with you. Sex is sex, and, yes, I agreed to a simple bump and grind. What you did to me was not acceptable. And, Isaac, I have it all on tape. So, listen up, you bastard." Elaine pressed the tiny button on the medallion hanging around her neck. Isaac's courtroom voice, filled with lust and passion, reverberated through the hospital room. "Tell me when you've had enough. Make sure you pay attention to my voice when I'm telling you to stop, when I'm fighting you, and you're telling me to shut up and take it like a whore. Once this goes public, if you force me to go that route, I am sure there will be many women, probably clients, who will come forward. Your call, sweetie."

"Turn it off. What do you want, Elaine?"

"Money. Lots and lots of money."

Elaine's mind raced. How much was too much? What if she lowballed it? She thought about her half of Gus's house, which, if she was lucky, would be $250,000 sometime in the future, possibly years, before the house could be sold. She straightened her shoulders and said, "I think three hundred seventy-five thousand dollars plus my retainer back will do nicely. What I want you to do is call your bank, your broker, or whomever you have to call, and tell them to wire the money into an account whose number I will give you when you're ready."

"That's blackmail!" Isaac blustered.

"Yes it is."

"You're insane! I'm not paying you four hundred thousand dollars for a roll in the sack."

"Sure you are. Because if you don't, I'll send copies of your performance to your partners, to the Bar Association, and to every judge in Sycamore Springs and in this part of Virginia. And I'll send it to the newspapers. I'm going to count to five, and if you don't already have the phone in your hand by the time I get to one, I'm walking out of here. And there are no second chances."

"Bitch!"

"Bastard. I'm going to start counting now."

"Wait just a damned minute. If I do what you want, how do I know you won't come back again and again? That's what blackmailers do. They try to suck you dry."

"Guess that's a chance you have to take. What's it going to be, Isaac?"

"Give me that thing," Isaac gestured toward the recorder.

"After you make the call, and I'm sure the money is in my account. Not one second before."

"How many copies have you made?"

"Enough to carry me through till the day you die, you son of a bitch. Do I start counting, or do you want to man up and pay for what you did to me?"

"Give me the damned phone."

An orderly opened the door and said, "Time for rehab, Mr. Diamond."

"Ooooh, can you wait just a few minutes?

Grandpa needs to make a phone call first. It will take just a minute."

The orderly ogled Elaine and backed out of the room. "Five minutes, Mr. Diamond. Your time is reserved with the therapist."

"Guess you better make it snappy, Isaac." Elaine handed the phone to the lawyer. She stood close enough so she could hear every word on both ends of the line. She held up her account number and the routing numbers.

Elaine could barely breathe as she listened to Isaac transfer $400,000 into her account. When he broke the connection, Elaine took one long, deep breath. She turned around just as the orderly came back into the room.

"Time to go, Mr. Diamond."

Elaine always prided herself on being able to think on her feet. She knew instantly what she had to do. "I'll just sit here and wait for you, Grandpa. I brought a book with me. Now, you do what they tell you to do so you can get out of here and back home to all of us. I'll just sit here and wait for you," she said playfully as she wagged a finger in Isaac's direction. Just for good measure, she winked at the orderly, who got so flustered he pushed Isaac's wheelchair into the door. She laughed when she heard Isaac curse.

Isaac Diamond glared at Elaine, but said nothing as the orderly helped him out of bed and into the waiting wheelchair.

Elaine waited until she heard the ping of the elevator before she got up to close the door. She moved lightning fast, checking the closet and the drawers of the night chest. She almost laughed out loud when she saw Isaac's car keys and wallet. What a fool he was to leave things like this in a hospital room. She helped herself to the $400 in the wallet, and to the Visa card. Four hundred dollars, another sign. She removed the car key. Time to go.

"Four, four, four," Elaine kept mumbling as she made her way out of the hospital. She headed straight for the parking garage, where she pressed the key to give her some idea of where Isaac's pride and joy, his favorite toy, a Mercedes Maybach worth $450,000, had been parked. She listened, heard the chirp coming from the upper level. She looked around to where she'd parked her VW to get her bearings. She walked over to her car and took a screwdriver out of her trunk, removed the license plate, and stuck it in her purse. She was glad she'd backed the little car into the parking slot. She then made her way up the ramp to the next level as she searched out the Maybach. She looked around for security cameras, but didn't see any. Nor did she see any people looking for their cars. She quickly removed the license plate and screwed the VW's plate onto the Maybach.

Elaine raced back down to the lower level and fixed the plate from the Maybach onto the VW, then back up to the next level, where she opened the car door with the remote, got in, and drove out of the parking garage. She was now $850,000 richer.

Time to get the hell out of Dodge.

Elaine drove the silver Maybach like she was born to do it. As she ate up the miles, a smile stayed on her face all the way home. She swerved into her driveway, bolted out of the car, and ran up to the deck. She checked the duct tape and saw that everything was the way she had left it.

Inside, she went to the front door, checked it, too, then backed into the house. All was well. She ran upstairs and changed into jeans and a T-shirt. Her heels were replaced with Gucci sneakers. She moved then, faster than she'd ever moved in her life. She carried boxes and boxes out to the cavernous trunk in the Maybach. Back inside, she packed all her designer clothes into her designer luggage and carried it all out to the car and jammed it to the ceiling in the car, being careful to leave the driver's side of the rear window free. She stacked the last of her things in the passenger seat and on the floor.

Back in the house, Elaine sat down at the table and typed out a text to Gus's cell phone. It was short and sweet.

> *Gus,*
> *I'm leaving town. You can have your house back. When I get to where I'm going, I'll sign a quitclaim deed for my half of the house and send it on to the courthouse. It's all yours, Gus. Check in with the courts to be sure it gets filed. With Mr. Diamond being incapacitated, it will*

*be up to you to file for divorce. I'll be in touch
at some point so you can send me the papers to
sign. I will lock all the doors and leave the new
key above the doorframe on the deck, since I
had the locks changed.*

*Sorry things didn't work out. For whatever
it's worth, you're an okay guy.*

Elaine

Elaine hit the SEND button and powered
down. She slipped the phone into her already
loaded shoulder bag. First chance she got, she
would ditch the phone and get a new one.

Elaine walked through the house to make
sure she hadn't forgotten anything and wasn't
leaving something behind. Satisfied, she walked
out of Gus's house for the last time. She kept
her word and placed the key above the doorframe.

Where to go? Maybe south, the Carolinas.
Time to take a few years off to recharge her
batteries before going out to find a good old
boy with a southern drawl who knew how to
treat a lady.

Yeah, time to head south.

Little did Elaine know, as she tooled down
the interstate, that the next mark she chose,
one Beauregard Levi MacNamara, would turn
out to be a Bernie Madoff wannabe, and that
for years after getting involved with him, she
would be back to driving a lemon yellow Beetle.

*   *   *

While Elaine was tooling down the interstate in Isaac Diamond's $450,000 Maybach, Gus and Barney were listening to the seniors' vote of confidence. The vote to go with Gus and Barney's plan was a hundred percent unanimous. Even Oscar, who had wanted to kill Gus, was in total agreement.

Gus and Barney walked among the group to shake each man's hand and to receive a motherly hug from the ladies, including the Blossom sisters.

Fresh fortune cookies and lemonade were served.

At the end of what Violet called the social hour to cement their new plan, the seniors dispersed, and Gus and Barney were left with each senior's résumé.

"Listen, Barney, we have to really read these so we get a clear idea of each person here. When we call them by name, that means we know them and their stories. And each of them has a story. I don't want either of us to think they're just a bunch of old people. I want each one of them to be my friend, and I want us to do what's best for our friends. Do you agree with me?"

"Hell, yes, and I couldn't have said it better. So let's get started. I'm glad it all worked out, Gus."

"Yeah, me, too. Hold on, I'm getting a text. It might be Jill or it might be my office." Barney stared off into space while Gus checked his text. His friend's joyful-sounding whoop almost toppled him off his chair. "Well, damn, take a look at this, Barney."

Barney's eyes popped wide. "Wow! Do you think this is another scam of hers? Or maybe she's trying to set you up for something or other?"

"Damned if I know. Want to take a break and ride out to the house to see if it's true? If she left the key, then I guess she's on the level. Give me five minutes to tell Granny, and I'll meet you out front."

Rose, Violet, and Iris behind her viewed the message. All three asked the same question at the same time. "Do you believe this?"

"It follows her pattern according to all the detective reports I've seen. But she's leaving without a payout. She's never done that before, so, yes, maybe it is a setup of some sort. Guess I won't know till I check out the house. Barney and I are going there now to do just that. We won't be gone long, if it's okay with you ladies."

"Go!" the sisters said in unison.

Gus felt detached when he walked up the steps to the deck that led to the back door. He was surprised when the key was precisely where Elaine had said it would be. He opened the door, expecting the alarm to go off. It didn't. He looked at Barney and shrugged. In the kitchen, he looked around. All was neat and tidy. There was nothing in the refrigerator.

The two old friends walked from room to room and couldn't find anything out of the ordinary. It just looked like a house that no one was living in. They walked upstairs and checked out the master bedroom. The bed was unmade, but that was the only thing to offset the impression of an unoccupied house. The closets were bare, the dresser drawers empty. The tons of makeup that used to dot the vanity in the bathroom were gone. Wet towels were hung over the shower stall.

"She's gone! Everything is gone. She had tons of stuff. I only had one small closet, and she had stuff in all the others. Tons of stuff, Barney."

"What do you make of this?"

Gus shrugged. "I honest to God don't know, Barney. If all her stuff is gone, I guess that means she has no plans to come back. She told me to go ahead with the divorce. I have to assume she'll be in touch. I'm going to put the house up for sale and give the money back to Granny. I don't need a house like this. I'm selling my car, too. I have my eye on a Mustang convertible. If I sell the Porsche, pay off what's owed on it—which isn't much—I can pay cash for the Mustang and have no car payment. The high taxes on this house were killing me, not to mention the homeowner's insurance. That will be a big load off my shoulders. And, no, Barney, you are not going to lend or give me any money, so get that stupid look off your face."

"But you love that Porsche."

"Well, guess what? I love my grandmother and aunts more than I could ever love some damned car. I'll learn to love the Mustang."

Barney wrapped his arms around his old friend. "You're one hell of a guy, Gus Hollister. You put me to shame."

"Nah. Hey, you're the guy who is going to buy a big yellow bus to help a bunch of new friends. I envy you being able to do that without blinking. So, Barney Beezer, you're a hell of a guy yourself."

The old friends left the house, their arms around each other's shoulders.

"You think we're making a difference, Barney?"

"Yeah, I do, Gus."

"Then let's head back to Blossom Farm and make all those dreams of those new friends of ours come true."

"How about heading for the DMV first, so I can pick up the application for bus driving?"

"Okay."

Fifteen minutes later, Barney climbed back into the car and waved the application under Gus's nose. "Guess what? I have a date tomorrow night!"

"Huh?"

"Yeah, they were out of applications, so the young lady had to send someone to fetch one. We got to talking, and I asked her out. She said yes."

"Did you tell her who you were?" Gus laughed.

"I think she thinks I'm going to be driving a

bus. I told her my name is Barney, and she didn't ask any questions."

"Well, you better hurry up and get that bus."

They were ten years old again as they laughed all the way back to Blossom Farm to work on making dreams come true for some wonderful people.

Epilogue

Two years later

THE SUN WASN'T UP YET, THE SKY JUST STARTING to pink up when Gus and Barney, followed by Wilson, walked through the sliding doors and out to the deck for their first cup of coffee of the day.

Wilson wandered off to water the bushes as the two old friends sat down at the table.

"Today's the day, Gus. You ready for it?"

Gus took so long to answer the question, Barney had to prod him.

"As hard as I try to stop them, Barney, my thoughts keep going back to the day I married Elaine. I was so excited, I actually threw up. I don't feel like that today. I feel . . . anxious. I think I'm afraid to unleash my feelings. I don't want to make another mistake. And yet I can't wait to marry Jill. I feel like she's my life partner. We don't have secrets. We talk out everything. I see us growing old together, like the seniors, and loving every minute of it. I guess I'm ready, but I am scared; I won't lie to you."

"I think that's normal, Gus, not that I'm any kind of authority."

"Well, that's for sure. You're still dating Priscilla from the DMV. Two years is a long time not to make a commitment. What's your game plan, Barney?"

"I don't have a game plan, Gus. Priscilla loves me, I love her, but she can't come to terms with who I am. My money scares her. She'd marry me in a heartbeat if I drove a bus. She said she would never fit in with the kind of people I hang out with. With the exception of you and the seniors. When I showed her my house, which is sitting empty, she started to cry and ran out to the car. She's been on her own for a very long time. She deals with a mortgage payment, a car payment, and one credit card she pays off every month. She shops at discount stores and doesn't recognize designer labels. She's honest, she's frugal, and she allocates a portion of her yearly salary to donate to various causes, what she can comfortably afford. In my eyes, she's as perfect as you can get. I am not perfect in her eyes. Oh, and one other thing. She wants a man who comes home for a supper that she cooks. And a paycheck that goes into a joint bank account. I've asked her to marry me a hundred times and, each time, she says no. Let's not talk about me; this is your day. For whatever it's worth, Gus, you did it all the right way. You found your path, and you stayed on it. I'll find mine, but it may take a little longer."

"Jill really likes Priscilla; they turned out to be great friends. The seniors love her, too. She's what Granny calls good people. We both know what that means."

"I'm happy for you, Gus."

"I know you are, and I have you to thank for it all."

"Nah, you should thank Elaine in a crazy kind of way. If she hadn't demanded a divorce, you never would have met Jill. By the way, have you heard from Elaine?"

"The last time I heard from her was more than a year ago, when I sent the divorce papers to a box number in Alabama. They came back in overnight mail. No note, no nothing. She must be moving around, because when she sent the quitclaim deed to the house, it was mailed from North Carolina. That was almost two years ago. Elaine is nothing more than a bad memory these days."

"Did the nibble you had on the house come to anything?"

"It was a lowball offer. I'm holding out because I want to return the money to Granny. The market is still bad, but I would at least like to get back the price Granny paid for it, so I'm going to wait as long as I can."

Barney shrugged. "I'm glad you and Jill

agreed to get married at Shady Pines. You guys made the seniors so happy. They've been working like beavers to make sure the garden is shipshape. And asking Albert to perform the ceremony put them all over the moon."

"Well, Al is a notary, and he casually said he could marry us if we wanted him to. I talked it over with Jill, and it seemed perfect to us. I hope he remembers the words."

"He's been rehearsing by pretending to marry Iris and Oscar six times a day. I think he has it down pat." Barney laughed.

Wilson trotted up to the deck, looked at Gus and Barney, and let loose with a bark that meant, *Where's my breakfast?*

"Did you make the bed, Wilson? Did you take the trash out? You need to work in this house, or you don't eat. Hop to it, buddy."

Wilson dropped to the deck and put his head between his paws. Gus shrugged.

Barney grabbed his own coffee cup and reached across the table for Gus's. He carried them into the house for refills. When he returned, he also had a Pop-Tart for Wilson.

"I closed on the house across the street yesterday, Gus. We're going to be neighbors. I bought a John Deere tractor, and they're going to deliver it later today."

"On my wedding day!"

"Yeah. I told them to put it in the garage. No big deal. Next week, Priscilla and I are going to shop for furniture, and, no, she is not moving in. She just offered to help me, so I don't get ripped off."

"Barney, what are you going to do about your business?"

"I'm not giving it up. It's what I do. I am cutting back on my travel, but I can't give it up entirely. I'm good at what I do, and people depend on me. If I can't get Priscilla to see my side, then she and I are not meant to be. I have to be true to myself. Granny taught us that, Gus."

Barney looked at his watch. "Five more hours, pal."

"Hold on, Barney. I have something for you. Groom has to give his best man a present. I got one for you."

"No kidding? You didn't give me one when you married Elaine."

"That's because I didn't know I was supposed to give you a gift. Elaine handled all the details. Granny and the seniors are doing this one, so they explained it to me." Gus got up and went into the house. He returned with a huge box and another Pop-Tart for Wilson.

Barney got up and stood over the box. He pried back the ends of the box and pulled out the slab of bark from the old sycamore tree. Gus watched as his fingers traced their names, then caressed the old bark. Tears rolled down his cheeks.

"Jesus, Gus, how the hell . . . ? I don't know what . . . you couldn't have given . . . this is . . . this is from our kid days. A memory I'll never forget. I don't know what to say," he said, throwing his arms around Gus. Then they both blubbered like little boys as their memories took them both back in time.

"I don't know what you're going to do with it—a doorstop maybe," Gus said, trying to lighten the intensely emotional moment. Barney just hugged him harder.

"I can't believe you gave me this. I guess my question would be, why didn't you keep it for yourself? And how did you get it, anyway?"

"Barney, I don't have a whole hell of a lot to give to show you how much I value our friendship and all you've done for me over the years. I thought . . . I hoped this would say it for me. I told Granny about how I wanted it, and she asked Mr. Younger when he was cutting the tree down. He had to do some serious cutting, but I think he understood how important it was to me to save it. The lightning strike ran down the side, right next to where we gouged out our names. You can see a little dark streak of it there on the side. You know, Barney, you have to stop squeezing me, or you're going to break my ribs on my wedding day."

"Oh, sorry, Gus. I'm just so overwhelmed. Listen, I'm going to take this over to my new house so it's the first thing I bring to my new life here in the neighborhood."

"Go ahead. Do you want me to make some breakfast?"

"No. I'm too excited to eat. Well, okay, maybe some toast and juice."

"Well, if that's all you want, you can make it yourself. I'm going up to take my shower. Now, if you want to cook something, that's okay with me." *Like that's going to happen.*

Gus made his way upstairs on wobbly legs, Wilson at his heels. He was getting married today, in less than five hours. He pinched himself to prove he wasn't still asleep, dreaming. In the bathroom, he gripped the edge of the vanity to steady himself. He closed his eyes and thought about the past two years and about how a warm friendship had turned into a deep and abiding love for the young woman he'd once called a fireplug. He had to be the luckiest man alive. He bowed his head and thanked Elaine. Because, in the end, Barney was right; if she hadn't kicked him out and filed for divorce, he wouldn't be standing here right now and looking forward to marrying the love of his life. "Wherever you are, Elaine, I hope you're as happy as I am right this moment," he whispered.

Barney drove to Shady Pines because Gus was too nervous. Both were attired in dove gray tuxedos as per Granny's suggestion. They told each other in jittery voices that they looked dashing.

As they drove down the long driveway to the main building, they took time to appreciate the seniors' hard work at sprucing up the grounds for this important day. The lawn had been mowed, and the scent of the newly mown grass permeated the air. It was not an unpleasant scent. Flowers of all kinds bloomed in profusion. There wasn't a weed to be seen. Lush, thick ferns moved gently from the rafters of the wide front porch, where the seniors congregated at night to talk or to play checkers or chess. The building itself looked clean and well kept. The shutters and trim sported a pristine white fresh coat of paint.

The wedding was being held at the back of the property, on the wide expanse of lawn, under a lattice arch. White roses and blooming Confederate jasmine climbed the trellis. Gus thought it looked beautiful.

Barney parked as close as he could to the south entrance to Shady Pines, the door Granny had told them to come to, where they could wait until it was time to see the bride.

"Did Granny tell you what's on the buffet for the luncheon?" Barney asked.

"Everything under the sun. Each senior's favorite, each of our favorites, and, of course, the wedding cake that Lewis Lippman made for the occasion, which Granny said was, as per the instructions, decorated with fortune cookies. One for each guest. Jill thought that the fortune cookie cake was the best idea she'd ever heard of and said she would have liked to have seen the look on Lewis's face when the request for the fortune cookies had arrived."

"They all love Jill. I told you that would happen, Gus. Jill loves having so many grandmothers and grandfathers. She adores each and every one of them. It turned out just the way we thought it would."

Gus laughed. "With a little help from Barney Beezer, who keeps feeding the coffers. I appreciate the help, Barney. The seniors would, too, if they knew. The twenty extra seniors we added the last two years ate into our reserve, but with your help and my creative accounting and Jill's expertise, it's working perfectly. We might have to cut back on the bonus each one gets next year. I don't think anyone will mind. I was also thinking of cutting back vacations from two weeks to one week. Again, I don't think anyone will mind. If we do that, we can take in ten more seniors. You prepared to commit to that?"

"It's done."

"You're a hell of a guy, Barney Beezer. I just wish you'd let me tell all of them how much you've done for them that they don't even know about."

"No. We agreed, Gus. I don't even want Granny or the aunts to know."

"It doesn't seem fair somehow."

"To me, it's fair. So, you ready to get out of the car? Do you think you can stand up? You're gonna be okay, aren't you, Gus?"

"God, Barney, I don't know. I feel like that night when we picked up our dates for our first prom. Remember that?"

"Jesus, is that how you feel?"

"Yeah."

"Well, get over it right now. You are going to marry the most wonderful young woman in this world. You have a huge family here to cheer you on and to wish you well. You have to stand up to that. So, let's put one foot in front of the other and head to the room that was assigned to just you, me, and Albert."

Gus climbed out of the car and stood upright. He started to laugh then and couldn't stop. "I'm getting married!" he bellowed.

" 'Bout time you got here, young fella. Thought you might be late for your own wedding there for a minute," Albert said, chuckling.

Gus gaped at the man standing in front of him. He knew it was Albert, yet it wasn't the Albert he knew. The beard was gone, his hair was trimmed, and he wore a stunning blue-and-white seersucker suit that had to be sixty years old. A white sash was draped over his shoulder. Not only was Albert marrying him, he was also going to do all the photography. They all shook hands as Albert paced and recited the words he would say once the wedding was under way.

Granny poked her head in the door. "Ten minutes, Augustus. Violet will escort you and Barney to the waiting area. May I be the first to tell you how beautiful your bride-to-be looks?"

Gus gulped. He felt as nervous as a cat on a hot griddle, a favorite saying of his grandmother's. Now he knew what that particular saying meant.

Violet swooped into the room, checked out Albert from head to toe, then she gave his tie a jerk to straighten it. "Okay, Albert, Iris is going to escort you to the trellis. You go first." Albert smiled as he left the room just as soon as Iris knocked on the door.

"Now, it's your turn, nephew." Violet leaned forward, her gaze soft and gentle. "I want to tell you how proud of you I am, Augustus. You truly redeemed yourself in our eyes. I want to thank you for that. Having said that, neither I nor my two sisters will ever apologize for our actions prior to your first wife's kicking you out of the house. We love you, dear, you're our family, and we care about you, and perhaps, back then, we cared too much. Whatever, that's all water under the bridge. This is now. I hope you will always be as happy as you are today." Then Violet pulled Gus close and whispered in his ear. Gus blinked, then blinked again, as Violet moved forward to lead the two men out of the room, down the hall, and out to the velvety lawn, where they would wait for Jill to make her appearance.

Gus was shaking so bad, Barney had to grip his arm in a viselike hold. "What'd she say, Gus?" he hissed in his ear.

Gus struggled to speak. "She said if I screwed up again, she'd personally help Oscar drag me out to the barn to do me in."

Barney let out a whoop of laughter. "That's Aunt Vi for you. She means it, you know."

"I do know that," Gus mumbled. "God, do I know that."

And then they were standing next to the trellis that smelled so sweet. Gus thought he was going to faint from the heady scent of the flowering jasmine.

"Three minutes and counting," Albert said.

"Two minutes and counting."

"One minute, and here comes the bride!"

The seniors burst into song as every male senior at Shady Pines escorted Jill to the trellis to give her away. They sang loudly, they sang off-key, they forgot some of the words, but their hearts were in the rendition. Jill smiled from ear to ear as Gus stared at his beloved. The gorgeous creature coming toward him loved him. Just him. (And the seniors, he added as an afterthought.) She was willing to spend the rest of her life with him. Just the two of them. Forever and ever.

Barney's arm snaked up to hold Gus erect. He looked at Albert and said, "Hit it, Albert, you're up!"

The ceremony was flawless, everything going off without a hitch. Albert had the words down pat and didn't miss a beat. The only time he screwed up was when he kissed the bride before the groom got to do it.

The seniors broke into another rendition of "Here Comes the Bride." They sang at the top of their lungs. They sang off-key again, but no one cared. They threw popcorn instead of rice because one of the seniors had read somewhere that when wild birds ate rice, it swelled in their stomachs and they got sick. Balloons of all colors sailed high in the air.

Everyone clapped hands as they all made their way back inside to the community room, where the buffet and the champagne toast awaited.

There were only two gifts, one large, one

small. The seniors clamored for Jill to open the gift that was from all of them. Tears in her eyes, Jill sat down and undid the wrapping. "Look, Gus, it's an album of our two years with all the seniors. Look, you're splitting wood in this one. Oh, my gosh, I'm cutting Annie's hair in this one. This is a group shot of all of us!" And on and on she went as she flipped the pages. Gus could feel his eyes start to burn. Jill was openly crying.

"Oh, my gosh, I don't know how to thank you. Look at Gus—he's speechless. You guys are the most wonderful family I could ever hope to have. I know Gus agrees." Gus was bobbing his head up and down.

"One more gift. Your turn, Augustus," his grandmother said.

Gus reached for the small package, unwrapped it, and opened the box. A key rested on black velvet. Gus's head jerked up as he looked at Barney. "This better not be a key to a new Porsche or even my old Porsche."

"Not even close, Gus," Barney replied, laughing.

The seniors were giggling and laughing and jostling each other, barely able to contain themselves.

Elroy Hitchens walked over to where Gus was, took his arm, and led him to one of the side windows of the community room. "Look!"

A big yellow bus stood right outside the window, with a big silver bow strapped to the top. "It's from Barney," the seniors shouted as one.

"My own bus!" Gus turned to Barney, who was laughing so hard he could hardly stand. "You son of a gun! How'd you know I wanted my own bus?"

"You talk in your sleep!"

It was chaos, then, as everyone started to talk, to kiss and hug the bride, and to offer congratulations. Gus received handshakes, accepted claps on the back, and listened to well-meaning advice.

Two hours later, Iris announced it was time for the bride to throw her bouquet. All the senior ladies and Jill's friend and former secretary, Louise, lined up and waited for Jill to toss the bouquet over her shoulder. A senior named Sadie caught the bouquet, immediately marched over to Elroy Hitchens, and said, "What do you think about this, Elroy?"

"They smell nice," Elroy said. It wasn't the answer Sadie wanted, but she took it with good grace and moved on so the other ladies could ooh and aah over the flowers.

Rose, Violet, and Iris appeared out of nowhere. "It's time!" they said in unison, the way they always spoke when they were together.

From somewhere, a whistle sounded. It was Albert, who then shouted as loud as he could, "Time to get ready, everyone! The bride and groom will be departing shortly."

The room cleared, as if by magic. Lynus and Lewis walked over to where Jill was talking quietly with Barney and said their good-byes. Before he left, Lewis handed her a small, flat package.

Inside, as she and Gus discovered later, were two framed pictures of their wedding cake, decorated all over with sixty fortune cookies.

Forty-five minutes later, everyone was dressed in casual, comfortable clothes. Barney led the parade out to the parking area. He put his arm around Rose and whispered, "This honeymoon is probably going to go down in history. The bride and groom are driving a big yellow bus to Las Vegas and taking along fifty-three seniors plus the best man and the maid of honor!"

"Are you sure, Barney, that the people you hired to clean up and put everything back in place are reliable? The seniors were a little worried about their personal belongings."

"Not to worry, Granny; they're bonded and licensed. There won't be any problems. You guys ready?"

"We are. None of us have ever been to Las Vegas before. Can you imagine Jill and Augustus giving each of us a fifty-dollar bill to gamble? And the casino will give us another twenty-five. Jill said it's customary to do that. I might be old, but I don't think I ever saw that in any of the etiquette books."

"You're slipping, Granny. Even I knew that," Barney said with a straight face.

"I guess I am getting old, but I'm glad I can learn something new each day. Thank you for enlightening us, Barney."

Outside, Albert's whistle blasted through the air. The seniors lined up, not sure which bus to get on. They waited for the bride and groom to make the decision. Gus looked at Barney and grinned. "We're going in my new bus. All aboard!"

Gus, Jill, Priscilla, and Barney were the last to board. The workers Barney had hired to clean up after the wedding waved from the front porch of Shady Pines.

"Isn't this great, Priscilla?" Barney asked the woman he hoped to marry. "Getting married, then taking your family along on your honeymoon. In a big yellow bus. I don't think it gets any better than that, do you?"

"You can't wait to drive this bus, right?" Priscilla asked.

"I take over for the second half of the trip. Got my license right here with me."

"Well, in that case, I'll marry you."

Unaware of what had just happened, Gus settled himself behind the wheel and turned the key in the ignition. The seniors clapped and whooped when the engine of the new yellow bus growled to life.

Before Gus shifted gears, he took a moment to look around at his big family, two of whom had their arms wrapped around each other and were oblivious to the rest of the world. Then he looked at his new bride, who was grinning from ear to ear. In that moment, he knew that if he lived to be a hundred, he would never ever be as happy as he was then. His fist shot in the air. The seniors clapped once again.

"Next stop, Las Vegas!" Gus shouted.

*In her powerful new novel, #1 New York Times
bestselling author Fern Michaels weaves a story of
betrayal, courage, and starting over . . .*

NO SAFE SECRET

From her silver Mercedes to her designer kitchen,
Molly's life is gleaming and beautiful—at least on
the surface. Married to Tanner, a top cosmetic
dentist, she has a wonderful daughter finishing
high school and twin stepsons from Tanner's first
marriage. No one in her exclusive neighborhood
in Goldenhills, Massachusetts, knows what living
with the demanding Tanner is really like. They
know even less about the life she left behind in
Florida almost two decades ago.

Back then, Molly was Maddy Carmichael, living
with her twin brother and neglectful mother in a
run-down trailer park amid the orange groves of
Florida. After the terrible events of her high
school prom night—and the act of vengeance that
followed—she fled north and reinvented herself.
But the veneer of Molly's polished existence is
finally cracking.

As secrets old and new are revealed, Molly must
face painful truths and the choices she made in
their wake—and find the strength to become the
woman she once hoped to be.

Turn the page for a special look!
A Kensington hardcover and eBook on sale now.

Present Day
Goldenhills, Massachusetts

MOLLY STOOD IN HER SPOTLESS, NEWLY RE-
modeled designer kitchen and checked her
shopping list one last time before driving
across town to Gloria's, her favorite market,
which specialized in organic produce, freshly
caught seafood, and everything in between.
She had ten people coming over tonight for
yet another one of Tanner's dinner parties.

This morning, as he was leaving for the dental clinic, he'd said one word to her: "perfec-

tion." He'd winked to soften his sharp command.

It was her warning that the outcome of this dinner party would determine their future. Everything must be perfect. Tanner was a true perfectionist. *A bit harsh*, she thought as she reached for the keys to her silver Mercedes, Tanner's gift to her on their fifteenth wedding anniversary. Now, nearing their twentieth, she continued to drive the same car. It had seemed like only yesterday that she'd gifted him with a photograph of the three children in an exquisite silver frame, an acknowledgment of the best part of their life together. The children. Holden and Graham, twins Tanner had from his first marriage, boys she'd raised since they were toddlers. Their mother, Elaine, had died in a tragic accident just months after they were born. To Molly, they were no different than Kristen, her biological daughter, who idolized her big brothers.

She remembered Tanner that day she'd given him the picture, all those years ago. He had been preoccupied with something and had only glanced at the framed photo, tossing it aside as though it were merely a flyer advertising a window-washing service or someone who was hoping to cut their grass. If he'd only known how hard it'd been to schedule the photographer and get all three kids in the same place for the scheduled appointment, maybe he would have actually appreciated her thoughtful gift.

She hadn't wanted or needed a new car then, didn't really like it all that much now. Her eight-year-old Range Rover had suited her just fine. She'd carted all kinds of sporting equipment when the boys played hockey, followed by football, stinky pads and all. Kristen had insisted on taking French horn lessons that she'd never quite got the hang of, but having such a large instrument was cool at the time, and she could fit it in the back of the Range Rover without a problem. Yes, she thought as she pulled out of the garage in her sleek and shiny car, her old Range Rover held many good memories, as did the other car, the one she'd had restored, which was now tucked safely away in a place where it belonged.

She glanced in the rearview mirror as she backed out of the driveway, aware that she looked older than her actual age. She put her foot on the brake and brought the car to a sudden stop, pulled the visor down, and looked into the vanity mirror. Her blond hair was more gray than blond, and her green eyes were lusterless. Her eyelids had begun to sag, and her once-full mouth drooped in a permanent frown. She traced the web of wrinkles around her eyes, then quickly raised the visor.

Shifting into PARK, she wondered when she'd begun to look so old. She had turned thirty-eight last month, had been dreading the big four-oh, but at thirty-eight she already looked much older than the ghastly forty. She was aging faster than Tanner, who at forty-eight looked much younger. Why hadn't Tanner mentioned this to her? He always critiqued her. What she wore, too much makeup, not enough make-

up, too tan, too pale, too fat, too thin, and on
and on it went. At least she had good teeth, she
thought as she pulled onto Riverbend Road,
the most exclusive neighborhood in Goldenhills. She ran her tongue across her teeth. They
were as smooth as the mother-of-pearl necklace
Tanner had given her on her thirtieth birth-
day. Of course, her perfect teeth were courtesy
of Tanner's expertise; he was one of the top
cosmetic dentists in the state.

Which brought her back to the reason for
tonight's dinner party. Tanner owned three
dental clinics, one here in Goldenhills and two
in Ocean Orr, and wanted to open a fourth in
Boston, near the Harvard School of Dental
Medicine, his alma mater. Tonight's guests
were potential investors.

Molly knew that tonight was very important
to her husband. She truly appreciated his hard
work and dedication, but there were times
when she thought he took his business drive to
the extreme. Tonight's dinner, for example.
He didn't need these investors any more than
she needed a snake for a pet, yet for Tanner,
having a clinic that actually drew in investors
was just another way to feed his already huge
ego, though she would never say anything like
that to him. Tanner strove to be a good husband and father most of the time, as well as a
dedicated medical professional. A tiny thought
crept into her head, a truth she rarely acknowl-
edged: in point of fact, he was neither a good
husband nor a good father. Right now, she
chose not to consider those truths.

Forgiveness. She must remember to forgive thy neighbor.

Isn't that what Father Richard Czerwinski, or Father Wink, as he preferred to be addressed, had shared with her just last week when she'd stopped by the church to light a candle? Religion was a very important part of her life. There was a time when she didn't believe in any formal religion or a higher power, and she felt guilty about that to this very day. But she reminded herself that she'd never really had an opportunity to seriously explore any religion. Her own day-to-day survival had been her top priority. Of course, when Tanner and his twin boys came into her life, all of that had changed. She rarely thought of her life before Tanner and the kids, and when she did, it angered her. For days afterward, she would be in the most dreadful mood.

GREAT BOOKS, GREAT SAVINGS!

When You Visit Our Website:
www.kensingtonbooks.com
You Can Save Money Off The Retail Price
Of Any Book You Purchase!

- **All Your Favorite Kensington Authors**
- **New Releases & Timeless Classics**
- **Overnight Shipping Available**
- **eBooks Available For Many Titles**
- **All Major Credit Cards Accepted**

Visit Us Today To Start Saving!
www.kensingtonbooks.com